CHRISTOPHER BUSH
THE CASE OF THE
DEAD MAN GONE

CHRISTOPHER BUSH was born Charlie Christmas Bush in Norfolk in 1885. His father was a farm labourer and his mother a milliner. In the early years of his childhood he lived with his aunt and uncle in London before returning to Norfolk aged seven, later winning a scholarship to Thetford Grammar School.

As an adult, Bush worked as a schoolmaster for 27 years, pausing only to fight in World War One, until retiring aged 46 in 1931 to be a full-time novelist. His first novel featuring the eccentric Ludovic Travers was published in 1926, and was followed by 62 additional Travers mysteries. These are all to be republished by Dean Street Press.

Christopher Bush fought again in World War Two, and was elected a member of the prestigious Detection Club.

He died in 1973.

CHRISTOPHER BUSH

THE CASE OF THE DEAD MAN GONE

With an introduction
by Curtis Evans

DEAN STREET PRESS

Published by Dean Street Press 2022

First published in 1961 by MacDonald & Co.

Cover by DSP

ISBN 978 1 915014 68 9

www.deanstreetpress.co.uk

INTRODUCTION

Rosalind. If it be true that good wine needs no bush [i.e., advertising], 'tis true that a good play needs no epilogue. Yet to good wine, they do use good bushes, and good plays prove the better by the help of good epilogues.

–SHAKESPEARE, Epilogue, As You Like It

THE decade of the 1960s saw the sun finally begin to set on that storied generation which between the First and Second World Wars gave us detective fiction's Golden Age. Taking account of both deaths and retirements, by the late Sixties only a bare half-dozen pre-World War Two members of the Detection Club were still plying their deliciously deceptive craft: Agatha Christie, Anthony Gilbert (Lucy Beatrice Malleson), Gladys Mitchell, John Dickson Carr, Nicholas Blake and Christopher Bush, the subject of this introduction. Bush himself would pass away, at the age of eighty-seven, in 1973, having published, at the age of eighty-two, his sixty-third Ludovic Travers detective novel, *The Case of the Prodigal Daughter*, in the United Kingdom in the spring of 1968.

In the United States Bush's final detective novel did not appear until late November 1969, about four months after the horrific Manson murders in the tarnished Golden State of California. Implicating the triple terrors of sex, drugs and rock and roll (not to mention almost inconceivably bestial violence), the Manson slayings could not have strayed farther from the whimsically escapist "death as a game" aesthetic of Golden Age of detective fiction. Increasingly in the decade capable of producing psychedelic psychopaths like Charles Manson and his "family," the few remaining survivors of the Golden Age of detective fiction increasingly deemed themselves men and women far out of time. In his detective fiction John Dickson Carr, an incurable romantic, prudently beat a retreat from the present into the pleasanter pages of the past, setting his tales in bygone historical eras where he felt vastly more at home. With varying success Agatha Christie made a brave effort to stay abreast of the times (*Third Girl,*

Endless Night), but ultimately her strivings to understand what was going on around her collapsed into the utter incoherence of *Passenger to Frankfurt* and *Postern of Fate,* by general consensus the worst mystery novels that Dame Agatha ever put down on paper.

In his detective fiction Christopher Bush, who was not quite two years older than Christie, managed rather better than the Queen of Crime to keep up with all the unsettling goings-on around him, while never forswearing the Golden Age article of faith that the primary purpose of a crime writer is pleasingly to puzzle his/her readers. And, in contrast with Christie and Carr, Bush knew when it was time to lay down his pen (or turn off his dictation machine, as the case may be), thereby allowing him to make his exit from the stage on a comparatively high note. Indeed, Christopher Bush's concluding baker's dozen of detective novels, which he published between 1957 and 1968 (and which have now been reprinted, after more than a half-century, by Dean Street Press), makes a generally fine epilogue, or coda, to the author's impressive corpus of crime fiction, which first began to see the light of day way back in the jubilant Jazz Age. These are, readers will find, "good bushes" (to punningly borrow from Shakespeare), providing them with ample intelligent detective entertainment as Bush's longtime series sleuth Ludovic Travers, in the luminous twilight of his career, makes his final forays into ingenious criminal investigation.

*

In the last thirteen Ludovic Travers mystery novels, Travers' *entrée* to his cases continues to come through his ownership of the Broad Street Detective Agency. Besides Travers we also regularly encounter his elegant wife, Bernice (although sometimes his independent-minded spouse is away on excursions of her own), his proverbially loyal secretary, Bertha Munney, his top Broad Street op, Hallows (another one named French, presumably inspired by Bush's late Detection Club colleague Freeman Wills Crofts, pops up occasionally), John Hill of the United Assurance Agency, who brings Travers many of his cases, and Scotland Yard's Inspector Jewle and Sergeant Matthews, who after the first of these final novels, *The Case of the Treble Twist* (in the U.S. *Triple Twist*), are promoted, respectively, to Superintendent and Inspector. (The Yard's ex-Superintendent George Wharton, now firmly retired from any form of investigative work whatsoever, is mentioned just once by Ludo, when, in *The Case of the Dead Man Gone,* he passingly imparts that he and Wharton recently had lunch together.)

For all practical purposes Travers, who during the Golden Age was a classic gentleman amateur snooper like Philo Vance and Lord Peter Wimsey, now functions fully as a professional private eye—although one, to be sure, who is rather posher than the rest. While some reviewers referred to Travers as England's Philip Marlowe, in fact he little resembles the general run of love and leave 'em/hate and beat 'em brand of brutish American P.I.'s, favoring a nice cup of coffee (a post-war change from tea), a good pipe and the occasional spot of sherry to the frequent snatches of liquor and cigarettes favored by most of his American brethren and remaining faithful to his spouse despite encountering a succession of sexy women, not all of them, shall we say, virtuously inclined.

This was a formula which throughout the period maintained a devoted audience on both sides of the Atlantic consisting, one surmises, of readers (including crime writers Anthony Berkeley, Nicholas Blake and the late Alan Hunter, creator of Inspector George Gently) who preferred their detectives something less than hard-boiled. Travers himself sneers at the hugely popular (and psychotically violent) postwar American private eye Mike Hammer, commenting of an American couple in *The Case of the Treble Twist*: "She was a woman of considerable culture; his ran about as far as Mickey Spillane" [a withering reference to Mike Hammer's creator]. Yet despite his manifest disdain for Mike Hammer, an ugly American if ever there were one, Christopher Bush and his wife Florence in the spring of 1957 had traveled to New York aboard the RMS *Queen Elizabeth,* and references by him to both the United States and Canada became more frequent in the books which followed this trip.

Certainly *The Case of the Treble Twist* (1957) features tough customers and an exceptionally cruel murder, yet it is also one of Bush's most ingeniously contrived cases from the Fifties, full of charm, treacherous deception and, yes, plenty of twists, including one that is a real sockaroo (to borrow, as Bush occasionally did, from American idiom). Similarly clever is *The Case of the Running Man* (1958), which draws, as several earlier Bush books had, on the author's profound love and knowledge of antiques. By this time Bush and his wife, their coffers having burgeoned from the proceeds of his successful mysteries, resided in the quaint medieval market town of Lavenham, Suffolk at the Great House, a splendidly decorated fourteenth-century structure with an elegant Georgian-era façade which he and Florence purchased in 1953 and resided in until their deaths. The dashing author, whom in 1967 *Chicago Tribune* mystery reviewer Alice Crombie swooningly dubbed "one of the handsomest mystery writers on either side of the Channel or Atlantic," also drove a Jaguar, beloved by James Bond films of late, well into his eighties.

The Case of the Running Man includes that Golden Age detective fiction staple, a family tree, but more originally the novel features as a major character a black American man, Sam, the devoted chauffeur of the wealthy murder victim. Sam, who reminds Ludovic Travers of Rochester, "Jack Benny's factotum of television and radio," is an interesting and sincerely treated individual, although as Anthony Boucher amusingly pronounced at the time in the *New York Times Book Review*, he speaks "a dialect never heard by mortal ear"—an odd compounding of "American Negro" and London cockney.

The Case of the Careless Thief (1959) takes Ludo to Sandbeach, "the Blackpool of the South Coast," as the American jacket blurb puts it, with "a dozen hotels, a race track, a dog track, a music hall and two enormous dance halls." Anthony Boucher deemed this hard-hitting, tricky tale, which draws to strong effect on contemporary events in England, "one of Ludovic Travers' best cases." Likewise hard-hitting are *The Case of the Sapphire Brooch* (1960) and *The Case of the Extra Grave* (1961), complex tales of murderous mésalliances with memorably grim conclusions. The plot of

The Case of the Dead Man Gone (1961) topically involves refugee relief groups, while *The Case of the Heavenly Twin* (1963) opens with a case of a creative criminal couple forging American Express Travelers Checks, concerning which Americans of a certain age will recall actor Karl Malden sternly enjoining, in a long-running television advertising campaign: "Don't leave home without them." In contrast with many of his crime writing contemporaries (judging from the tone of their work), Bush actually learned to watch and enjoy television, although in *The Case of The Three-Ring Puzzle*, a tale of violently escalating intrigue, Travers dryly references Scottish philosopher Thomas Carlyle's famous observation that England's population consisted of "mostly fools" when he comments: "I guess he wasn't too far out at that. But rather remarkable an estimate perhaps, considering that in his day there were no television commercials."

Of Bush's final five Ludovic Travers detective novels, published between 1964 and 1968, when the Western World, in the eyes of many, was going from whimsically mod to utterly mad, the best are, in my estimation, the cases of *The Jumbo Sandwich* (1965), *The Good Employer* (1966) and *The Prodigal Daughter* (1968). In *Sandwich* a crisp case of a defrauded (and jilted) gentry lady friend of Ludo's metamorphoses into a smorgasbord of, as the American book jacket puts it, "blackmail, black magic, a black sheep, and murder." It all culminates in a confrontation on a lonely Riviera beach in France, setting of some of Ludovic Travers' earliest cases, between Ludo and a desperate killer, in which Bernice plays an unexpectedly active part. Ludo again travels to France in the highly classic *Employer*, which draws most engagingly on the sleuth's (and the author's) dabbling in the world of art and is dedicated to his distinguished Lavenham artist friends, the couple Reginald and Rosalie Brill, who resided next door to Bush and his wife at the fourteenth-century Little Hall, then an art student hostel for which the Brills served as guardians. In *The Guardian* Francis Iles (aka Golden Age crime writer Anthony Berkeley) pronounced that *Employer* represented Bush "at his most ingenious."

Finally, in *Daughter* Travers finds himself tasked with recovering the absconded teenage offspring of domineering Dora Marport, sober-sided head of the organization Home and Family, which is righteously devoted to "the fostering, so to speak, of family life as the stoutest bulwark against the encroachment of ever-more numerous hostile forces: sex and violence in literature, films and on television; pornography generally, and the erosion of responsibility and the capability for sacrifice by the welfare state." Can Travers, a Great War veteran who made his debut in detective fiction in 1926, bridge the generation gap in late-Sixties London? Ludo may prefer Bach to the Beatles, but in this, the last of his recorded cases, he proves more "with it" than one might have expected. All in all, *Daughter* makes a rewarding finish to one of the longest-running and most noteworthy sleuth series in British detective fiction.

Curtis Evans

1
FIND THE MAN

As soon as Bertha Munney, our secretary-receptionist, opened the door to my room, I could see at once that the lady was out of the ordinary. Bertha, who's practically grown up with the Broad Street Detective Agency, has gradually acquired over the years a fine facility in social discrimination. Bertha could spot a duchess at the end of the street—not that I recall many duchesses. To be frank, we do quite a small amount of private business these days. Work for two insurance companies and some of the bigger stores gives us almost all the work we can comfortably handle.

But, as I said, Bertha discriminates. I hate snobbery myself but Bertha's occasional manifestations give her obviously so much pleasure that it would be stupid now to interfere with a procedure that's become established. Norris, my general manager, is a retired inspector from the Yard, so not for him the social cream. I'm a president-proprietor whose parents could afford to send him to public school and Cambridge, and so, if a duchess happened to turn up, Bertha would ensure that she was manoeuvred into my room. Norris gets the lower shelves. I don't think he's actually aware of the way things work. Or maybe he prefers things Bertha's way.

"Mrs. Wilson, sir, for her appointment."

I ran a quick eye over Mrs. Hugh Wilson as Bertha gently closed the door. I'd never seen anyone quite like her in our office. She was tall for a woman, and about her figure and bearing there was something I can only call voluptuous. I know no more than the average, reasonably well-off man about women's clothes, but I knew that hers hadn't come off any ordinary hanger. It was a fine but very cold day of December, and she was wearing a black coat trimmed at neck and cuffs with expensive-looking fur and the same fur was used for the latest in upturned pail hats. The costume had a black-and-white motif and the handbag had white ivory trimmings. If that ensemble had left much change out of a couple of hundred guineas, then my name wasn't Ludovic Travers.

I came from behind the desk to greet her. "Glad you could come, Mrs. Wilson. Would you care to take off your coat? It's quite warm in here."

"Just loosen it. I think," she said, and gave me quite a nice smile. "I don't think our business will take very long."

I caught the faint perfume of her as I held the chair. She was probably about thirty: a brunette with as lovely a complexion as one would see even on a long Irish day. Her voice had been quite pleasant and very assured. Of the usual client nervousness there was never a trace.

I took my seat behind the desk.

"You'll pardon me if I ask what may be a rather foolish question." she said, "but are you a detective yourself? Or do you employ people?"

I smiled.

"I suppose you might call me a working employer. My name's Travers, by the way."

"Yes, your receptionist told me. But she didn't say you were an actual detective." She gave me another charming smile. "I mean . . . well, you don't look like one."

How true she was. I'm well over six feet and what my old nurse used to call "one of Pharaoh's lean kine". I also have a toothbrush moustache and wear heavy, horn-rimmed glasses.

"Maybe not," I told her. "I don't look much like the television detective but the criminals also these days have a habit of not looking like criminals. So you see it's a sort of Greek meet Greek."

"How nicely put," she said. "And you yourself could handle whatever it is I'd like you to do?"

I tried another smile. "Naturally that depends on what the assignment actually is. I never disguise myself these days and go into opium dens, for instance."

She laughed. "I'm afraid you're making fun of me. But, seriously, it's quite a simple thing I'd like you to do. I want you to find somebody."

"I see." I drew the pad towards me. "Would you care to give me the fullest possible particulars?"

"This will be in the strictest confidence?"

"Absolutely so. If you wish it. it can remain something between you and just myself. Integrity, Mrs. Wilson, is the absolute life-blood of an agency like this. Which reminds me. Why did you actually come to us? Were you recommended, or what?" I tried yet another smile. "We always like to know. It sort of boosts our morale."

"Actually you were recommended by a former client," she said. "I'm afraid I'm not allowed to tell you her name."

"In any case it's nice to hear. And now about this person you want us to find."

"I'm doing this on behalf of a relative who'd never be able to afford your fees. I've let him understand simply that I'll do my best to find this man who once did him a great favour. The name of the man is Richard Sambord. He was a music-hall artist and called himself The Great Sambrino."

"Wait a moment," I said. "The Great Sambrino. I think I actually saw him some years ago. Didn't he do a kind of Houdini act?"

"Something of the kind, I believe. Later I think he was sent to prison for some offence or other, and after that he seems to have disappeared."

"And what would his age be now?"

"Well, I imagine about fifty. He was rather on the short side. I'm told, and spare in build. Apparently he had to be that way on account of his act."

"And you haven't the least idea where he might possibly be?"

"No idea whatever. As I told you, he seems to have dropped completely out. We're practically certain he's no longer doing any music-hall act."

That assignment was almost child's-play. I couldn't tell the client so, but I had sources of information that ought to unearth the missing Sambrino inside forty-eight hours. It doesn't do to make a job too easy, and it isn't ethical to spin one out for the sake of a fee. And this was one of those jobs, and I had to think pretty quickly in case she mentioned our charges. And she did mention them, straight away.

"Well," I told her reflectively, "I think we can find this man for you inside a week, so may I quote a kind of flat rate? Seventy-five pounds. If we find him quickly, well, that'll be our good fortune.

If it should take a bit longer, that'll be just our bad luck, though I should tell you that if we haven't found him after, say, ten days, then we'll have to throw the case up. If we haven't found him by then, in my considered judgment we'll never find him. That strikes you as fair?"

"Very fair indeed. The seventy-five pounds is inclusive of everything? Things like expenses?"

"Absolutely so. And now, Mrs. Wilson, I don't think you gave our receptionist your address when you telephoned."

"There isn't an actual address," she told me calmly. "I do an enormous amount of travelling. I'm flying to Paris, for instance, this afternoon and then touring the French provinces almost at once. What I suggest is this. I definitely shan't be back in ten days, and so you might put the address, when you have it, or the man's whereabouts, with the name Wilson, in the *New York Times*. It's being published now, as you probably know, simultaneously in New York, London and Paris. I can always acquire a copy anywhere in France. You insert the notice through London."

"I'll do exactly that," I said. "Just that Wilson's new address is so-and-so."

"That'd be just perfect," she told me delightedly.

She took some banknotes from her bag and laid them on the desk. "I think you'll find that just right."

I typed an official receipt. It was also a form of contract in which, for the sum received, the Broad Street Detective Agency agreed to spend not more than ten days in finding the whereabouts of a Richard Sambord. She read it and still seemed quite happy.

"Just one other thing, Mr. Travers. This man Sambord is on no account to know that anyone's looking for him. Can you guarantee that?"

"Most certainly."

"And, of course, I'm not to be mentioned in any way whatever."

"You can rely on that, too."

"Thank you," she told me quietly. "I'm very grateful to you."

"It's a pleasure to have so amenable and—if I may say so—so charming a client."

She smiled but she didn't blush. Somehow she struck me as the kind of woman who didn't do much blushing. After that we rather solemnly shook hands, and I pushed the bell for Bertha. The last I saw of Mrs. Hugh Wilson was the swirl of a fur-trimmed coat as she went through the door.

It's a good thing in my job to deduce what one can about a client. A failure to do that has more than once involved us in quite a lot of trouble. Not that there seemed a lot of deduction crying out to be done in the case of Mrs. Hugh Wilson. The whole thing, too, had been a cash transaction. Whatever happened, nothing— from our point of view—could go wrong.

All the same, she'd been quite an unusual client. No nerves, as I've said, and a refreshing candour and directness about what she wanted. I'd heard from her just as much as was needed, and I'd made no enquiries about her private life because, in the circumstances, that would have been as good as impertinent. For all that, I couldn't help wondering just what she was, and my final guess was some business executive. That tour of hers in France sounded like a business one, and there'd been her general manner to back the theory up. Throughout, she'd used a minimum of words in coming directly to a point.

Naturally I wondered for a moment how a woman like that could have a relative who wanted to repay a favour from The Great Sambrino, but when I dissociated the woman herself from the half-hour she'd spent in my room, it didn't seem all that unusual. People do have queer relatives: I've one or two myself. In any case I began thinking about Sambrino himself and that night when I'd seen him. As far as I remembered, it was at the Palladium and not too long after the last war. I remembered I was entertaining a client and he, like myself, was a music-hall fan.

The Great Sambrino had been the star turn. I seemed to remember that when the curtain went back, he'd been on the stage clad only in a bath-robe and bathing trunks and behind him was a tank of water and, behind that, an enormous white-faced clock with just one hand—a second hand. A couple of attendants in elaborate Indian costumes stood on either side and, when the initial applause had died down, one took the bath-robe and the other placed a stool in front of the tank. Sambrino made the usual theatrical gestures, mounted the stool and entered the tank, and concealed Lights came on to show him as he swam. A minute went by and he was still swimming. Two minutes and you could feel the tension. Three minutes and it was getting unbearable, and yet Sambrino swam slowly round and round that tank like an immense fish. Applause, maybe to relieve the tension, burst out and, as the clock showed four minutes exactly, Sambrino emerged.

The tank was removed and what looked like a huge box with stout glass sides was wheeled on in its place. The lower foot of the interior was verified as ordinary earth by two observers invited up from the audience. Sambrino reappeared and another smaller box was brought on. It was examined and pronounced to be merely a stout, wooden box. Sambrino squeezed his body into it and the box was tilted to show how tightly he fitted. The lid was put on and looked to be as good as air-tight.

That box was put in the centre of the larger one, then the attendants brought on sacks of earth till Sambrino was enclosed by a foot of earth all round him. The huge container was made to revolve while once more the seconds ticked by. When four minutes had gone, sufficient earth was removed for the smaller box to be taken out. The lid was lifted and Sambrino slowly uncoiled himself. When he had entered that box he had been wearing just a green loin-cloth. Now he was wearing a red one and he was also smoking a cigarette!

My description, of course, is just a bit bare. What you have to add is the slick presentation, the skilful lighting and the music. At any rate, that was Sambrino's act as I remembered it, and now he was a man I had to find. It was a job I wanted to do myself, not so much because we were short-handed as that I hadn't had a worthwhile outdoor job for over a month. Also I knew already of two methods of approach, so I went through to Norris's room and told him what I knew about the new assignment.

"Couldn't you do something about that prison term Mrs. Wilson mentioned?" I said to him. "Some old friend of yours at the Yard might know something."

"As a matter of fact I remember something myself," he said. "I didn't have anything to do with it personally, but—well, give me a minute while I think back."

I lighted my pipe while his brow puckered in thought. He gave himself a congratulatory nod.

"I think I've got it. This Sambrino, or whatever he called himself, used to throw his weight about a lot, and one night he'd been drinking in one of those posh bars in the West End and he got into an argument with some fellow or other and ended up by striking him on the head repeatedly with a heavy, gold-headed walking-stick he used to carry. This chap died in hospital and Sambrino got two years for manslaughter."

"Must have been about ten years ago when he went in," I said. "You find out where and if he had any special visitors. Just possible the Prisoners' Aid Society might tell us something about when he came out. We've got to follow him up from the day he was turned loose."

I went back to my room and rang Tom Holberg. Tom's a very old friend indeed, but I wanted him because his is the best theatrical agency in town. I was lucky to catch him between clients, and Ruth, his secretary, put me through. I asked him if he could lunch with me. Something was temporarily wrong, he said, with his insides and he was having a sandwich and milk in his room. I offered to bring a sandwich myself and keep him company. Maybe it was the novelty of the idea that made him tell me to come along.

For years Tom and I have done each other favours, but somehow he always insists that his is the credit balance. I'd taken him one of those enormous cigars he favours, and when he'd lighted up after our rather amusing scratch meal, I told him what I wanted. He went across to one of the filing cabinets and came back with a photograph.

"That's Sambrino as he was ten years ago."

The photograph showed a man of the build my client of the morning had briefly described: probably five feet seven or eight in height and a hundred and forty pounds weight. That night when I'd seen him in person I'd been in the upper circle so that everything on the stage had been fore-shortened. In the photograph he was fully clothed: to use a term of the nineties, he was dressed up to the nines—light topper at an angle, dark jacket with handkerchief showing from the breast pocket: light, flowered waistcoat and light trousers with white spats. The quite handsome face was tilted superciliously back, and the gloved hands were on the handle of a walking-stick.

"A professional take," Tom said. "I nearly handled him myself once. Not that I lost very much. He didn't last all that long."

"Who *was* his agent?"

He had a look at some notes on the back of the photograph and told me it was Benny Rose.

"You ever meet Sambrino personally?"

"No," he said. "Maybe I know plenty about him. It always pays to make enquiries. The publicity they send you—" He shrugged his shoulders to show what it was worth.

"I've taken on the job of finding him," I said. "That's just between ourselves, by the way. You've no idea where he is now?"

He shook his head, thought for a moment, then picked up the receiver. "Ruth, get me Benny Rose."

He cupped the receiver and leaned forward. "Like me, Benny has ulcers."

Ulcers or not, Benny was available. I gathered that Sambrino's whereabouts were unknown.

"Tell me all about him." Tom said. "No. I've got plenty of time. . . . Maybe he comes into some money and I've got a lawyer here who wants to give it to him."

Tom listened for a good five minutes, said he was much obliged and hung up.

"Now," he told me. "we can put together what I know and what Benny knows and maybe it will help."

Sambrino, it seemed, was English. His father had been a baritone and his mother a soubrette. They'd had relatives in America and had gone there when their son was in his early teens and had tried their luck as a double act. The young Sambord had made a modest start in the profession by becoming assistant to a certain Lambelli, who'd then had the act which Sambord was later to use himself. Sambord progressed sufficiently to act occasionally as

Lambelli's understudy, and when Lambelli died in 1948, Sambord brought the act to England and, with certain modifications, used it as his own.

He did uncommonly well. At the height of his short career he was making two hundred and fifty pounds a week, which must have left him plenty after expenses, even if he did run an office with a secretary to handle correspondence. But, according to Rose, he was an exhibitionist and spent lavishly, and he soon began to drink more than was good for his act. He'd got married—Benny thought it was to his secretary—but his wife left him almost at once, which might have accounted for the drinking. Then came that brutal assault and two years, less remissions, in jail, after which he was finished as far as England was concerned. Benny was positive he'd gone to the Continent, and the very last heard of him was that he was working with a second-rate circus in Germany.

"And there was I, thinking I had a pretty soft assignment on my hands," I told Tom ruefully. "Lord knows where I'm going to begin. What do you suggest? Trying the German agencies?"

"If you've got only ten days, you might as well give it up now," he said. "I mean if you're going to try Germany." He shrugged his shoulders. "My idea is he might have gone back to the States."

"Or drunk himself to death long ago."

Tom shrugged his shoulders again.

"Who knows? You can wait a day or two while I make more enquiries?"

That was how we left things. I went back to Broad Street to see if Norris had had more luck than I. He hadn't. The P.A.S. knew nothing about Sambrino. As for finding out what visitors Sambrino had had while in jail, a lot of red-tape would have to be cut through before the prison authorities would part with information like that. But for the fact that Tom Holberg was probably doing the same thing, I'd probably have spent the rest of the day ringing London and provincial agencies.

And so to the next morning: mid-morning to be precise, when Bertha had brought me coffee. Her buzzer went and Tom was on the line.

"I think I've found your man for you." he told me in his mild way. "It's largely hearsay, so maybe you'd better verify it, but I'm told he's with Fred Granding's circus. They're in winter quarters. A little place called Wishington, in Essex."

"I can't thank you enough, Tom," I said. "How you did it I don't know. But thanks again, Tom. Some day I may try to do as much for you."

"It was nothing," he said. "Just let me know if you find him."

It was quite a long time later that Tom Holberg told me just how he'd unearthed Sambord. Benny Rose, as Sambrino's agent, would be responsible for the whole act, so Tom had had the idea that Benny might know the names of those two fake Indian assistants. Benny checked and one was named Granding. Benny didn't spot the significance of the name, so Tom, having in mind what I'd said about secrecy, had a friend get into touch with Granding. Even though the friend said he was an American buddy of Sambord, Granding was cagey. All he would say was that he *might* have seen Sambord recently.

"It was a fine job all the same," I said, and then I had to laugh. I'd been supposed to be the detective, so, if at any time Tom wanted a new job. . . .

He just smiled dryly. He said it was nothing. Just a routine job. He was always making enquiries about this and that.

"Besides," he said, "one or two other people had the brains to find him sooner than we did."

He shook his head slowly as he thought of something else: something that ended with a kind of epitaph.

"Too bad Sambord had to die the way he did. He used to have a pretty good act."

2

ASSIGNMENT FINISHED

I often envy some of our own operatives. Perhaps it's a kind of carry-over from the exploits of detectives about whom I used to read in my youth: at any rate, I still have a secret urge to don false whiskers and do some tracking and trailing on my own. Strictly between ourselves, I've even thought of using contact lenses instead of the horn-rims which would be sure to betray me. I'd also have a clean shave. Provided my wife was away on a long holiday. I'd even have a Yul Brynner done to my head. I could pad myself to disguise the spareness and I could acquire a stoop to lessen my height, but the trouble is that I could never rise to all those efforts at one particular time. And there's often more fun in day-dreams than in reality.

But I did do a modest amount of disguising for that visit to Wishington. The village was so small as not to appear in the motoring handbook and the railway that passed just north simply ignored it, but once you were clear of the outer suburbs, it was only a drive of some twenty-five miles. I wore for the occasion an old tweed suit that Bernice, my wife, had ordered me to discard quite a few years back, and I unearthed an old fishing hat to go with it. My garage lent me an oldish car, and all that to be in keeping with a none-too-prosperous free-lance journalist. We have a little printing press at the office and Bertha ran off half-a-dozen appropriate cards. L. Travers was the name, and the address had to be my own flat and the telephone number my own. No one in Wishington would be likely to check any of that in town: on the other hand I might want someone down there to ring me up.

I'd also done some research on the Granding Circus. It was smallish but select. It didn't tour the big cities but kept itself to medium-sized provincial towns. It didn't run to more than a couple of elephants but it had lions, and its ponies were specially good. It also managed to have good acts—trick-cyclists, illusionists, acrobats and performing animals—and I was assured that quite a few of the topliners, now with the world's biggest, had begun in the Granding Circus.

It was about half-past ten that morning when I drove slowly into the little village. The core of it was nothing more than a scattering of houses along the side road, with a post office, a couple of shops and a pub, the Jolly Waggoners. A smaller side road, little more than a track, led to the church. In the flattish country as I'd neared the village, I'd also seen one or two farms. It had been a shocking summer and plenty of stubbles were unploughed.

I drew up at the post-office-general-store and bought some stamps. I had a word or two with the woman in charge about the weather. Off-handedly as I could I mentioned the Granding Circus. I gathered it had winter-quartered near the village for the last five years.

"How's Fred these days?"

"Fred?" She smiled. "Oh, you mean Mr. Granding. He's just his usual self. He comes in pretty regularly."

"I'd rather like to see him again. Which way is his place?"

"Oh, you keep on for about half-a-mile and take the Winterford road. It's what used to be a farm, Drove Farm, on the left."

Five minutes later I was at a gate to the top bar of which was fixed a large notice—STRICTLY PRIVATE. I drove on a bit. reversed and came back to the gate. A private road went round to my left and through the bare-leaved gaps of elms I could see quite a few buildings. I moved the car on and left it on the verge in the lee of a tall straggling thorn hedge. The gate wasn't locked. I had about four hundred yards to go and I walked pretty briskly. It was cold with a north-east wind, but there'd been no ancient overcoat to match my suit.

As I neared the buildings and the road went even more left, I could see the transport park: the huge trucks and conveyers that got the circus around. More towards the cluster of buildings there were half-a-dozen caravans. From the shelter of a nearer hedge I wasn't fifty yards from the old farmhouse and could read the notice above the front door.

THE GRANDING CIRCUS
OFFICE

F. GRANDING, PROPRIETOR.

As I stood there the wind brought a farmyard whiff of animals and dung. From somewhere behind the house a horse suddenly neighed and I could hear women's voices.

I sheered away to the right and came round the end of an enormous barn. In an open space between it and a range of large

Nissen huts, a couple of young women were exercising a team of tiny pinto ponies in a straw-covered ring. I walked on towards the Nissen huts. A girl in jeans and pullover emerged from the nearest door. She was carrying a pitchfork. I must have looked rather startled, for she laughed.

"Looking for anyone? Or do you want the office?"

She had a perky, Cockney voice.

"As a matter of fact I was. Mr. Sambord about anywhere?"

"Oh, him," she said. It might have been my imagination, but the voice had a certain contempt. "Probably in that caravan over there. The small blue one."

It was an old-fashioned caravan of the gipsy type. The half-door was open, and as I began mounting the steps, a man looked out and I knew it was the man I'd come to find. The man of the photograph was there, and no more. His hair was almost white and his cheeks thinner. The veining of the slightly bulbous nose showed a heavy drinker.

"Mr. Sambord?"

His head went back in that same imperious gesture of the photograph.

"Yes. What d'you want?"

"I want to give you some money."

He stared.

"May I come up?" I said. "Then I can explain it."

Maybe I ought first to explain something to you. I'd found Sambord, so why didn't I make some excuse and get back to town instead of going up those steps and into the caravan? Behind everything, of course, was my insatiable curiosity: interest in Sambord himself and the thought that perhaps he might let fall something about that client of mine of the previous morning. But whatever the cause, I went up and in. It was a tiny place: just room for a bed, a chair, a cupboard for crockery and a miniature kitchen at the far end with a sink, a cooking ring and a tiny electric stove, both fed by a wire from outside. Everything was clean. Sambord himself was clean. He'd shaved, and the only dirty thing about him was his nails.

He began moving the chair for me and, as soon as he looked round, I handed him my card and began talking fast. As he saw, I was a free-lance journalist, engaged at the moment in writing a series of articles on the great music-hall acts of the past. I ran off a string of names: conjurers or illusionists every one of them.

"And you, Mr. Sambord—or should I call you Sambrino?—were one of the greatest. I saw you at the Palladium and I've never forgotten it, so what I'd like you to do is give me a few facts about your career."

I'd counted five one-pound notes and I laid them on the bed, within my reach, not his.

"I'm not that well-off myself," I was running on, "but you're entitled to compensation for the use of your time and—well, that's just about as much as I can afford. So will you tell me about your-self, and why you retired and what your plans are and so on?"

I don't know what there is about me that makes people confide in me, but they do. Sambord talked and talked, and every now and again his look would shift from me to that small pile of notes. As far as he knew, I was taking everything down in shorthand, and more than once he told me to be sure to remember this or that. He still had a slight American accent, and in some queer way it made the whole egotistical recital less bizarre. But it still remained pathetic. If ever a man was professionally dead, it was Sambord, but he just wouldn't lie down.

"Why did you suddenly disappear from the English music-hall scene?" I asked him during one brief pause.

He gave me a quick look, then made up his mind that I didn't know. He gave a sad shake of the head.

"A whole train of misfortunes. First my wife died suddenly. We were a devoted couple and it brought on a nervous break-down. When I slowly recovered I found that my nerves had been affected. You saw my act, sir, and you know what that meant to anyone like myself. Since then I've been slowly recuperating. Every day I feel myself getting—well, back to what I used to be."

"And you're still recuperating here?"

"Convalescing is the word," he told me reprovingly. "Getting into shape for a come-back. My old friend Granding invited me here for just that purpose."

"This is wonderful news!" I told him. "You mean we're actually going to see you in public again?"

"That's strictly between ourselves," he said. "Can't mention any dates of course. And there's the question of expenses. It costs more than peanuts to get an act of mine going."

"Too true," I said, and smiled. I passed him the notes. "This is only a small contribution towards it. And may I wish you the best of luck."

"There's nothing else you want to know?"

"You've got my address and telephone number, so if there's anything else you'd like to have me mention, just write me or telephone."

His head suddenly moved and his tongue went slowly across his bluish lips. He craned up as if to peer round the partly opened top of the half-door. His voice was urgent.

"How'd you come here? By car?"

"Yes," I said. "Why? You want a lift to town?"

"Where'd you leave it?"

"Near the main gate."

His voice had been getting lower: now it was almost a whisper.

"I'll meet you there as soon as I can."

He made a gesture of warning and waved for me to leave. As soon as I looked out of that door I knew why. A middle-aged man in riding breeches and turtle-necked pullover was practically on us. Sambord was giving me a gentle push as if to urge me down the steps.

"No, sir, I can't show you round without Mr. Granding's permission. You'll have to see him if you want—" He broke artistically off. "Ah, there you are, Fred! I was just telling this gentleman—"

"That's all right, Dick." There was something ironic about the smile. "I'll see to it. Come along with me, sir, will you?"

Granding had broadened out since his days with Sambrino. He was about five feet ten and his red face had a country look. He didn't say a word till we were round the near end of the barn and a stone's-throw from the back of the house. Then he stopped dead in his tracks and turned to face me.

"What's all this about?"

I gave him a card and handed him the same spiel I'd tried on Sambord.

"I see."

He looked at the card again, stuck it in his hip pocket and gave me a nod.

"Let's go to my office."

There was an alert-looking woman of about forty working at one of the desks as we went in. Granding asked her to bring us some coffee.

"Now what's all this really about?" he wanted to know, and waved a brusque hand at a chair.

I told him just what I'd told him before. I added that an American friend who'd known Sambord in the old days had given me the tip that I might find him at Wishington. It seemed a lucky piece that fitted the jigsaw to his satisfaction.

The coffee came in. The secretary waited. Granding said he'd let her know when he was free.

"You look as if you might be a square-shooter," he told me. "You and I are going to make a deal. Tell me what Dick Sambord told you."

I shrugged my shoulders resignedly, took out my notebook and made as if reading. Granding listened impassively. Once or twice there was a slight frown.

"Now let me talk," he said. "Sambrino never was in the same class as Houdini and those others you've mentioned. He might have earned big money for a couple of years, but what's that? Did you pay him anything, by the way?"

"Just a small sum. After all, I was using his time."

"His time!" He gave a dry laugh. "All right then, Mr. Travers"—he pronounced it Trayvers—"I'll come right to the point. I'm prepared to pay you ten pounds for your time and so on if you don't go on with this . . . after you've heard what I've got to tell you."

"I don't want your ten pounds," I told him with a pretence of indignation. "I've got my own ideas about what's right and what's not, and I'm not so hard up as all that. All you've got to do is convince me, and that'll be the end of it. And I'll give you my solemn word."

I liked Granding. There was something John-Bullish, some natural integrity about him. I won't go over the things you already know but pick up his story much later.

"I missed him when he came out of jail. I'd intended to meet him but I got the date wrong and lost him altogether. I did hear he was in Frankfurt but I wasn't in any position then to throw up a job and go hunting for him. I had a job with my Uncle Bill. He started this circus—much smaller then, of course—and always wanted me to work for him, so when Sambord faded, I did. Two years later my uncle died in an accident and I came in for the circus. He also left a bit of money and I used it to expand. That's really how I came to run across Dick Sambord again."

"I wonder if you could tell me something," I cut in. "What in heaven's name made him run amuck in that bar?"

"I never did get the real truth about it," he told me. "He had a little office in town and a secretary and we—that's the other chap I worked with—never had any reason to go there. He married his secretary, you know. All very hush-hush. No one knew a thing about it till it was all over. I do know that she left him flat about a month afterwards and word got around that he'd got himself into some mess or other with a woman in America before he came over here. Reckon his wife found out about it, but you can bet that's what it was that drove him crackers. I seem to remember a rumour that he employed a detective agency to find her but he had no luck. We'd known something was wrong a week or two before it happened."

"I get it. And how'd you happen to run across him again?"

"I'll tell you. But don't put me down as one of them Good Samaritans or anything like that. Sambord was a good boss. He always treated me right, and more than right. At any rate I was in Hamburg looking over an act or two I was hoping to bring back here, when I happened to ask about Sambord. Don't ask me why: I just happened to ask, and before you could snap your eyes I found out where he was—in a German doss-house. That was just over two years ago. He was soaked in drink so I got him into a German version of Alcoholics Anonymous and said I'd pick him up when they gave the word, which they did. That was about nine months ago. I had him with me on the road—had him do odd jobs—and now he's here. Sometimes I wish he was a million miles away, and then I know if I kicked him out I'm that damn soft-hearted I'd go and fetch him again."

"He's let you badly down?"

He shrugged his shoulders. "Had one relapse, or nearly a relapse. Slipped away to the Waggoners one evening and was just through his first double whisky when I got there. Now I have a private arrangement with the landlord. He's allowed one pint of beer any morning and no more. Any funny business and I'm rung up at once. So far he's kept to that pretty well. No use in making him go absolutely teetotal. If I can get him to stick to that pint of beer, then I reckon he's cured."

"Makes sense to me," I said. "Is he any help to you here?" He smiled a bit ruefully. "To tell the truth, he's little more'n a damn nuisance. I had him helping with the ponies, then I had to switch him to giving a hand in the stables. He's like the husband who doesn't want to wash up. You know, keeps on breaking plates. And he will throw his weight about. Keeps on reminding my staff what he was. People don't like that. Now I let him loaf along in that caravan. Oh, and another thing. He tried to get you to think he was making a come-back. Did he go into details?"

"Just hinted at it: no more."

He snorted. "You saw him. He's got as much chance of getting back as I'd have of doing a Blondin. But that's what he's been doing lately. He tried to get Bob Fisher, my head man, to find out what a set of props would cost like what he used to have for his act, and Bob passed the word to me. Something's happened to him. I can't put my finger on it. or anywhere near, but he's up to something. I wouldn't be surprised if he's got hold of some money somewhere."

"You know him better than I do, Mr. Granding, but he's a pretty crafty customer. Look at the way he tried to hoodwink you about why I was in that caravan."

"Well, I don't like it," he said. "George Farmer—that's the landlord of the Waggoners I was telling you about—George reckoned there was some other stranger he saw Dick hobnobbing with. A fellow about your own age. One thing I'm afraid of is there's a swindle being worked: someone being kidded there's money in that old act, or something like that."

"Might be just that," I said. "After all, it was a good act." He gave me a quick look. The dry smile came again. "Like most illusions it kidded the public pretty cleverly. You'll keep it under your hat if I tell you something?"

"I certainly will."

"Well," he said, "the original act belonged to a freak named Ed Lambert. Three-and-a-half minutes is the proven record for staying under water, but this Lambert is reckoned to be the only man who could stay four. He was in show business and he developed the act. Called himself The Great Lambelli. Toured the States with it for years, and part of that time Dick Sambord was his chief assistant,' only Dick could never make the four. So over here he had to work by that clock that showed the seconds. The audience would be concentrating on him more than the time, if you know what I mean, so they wouldn't check by their watches. Only the stage was lighted in any case."

"The hand of that clock was made to go fast?"

He laughed. "Isn't that what I've been trying to tell you? He was actually in that tank for under three-and-a-half minutes, which was just what he'd been timed to make."

I had to laugh too. I was one of those who'd been fooled. "Everything's legitimate," he reminded me. "Your job is to gull the public. The same with that buried-alive act. That depended on manoeuvring a couple of the right kind of people on the stage for the simple reason that the inner box was a trick one. Just before it was covered, a signal was flashed to show it was working, which meant that slats in the inside would slide back and leave very fine-meshed wire for air to come through. Also, he wasn't so tightly packed as it looked. That was another illusion. He actually had quite a lot of freedom of movement. Even I could have done it, as I was then. Couldn't do it now, of course."

"Just shows you," I said. "I'd have sworn on a stack of Bibles everything was genuine. But couldn't you use that act yourself? With Sambord's permission?"

"Not all that easy. I'm not so sure now that he didn't pull a fast one bringing that act over here at all. There was some talk about it being the property of Ed Lambert's widow. You'd never get the facts out of Dick Sambord."

Something just a bit theatrical seemed called for. In the brief silence I went across to the open fire, ripped some pages from my notebook and watched them burn.

"Well, that's that," I said resignedly. "There'll be no article about The Great Sambrino.

"It's been a pleasure meeting you, Mr. Granding," I went on, "and I'm only too sorry if I've caused you any trouble."

"No trouble at all." He held out his hand. "Now let me pay your out-of-pocket expenses."

"Well, if you insist. Ten bob for my petrol. That'll be plenty."

"Let's make it a quid."

Before I could stop him he had a note in my hand and his hand over it to keep it there. Then he showed me out by the front door.

"Time I went back on my rounds." he told me. "Might see what his lordship is up to. Mind you drop in, by the way, if you happen to be anywhere near."

It had been one of the most interesting mornings of my life and I couldn't help chuckling to myself at how well everything had worked out. Then, as I realised how cold that wind was after the comfort of Granding's office, I began to wonder. There ought to be money in that act, whoever owned it. Was some syndicate or other trying to acquire it? And—I as good as stopped in my tracks at the thought—was my client of the previous morning anything to do with that syndicate?

When I saw her again in my mind's eye, the idea wasn't so good, and, in any case, I was nearing the gate. I went through, closed it carefully and moved on to my car. A man emerged through a gap in the hedge.

"Thought you were never coming," he told me reproachfully.

I'd hardly have recognised him. In the caravan he'd been wearing the standard pullover with flannel bags and slippers: now he had a dark overcoat below which were dark blue trousers and clean shoes. The coat collar was turned up against the wind but he had no hat.

I waved for him to get in, started the engine and said I'd been engaged.

"What did Granding want to know?"

I didn't like his tone. I drove as far as the turn to the main road before I answered him.

"Is it any real business of yours what Mr. Granding and I talked about?"

"It was if you were talking about *me*."

"Oh, for heaven's sake! Why should we want to talk about you? You told me all I wanted to know."

He hunched himself back in his corner and we were almost at the pub before he let himself be placated.

"About that article. You'll let me have a copy? I can pay for it, you know."

"No need for that," I told him, and slowed the car down.

"Got the time on you?"

"A quarter-past twelve."

He clicked his tongue annoyedly. As the car stopped in the parking place outside the pub he had the window down and was peering out. A dark saloon car that looked like a '57 Jaguar was just beyond us by the side of the road, and headed west.

"Thanks for the lift," Sambord told me hurriedly. He made his way, cautiously it seemed to me, towards that dark saloon. A man in a Homburg hat—I got the impression he was elderly— just peered from the car's opened window, then waved a hand. Sambord got into the car and at once it moved off.

It was no skin off my nose—or was it? I decided to think it over. Maybe Sambord had gone somewhere for good. Or had he? The test would be if he came back, and that was why I decided to have a meal. The landlord found me cold ham and bread, and I sat in a corner with a pint of bitter and watched some dart players and listened to the general talk. A quarter of an hour went by and Sambord hadn't come back, at least not in that car. I knew. From my seat I could see the whole stretch of road through the window. And if he had gone for good, then, I kept telling myself, the whole morning was wasted.

I managed to stay on till nearly one o'clock and then Sambord did come back. The car dropped him just short of the pub, reversed and moved off in the direction of town, and I'd caught just another glimpse of the heavy-jowled man who was driving it.

I slipped out of the room just as Sambord was coming in. The post-office had closed, so I couldn't telephone from there. In any case there didn't seem all that hurry, so I left it till I came to a callbox in the next village. Granding himself came on the line.

"Very good of you," he said. "I thought something was up when I was told he'd been slipping round behind the huts."

"Any connection, do you think, with that other man you said he'd been seen with?"

"Oh, no. This is something new. That other man was the kind we're often bothered with. Trying to pump Sambord about me supplying an act or two for some charity do or other. George Farmer rang me about that not long after you'd left. This is different. I don't like that business about going off in a car. Between you and me we'll keep a pretty strict eye on him from now on."

That, as I knew, concluded the case of Richard Sambord. Only one thing remained. A special ad. appeared two days later in the *New York Times*.

> *WILSON sends birthday greetings from Drove Farm, Wishington, Essex.*

3
UNEXPECTED CALL

IT WAS a Monday morning five days later and I was in my room at the agency when a call came for me. I spotted the voice at once: that of a very old friend of mine, Superintendent Jewle.

"Haven't seen hide or hair of you for a long time," I said. "Where've you been."

"Oh, here and there," he told me rather quickly. "Want you to do something very urgently. I'm speaking from Ambourne. You know it?"

"Been through it dozens of times. Why?"

"I'll tell you when I see you, but I want you to get down here as fast as you can make it. Turn sharp right at the Hare and Hounds and go on to the T-head at the river, then turn right again. I'll be at River Cottage, about a couple of hundred yards on. All right?"

I mumbled something and then he rang off. A minute or two later I told Norris what had happened.

"Time to try and find out anything?"

He said he'd see. I went back to my room, had a wash, put on overcoat and hat, waited another minute and then went back. Norris was just ringing off.

He's somewhat secretive about his sources of information at the Yard.

"Says it's something serious. Might be murder. They haven't the facilities down there, so anything important and the Yard's practically automatically called in. Jewle and Matthews left just after ten o'clock so they can't have been there long."

It was lucky I'd brought my car along that morning. As soon as the northern traffic thinned I tried to do some thinking but there was nothing whatever to go on and I gave it up as a waste of mental effort. I turned into the arterial road and made faster time. It's only twenty miles to Ambourne from town and only forty minutes had passed when I turned right at the Hare and Hounds. Another two minutes and I was drawing my car in behind a couple of others at River Cottage.

It was a quiet road with houses well spaced to the right and the river immediately to my left. Trees ran along that pleasant road to the right with the gardens of the houses set well back. In the summer it must have been quite a charming spot. That morning a north wind was blowing clean down it and there wasn't a tree that had a leaf.

You couldn't call River Cottage a cottage in the accepted sense. It had traces of an old, half-timbered building with fairly recent modernisations. A wing thrown out towards the back was very definitely almost new, as was the largish garage to the left. The whole property lay back some twenty yards from the road and only a long bed of flowers, now blackened by frost, separated its stretch of lawn from the quiet road. Everything about the house looked in good order. There wasn't a weed on the gravelled drive to the garage or on the path that turned sharp right from it to the front door. It was open. The plain-clothes man on guard held up a hand.

"Travers," I said. "The superintendent's expecting me."

"Through to the left, sir."

I went through to a comfortably furnished lounge. Not a soul was there, but as I halted just inside I heard voices above me and the movement of feet. From where I was I took a look round. I suppose it was a kind of instinct to be cautious, but all I could gather was that the french window led to a rain-soaked garden and that one could get to where I was by a path between garage and house.

I went through the door to my right and was in an incongruously placed cloak-room. At least it seemed so till I recognised that the new wing in which I stood had been added in order to provide amenities for what had once been just a small, four-roomed cottage. Stairs led upwards and the voices were now fairly clear.

"Anyone there?"

My voice seemed startlingly loud. There was a hush and then quick steps, and Matthews was looking down at me from the landing.

"Hallo there, sir! Be with you in a moment."

I'd known Jewle, and worked with him, since he was first made inspector and Matthews even before he was made sergeant. Both had moved well up since then. Something had gone, perhaps, from the old free and easy relationships, but underneath was something that even red tape couldn't quite strangle. Who the third man was that came with them down the stairs I didn't know till Jewle had introduced him—Inspector Brass of the local C.I.D.

"Well now, what's all this about?" I asked the three of them.

"We'd just like you to see if you can identify a certain individual," Jewle told me quietly. He's one of those big, burly men who seem unaware of just how big they are. He's rarely flustered and you just as rarely hear him raise his voice. Matthews, tall and lean, is a more mercurial type—or was. He's sobered down a lot since I first knew him.

"Glad to help," I said. "Where is he, or she?"

"Quite handy," he said. "Just through here."

He led the way through a door at the far end of that cloakroom and, just as I followed him through, I was suddenly shooting through space. If I hadn't hurtled into Jewle's back I'd have taken a real purler. Everyone was solicitous as I dusted my knees.

"Damn that threshold!" Jewle said. "That parquet has worked itself up. I nearly came a cropper there this morning. You sure you're all right?"

I was, and I was taking a quick look round. The room was obviously a study or den. Another door to the left opened on the back garden which was overlooked by a large window. There were a couple of leather-covered easy chairs and, by the far wall, a desk. In the angle beyond it was a stout safe, of the kind that opens with a key. Its door was partly open. Then I saw two other things: first a swivel chair standing against the wall beyond the flat-topped desk and, between desk and chair, a something on the floor: a shape covered by a travelling rug. Jewle went forward and drew the rug carefully off.

The man looked about fifty. The right eye had gone where probably a bullet had struck it, and blood disfigured the whole upturned side of the heavy, greyish face. The dark clothes looked expensive as did the gold watch on his out-flung wrist. As I saw it, in the brief moment before Jewle spoke again, that man had been behind the desk when the bullet had hit him. In his fall he'd knocked the chair back, but not overturned it. He'd died as he now was, and virtually without knowing it, on his back.

"We'd like you to have a real good look at him." Jewle told me. "Doesn't matter about moving him now, so let's get him to the light."

They laid him just below the window. Jewle held the greying hair and turned the head towards me. I got down on one knee. "No," I said slowly. "I'm afraid I'm no use to you."

I got up after another look.

"Funny," Jewle said. "I could have sworn when you first had a look at him there was a sort of flash of something."

I stared. I was thinking of something apt and indignant.

"Now don't take this in the wrong way," Jewle was going on.

"You have clients and you have to protect their interests. This"—he pointed down—"couldn't possibly be one of them?"

"Very well." I told him stiffly. "I'll put it so that even you can understand. He isn't a client of mine. I haven't the faintest idea *who* he is. So if you've discovered some connection between him and me which made you want to see me, I think I ought to know what it is. At the moment I can't possibly think of one."

"Fair enough," he said mildly. He smiled. "Sorry if I got you slightly ruffled, but in a minute or two I think you'll see we had reason. Any apologies needed, you have them now."

"Forget it," I said. "Who is he? Tell me that."

"His name's George Peplock. *What* he does we don't yet know. If there was any clue to it, it was taken away by whoever went clean through the house after he shot Peplock. All the facts are these. He was killed between four o'clock and six yesterday, Sunday afternoon. He isn't married but a daily woman looks after things. He has a reasonably new three-point-four-litre Jaguar which he drives every morning to the local station to catch the half-past nine. He has a first-class season ticket to Liverpool Street. Two years ago he bought this place when it was what they call 'old-world'. I'd say he spent more on additions and modernisation than he gave for it. Oh, and something else. He usually got back here on the six-thirty when his dinner would be ready for him and his woman would have everything washed up and so on, and be out of the house an hour later. In the morning she'd be here in time to catch him before he left for the station, so as to get any change of plans. There very rarely were any.

"What Peplock did with his time of an evening we don't know, and Mrs. Keate, his woman, doesn't know. You may have seen the radiogram and the television set in the lounge, but as far as we know he had no interests in Ambourne and no friends. And he didn't bank here. He never talked about himself to Mrs. Keate, and the only unusual thing about him she could think of was that he had an American accent. In the telephone directory he appears locally as G. Peplock. In the London directory he doesn't appear at all."

"You've certainly been busy," I told him admiringly. "I take it he wasn't discovered till his woman got here this morning?"

"That's right," he said. "The inspector here has been handling things even better than we could. He has a couple of men still making enquiries. Mrs. Keate was so distressed, we had to send her home. Maybe we can get some more out of her this afternoon."

"Now we're back where we started," I told him ironically. "That is if the *we* means me."

"Naturally it all depends," he said. "Let's go somewhere more congenial, and Matthews might roust us out some coffee. The kettle should be on."

We went back to the lounge. As I said, it was comfortably furnished and had an open fireplace. It hadn't a thing that I envied and practically nothing to dislike. The whole thing was just middle-class comfort.

"Nothing among those ashes?"

"No," Jewle said. "The man who shot him was in no hurry. I'd say he searched the house methodically and burnt every scrap of paper that was incriminating. What he took away we don't know."

Matthews brought in four breakfast cups of coffee.

"Ought to warm us up," Jewle said. "Daren't light a fire because we want to go over that charred paper again. Which reminds me. The killer went through Peplock's pockets but he overlooked just one—a little slit of an interior fob pocket. In it we found this. It had various confused prints that don't add up to a thing, so you can handle it."

It was a visiting card. When I saw what was on it, I sat there for a moment gaping like a fool.

"It's you all right" Jewle said. "Name, address and telephone number. I'd say it's one of those things Bertha runs off for various occasions, hence the free-lance journalist."

"True enough," I said. "But how it got here, God knows."

"Well, tell us all you know. Who *did* you give cards like this to?"

Jewle had been right about that flash of something when I'd first looked at Peplock, but even in that brief moment I knew I had to be cagey. Mind you, I was far from sure till Jewle mentioned the Jaguar, and then I knew. And there was another consideration. It's become a kind of second nature to protect a client, and something had been telling me that Mrs. Hugh Wilson couldn't help but be involved, however indirectly or obscurely, in what had happened. Now once more I had to think fast.

"It's an extraordinary story." I got up from the chesterfield and put my empty cup on the mantelpiece, and I stayed there, facing the three of them. "You'll realise that I can't tell you the actual name of the client. Also at the moment I can't see any possible connection between her and what's happened here. However, here are the facts."

It took me a good ten minutes to tell them only what I thought absolutely necessary. What I kept to myself for future eventualities was that meeting between Sambord and the man in the Jaguar. That's where I was wrong. Many a time I've had cause to regret what the poet calls the tangled web we weave when first we practise to deceive, and this was to be another one of them.

"I saw this Sambrino myself," Jewle said. "After all, it was only about ten years ago. He was a marvel. How he did it I'll never know. But about those cards. You parted with only two. One you gave to this Sambrino, or Sambord, and the other to Granding. You're dead sure of that?"

"Dead sure."

"And the cards were specially run off for the occasion? You'd never used any like them before?"

"Never."

"Then that simplifies things," he said. "Either Sambord or Granding gave his card to Peplock."

"But, for heaven's sake, why?"

"No hurry," Jewle told me. "We haven't even begun this case yet. Plenty of time for reasons so let's make a start with facts. Let's go back to the other room and you can ring Granding and he can question Sambord."

Brass had a private word with Jewle and left. The three of us went back to the den. Ambourne was a good thirty-five miles from Wishington and the two were in different counties, so Jewle had to call the Yard to get Granding's number. When at last I was able to ring, I got only the secretary. She said she'd find Granding if I'd hang on.

I had only a couple of minutes to wait. After a friendly word or two I had to plunge right in.

"Don't get alarmed about this, Mr. Granding, but I'm with the police. They've apprehended a man who had one of my cards in his pocket and they're trying to trace every person to whom I gave a card. There's just the possibility he might have given it to someone else. What about the card I gave you? You still have it?"

He asked me to wait a minute.

"I've got that card in my hand right now," he told me. "Far as I know it can't have been out of the drawer in the desk where I put it."

"What about Sambord? Could you ask him? He was the only other person to whom I gave a card like that. They only arrived from the printer's that morning."

What he told me then was an absolute facer. I'd landed myself in a pretty deep hole. My only hope was to let him do the talking. I was giving a wry shake of the head when at last I hung up.

"Not so good," I said. "Granding put the card I gave him in a drawer of his desk and it was still there. He can't question Sambord because Sambord is missing. He left the farm to go to the Waggoners for his usual pint at about half-past twelve yesterday and he hasn't been seen since. His bed wasn't slept in and what few possessions he has are still in the caravan."

Jewle frowned. He looked at Matthews. Matthews frowned, too. I was hunting for words to explain away something else now that both might soon be interviewing Granding.

"One other thing," I said. "It might be important now but it didn't seem the least bit so when I was telling you about Sambord. When I went back to my car after talking with Granding that morning, Sambord was waiting for me and asked for a lift to the village. He wanted to know the time, which made me guess he had some kind of appointment. I dropped him at the pub and, instead of going in, he went on a bit and got into a car that drove off straight away. In view of what Granding had been telling me about how queer Sambord had been behaving, I suddenly made up my mind to tell him about it, so I rang him from a callbox in the next village."

"You saw the car that Sambord entered?"

"Saw it and that's all," I said. "It was no business of mine. Not, that is, till I began to think things over. All I can swear to is that it was a black saloon. All I really saw was the back of it and it was quite a distance away."

"Right," Jewle said. "Let's take a look at Peplock's car." We went out by the den door and along a concrete path and round between garage and house. Jewle told me to go on to the road while he opened the garage doors. When I turned round I could see the back of the Jaguar.

"I wouldn't swear to it but I'm pretty sure that's it."

"Fine," Jewle said. "It's good enough for the moment. The next thing is to make it dead sure. Probably someone down there saw Peplock in the car. That'll be a job for Matthews."

"What about Sambord? You'll keep in touch with Granding in case he comes back?"

"We certainly will. Hope to heaven he does come back. Strikes me at the moment as if he might be a key person in all this."

He glanced at his watch. "Half-past twelve. You go back to the Hare and Hounds and get yourself some lunch."

"At whose expense?"

He laughed. "I wouldn't worry. Have a good lunch and get back here at, say, two o'clock. And don't ask me who's paying for your time."

I did myself quite well at the hotel. Ordinary lunch was eight shillings but roast duckling, as an extra, was on the menu. I had the duckling. I didn't want to overdo things or I'd have had a half-bottle of white Bordeaux: I just had a Carlsberg instead.

And I was feeling easier in my mind, even if I did have a cold shudder as I thought of what might have happened if Jewle himself had rung Granding. I could hear Granding talking.

"Didn't Mr. Travers tell you about Sambord meeting a man at the Waggoners and getting into his car?"

And there was something else that made me feel considerably better—the realisation that my client could have had nothing whatever to do with that car business. At that time neither she nor the relative for whom she was acting could have had any idea where Sambord was to be found. She couldn't have seen my notice in the *New York Times* till its publication two days after I'd been at Wishington.

I pointed that out to Jewle as soon as I got back to River Cottage. He was alone. Matthews had already left for Wishington to begin enquiries.

"I don't know," Jewle said dubiously. "The older I get, the less I believe in coincidences. A woman comes to you and asks you to find Sambord. All right, you find Sambord, and you give him a card. Not an agency card, mind you, but one that makes you a journalist. Then Sambord sneaks away from the farm and contacts Peplock and he gives Peplock your card. Why?"

I said I hadn't even the beginnings of a clue. Why anyone should want to cultivate the acquaintance of a has-been like Sambord was beyond me. As I, and Granding, saw it, Sambord had nothing to give.

"All the same I'm of your opinion," I said. "There must be some connection between Sambord and Peplock's murder. You can't rule out the chance, now Sambord has disappeared, that he wasn't the actual murderer."

"I know," he said. "That's why Matthews is now at Wishington."

There'd been a change or two while I was away. Peplock's body was now in the local mortuary. Nothing in the least legible had been found among the ashes of the grate, so Jewle had lighted a fire, and we were warming ourselves in the lounge when one of Brass's men arrived with Mrs. Keate. She was a middle-aged widow who'd been a cook-general before her marriage, and had been with Peplock ever since he'd been in Ambourne.

"You feel equal to answering a few questions now?"

She did. Jewle got her comfortably seated. She smiled. "Doesn't seem right, somehow, me sitting here."

"These things happen," Jewle told her. "I take it he was a good employer?"

"Couldn't have been better, sir. Always the perfect gentleman."

"Did he have any visitors? Anyone, say, who called while you were here alone?"

"No, sir. Only tradesmen bringing anything I'd had to order."

"Any telephone calls?"

"Not while I was here. Also when he was here I had strict orders never to answer the telephone. Wherever he was I had to call him."

"Any traces of visitors when you began cleaning up after he'd left of a morning?"

She didn't quite understand.

"Any dirty glasses, for instance, or cigarette ends in the ashtrays?"

"There'd been no glass except the one Mr. Peplock always had his whisky in. As for cigarette en

ds, he smoked a lot of cigarettes himself."

"We knew that," Jewle said. "But you never found one with lipstick on?"

"Never, sir." The denial was almost indignant.

"And about that American accent of his. Did he ever talk about America?"

"Never, sir. You can't say he ever talked at all, not to me. Just gave me my instructions or told me anything I wanted to know about meals. He was quiet, you might say. Not exactly pleasant but always the gentleman. There was never a cross word all the time I was here."

"And how *did* you come here?"

"Answered an advertisement he put in the *Ambourne Herald*."

"Well, that's all." Jewle got smilingly to his feet. "Let me have an account of anything that's owing to you and we'll see you get it sooner or later out of the estate. And if anything occurs to you you think we ought to know, you'll let the police know?"

"I certainly will, sir."

"That's fine," Jewle told her and began showing her out.

"Our Mr. Peplock seems to have been pretty close-mouthed," he said when he came back. "I don't want to sound theatrical, but doesn't it look as if he must have had something to conceal?"

The telephone suddenly shrilled. Jewle nipped across to the lounge extension. He gave a quiet, "Hallo?" and then did some listening.

"Let's say I'm the doctor. What did you say your name was? . . . Well, I think you ought to get down here as soon as you can make it. . . . No, he's not dying, Mr. Dorlish. All the same, you ought to get here at once. . . . That's fine. I'll expect you in about an hour."

He told me what had happened.

"What the devil's happened to you, George? Why weren't you in? I just got back and they told me you hadn't turned up."

That's what Jewle had heard. What emerged was that Dorlish or Dawlish was a business associate. In view of what we knew or suspected, Jewle didn't want to do any more questioning. And it wouldn't have been in keeping with the fact that Jewle was supposed to be a doctor.

"Well, no need for any more enquiries about Peplock. Another hour and we ought to know a whole lot of things." He glanced at his watch. "Don't know about you but I'd like a cup of tea."

The remaining part of the ground floor of that new extension was an extremely up-to-date kitchen—a housewife's dream, Jewle called it—and dinette. He brought the tea and his packet of sandwiches to the lounge and then the telephone went again. This time it was Matthews. He and Jewle must have talked for a good three minutes.

"Don't expect you got the hang of all that," Jewle told me, "but Sambord still hadn't turned up. How much money did you say you gave him?"

"Five pounds. In pound notes. The new ones."

"Well, they found a private cache in that caravan. Two tenners, a fiver and four pound notes. He probably broke into one of those you gave him. And you weren't the only one. The car you saw that morning was definitely Peplock's, and Matthews is having the route from here to Wishington gone over in case it stopped at a garage and we could prove Peplock himself was driving it."

"Proof or no proof. I guess we know who was driving it," I said. "And that it was Peplock who gave Sambord that money. What worries me is why. Sambord was a down-and-out. What had he got to sell?"

"Might have been information about something."

He broke off as the constable now on duty just inside the front door was heard speaking. Jewle went to have a look.

"Hallo, Rodey. What brings you here?"

"Ask me in," a man's voice said amiably, "and I'll tell you."

4

DEAD MAN GONE

RODEY was a man of about forty, dark-haired, hook
-nosed, clean-shaved, of just above average height and, from the pens and pencils discernible in the jacket breast pocket beneath the worn waterproof, some sort of writing man.

"You know Mr. Travers?" Jewle said.

"I've seen him enough times," Rodey said, and held out a hand. "Never actually had the pleasure of meeting you, sir."

"Max Rodey's crime reporter for the *Record*," Jewle explained. He waved a hand at a chair. "Might as well sit down, Max, even the short time you'll be here." He smiled dryly. "I'd hate for you to print in that sheet of yours that the police had been uncooperative."

"Very nice of you. Super." Ever since he'd entered the room, an ironical smile had never left his mouth.

"Why'd you come here?" Jewle asked bluntly.

"Well, I may get shot at dawn for this, but I'll confess," Rodey told him. "You've got traitors at the Yard. People who for filthy lucre, or other considerations unknown, are prepared to pass on information, so when I got the news that you and a colleague had left suddenly for Ambourne—well, here I am."

"I see. And what about finding this location?"

"Well, *I could* have rung the local police from a call-box as soon as I got here and allowed them to think I was someone at the Yard."

"Very ingenious," Jewle said. "Not exactly ethical; still, there we are. And what do you want now you are here?"

Rodey looked surprised. "Why, everything you can tell me!"

"Sorry," Jewle said, "but I'm telling you nothing. I hope to be in a position to make a statement later in the day. You jumped the queue Max, and now you've got to get back into line."

Rodey looked reflectively at the ceiling. He quietly began singing:

"I can't give you anything but love, baby."

One line was enough.

"Didn't expect this from you, Super, not after all the trouble I've taken. You know I'll be absolutely discreet."

"Like hell you will," Jewle told him. He moved across from the fireplace. "Sorry. Interview ended."

Rodey hoisted himself up from the deep chair. He was taking it pretty well.

"You hold the aces, Super. But what about anything I find out independently? You know and I know that I'm not going to sit on my backside now I'm here."

"You know the rules," Jewle said evenly. "Print what you like. Only one word of warning. Don't do anything—and I mean anything, Max—that I can construe as hampering the cause of justice. Beyond that, help yourself." He smiled. "Of course you've no intention whatever of approaching any possible witness. You wouldn't do anything so dangerous as that. Otherwise just go and enjoy yourself. And don't forget there may be a hand-out tonight. I can't guarantee it'll be from here. I may have to get back to the Yard."

"Thanks a lot," Rodey told him amusedly. "And congratulations, Super. You can choke a man off in the fewest number of words of anyone I know."

He made a little sound of pain and winced as he got up from the chair. He rubbed his wrist.

"What's up?" Jewle said. "Stuck a pin in yourself or something?"

"No," he said. "Trying to do a kindness to somebody, like it might be you and me. Cranked a neighbour's car up for him this morning and it back-fired on me." He switched on that ironic smile again. "There's a moral in it somewhere, but damned if I know what it is."

He waved a cheerful hand at me from the lounge door. Jewle went out with him. He was smiling to himself when he came back.

"So that was Max Rodey," I said. "I've read some of his stuff."

"Max knows his job," Jewle told me. "He isn't always so brash as he was just now. When he likes he can be as nice a fellow as ever you met. You know anything about him?"

"Personally, no."

"You get to know these fellows," Jewle said. "I believe he spent some time in the States. A private eye or something like that. I seem to remember he came back here about seven or eight years ago and got a job with the *Record*. Now he's their top crime reporter."

"He seems to have a very ironic view of life?"

Jewle smiled. "Just his way. He knew very well he couldn't hot-stuff me but there wasn't any harm in trying. I might have let something useful slip. Did you notice his eyes wandering round? I'll bet he memorised every detail of this room—just in case." He smiled again. "I don't know why, but I've always had a soft spot for Rodey."

The tea was now tepid, so we didn't have a second cup. We did the little spot of washing-up, then Jewle looked through the local telephone directory—again just in case. It didn't have a Dawlish or Dorlish.

"About time he was here," Jewle said. "Traffic isn't all that heavy this time of day. Might be a good idea to let him in ourselves."

The constable was told to make himself comfortable in the kitchen. We sat on in the lounge with the front door just ajar and there was nothing to do but gossip about old times and every now and again make up the fire. It was a quarter to five and dusk was well in the sky when at last we heard the sound of a car as it sharply braked. Jewle went to the door.

Dorlish—that was the way he spelt his name—was a trim, fit-looking man in the forties. There was something of the soldier about his bearing, and, from the way he threw quick looks around that room, he was the nervous, quick-thinking type.

"My colleague," Jewle said, and waved a hand at me.

"Two of you, eh, Doctor? Must be something serious. Where is he? In his bedroom?"

"No hurry, Mr. Dorlish. Make yourself comfortable, and then we'll talk."

He didn't want to make himself comfortable. He stood four-square where he was.

"Look. Doctor, I'm a busy man. I didn't come here to talk. You tell me what's happened to George Peplock."

"Very well. But I've a surprise for you. The doctor left long ago. I'm Superintendent Jewle of Scotland Yard."

The mouth gaped. To my mind there was as much alarm as surprise. He shot a look at me, then back at Jewle. The smile was a bit feeble.

"I don't understand it. What's been happening?"

"Sit down," Jewle told him quietly, "and we'll have that talk. You look like a man who can face bad news, so here it is. Mr. Peplock was murdered yesterday and his body was discovered this morning."

"My God, no!" This time there was no doubt about the surprise. "I just can't believe it! Who the hell would want to kill George Peplock?"

"That's what we were hoping you might be able to tell us. Who was he exactly?"

"My partner. But tell me. Superintendent. How was he killed?"

"Shot at point-blank range through the head."

"Oh, my God!" He moistened his lips. "And you don't know who did it?"

"At the moment, no," Jewle told him. "But tell us about this partnership of yours. Partnership in what?"

We were the ones to get the surprise. I knew that Harry Frimmer had sold City Investigations two years ago—about a year before he died—but it was a smallish concern with which I'd had no contacts. I didn't even know the names Peplock and Dorlish. London's quite a big place with a goodish few private investigators scattered around. Also, they come and they go.

"Your partner was American, wasn't he?" Jewle asked.

"No, Superintendent—Canadian. He came from Vancouver, British Columbia. He happened to be in England at the time Frimmer was selling, so he had a look at the place and made an offer. He'd had his own agency and had just retired, and then he had the urge to get back in the game again, this time over here."

"And you?"

"Well, I joined the force just over twenty years ago at Mainford. C.I.D. Sergeant six years later and was about due for Inspector when there was a disagreement. I didn't like the way a certain case was being handled, so I resigned and then got a job with Harry Frimmer. I was his head man when Peplock bought the business. He offered me a partnership if I could find the money, which I did. I'm not married and I always lived pretty quietly."

"I see. And now about Peplock. Any particular reason why he should live here instead of town?"

Dorlish smiled. The smile gave a kind of Mephistophelian look to the spare face with its thinnish line of dark moustache.

"You know what colonials are like, Superintendent. There's nothing very old in Canada, or the States, so they're keen on what we call 'old-world'. George saw this place when it was just a cottage. Told me it was his dream house. Handy enough for town, too, if it came to that. He's a bachelor, like myself." He made as if to rise. "Where is he now? I can see him?"

"Just a moment," Jewle said. "I'll try to find out."

He could have rung from where we were. Maybe he was making a deliberate mystery of things. I kept the ball rolling. "You've been here often, Mr. Dorlish?"

"Only once," he said, "and that was just after it was finished and he wanted to swank a bit about the way it turned out. But tell me—by the way I didn't catch your name."

"Wilson." It was the first I could think of.

"Well, tell me what happened. What time was it yesterday?"

"In the late afternoon," I said. "His woman doesn't come in on a Sunday so he had his midday meal as usual at the local Hare and Hounds. He didn't leave there till after two, and at some time he had a cup of tea and a slice of cake. According to when he had that you get the basis for time of death—say between four and six."

Jewle came back. "They're not quite ready yet, Mr. Dorlish. Another quarter of an hour and you can see him. He's at the local mortuary. You're familiar with all this routine, so do you mind if I ask a few more questions?"

"Go ahead, sir."

"Cigarette?"

"Thanks."

I pulled out my pipe. A minute and we were snug as three bugs in a rug.

"First the routine question," Jewle said. "Where were you yesterday afternoon?"

"At the Maryland Hotel, Brighton, keeping an eye on a husband. I had tea in the lounge there at about half-past four and took a cue in a foursome of snooker, with the husband, just before six." He held up a quick hand to check Jewle's question. "We're a bit short-handed so I did the job myself. Also it's a case that's going to make a stink when the facts come out. When I'd got as much as I needed this morning, I came back to town. I expected to find George there, dealing with another client, and that's why I rang."

"That clears that up," Jewle told him. "Nice for once to be dealing with someone who knows the ropes. Now about enemies. You know of any?"

Dorlish shrugged his shoulders. "In our game you're bound to make them. The husband I was telling you about isn't going to be very pleased when he finds out who I was. but that's a long way from saying he'll think of killing me."

"You can think of no one off-hand?"

"No, sir, nor at any other hand." He smiled. "In all your experience have you ever heard of an enquiry agent being murdered?"

"Can't say I have. I've known of more than one I wouldn't have minded murdering."

That was a joke and we laughed.

"Something else I should have mentioned," Jewle went on. "Whoever killed your partner searched the house thoroughly. I think we can prove that every piece of correspondence was burnt in that grate. Nothing was left to show who Mr. Peplock was or what he did. Can you explain that?"

Dorlish had been listening intently, and it seemed to me that when Jewle spoke of nothing having been left, there was a quick look of relief. All my life I've been questioning or watching witnesses. A snap of the eyes, a movement of the mouth or even of the hands can reveal some new emotion. It isn't quite so easy to know just what that emotion is.

"It's incredible," Dorlish said. "Never knew anything like it. You're an infinitely older hand than I am, sir, but doesn't it suggest what you said? Someone who thought there might be incriminating evidence here about a former case?"

"A good idea," Jewle told him. "Maybe if you go through your files you might come up against something that'll help."

"I'll certainly do that."

"Fine," Jewle said, and got to his feet. "Where *is* your office, by the way?"

"Five, Whitmore Court, W.C.2."

"We'll keep in touch." He held out his hand. "Meanwhile thank you for your help. Sorry things had to happen this way, but there it is. You know your way to police headquarters?"

I heard Dorlish's car move off. Jewle came back, gave me a quick nod and went on to the den. He was there about five minutes.

"I knew there was something just a bit familiar about that name Dorlish," he told me. "While he was talking, it struck me things about his retirement weren't quite what he said. We're trying to get the facts of the case now, not that it necessarily matters. Did you gather anything? I noticed you were watching him pretty close."

I mentioned one or two things. "Also I don't think he needed to have told us about that retirement business. I may be wrong, but it struck me he was trying to keep you from making your own enquiries."

"Could be so," he said. "If so, he was a fool, and I don't think he's that. And Peplock," he shook his head slowly, "the last thing I'd have expected him to be. What sort of business was Harry Frimmer's, by the way? I never actually ran across him."

"Quite small," I said. "Probably only two or three operatives. Peplock might have seen possibilities, of course. You might do worse than see what advertising he did."

Jewel went slowly across to the chesterfield. He lighted a cigarette. I gave the fire a stir and put on more coal.

"As I see it," he told me, "the fact that Peplock was what he was changes things quite a lot. It makes some sort of a tie between him and Sambord. Sambord, by the way, hasn't come back yet. Matthews is staying down there tonight."

"What sort of a tie?"

"Don't know," he said, "except that Sambord might have had some information that Peplock wanted, and was prepared to pay for. . . . It's logical to assume that Peplock gave Sambord those notes. And my guess is they were only earnest money."

"And what about the fact that Sambord has now been missing well over a day? Could it be that Sambord killed him during some dispute here, then took to his heels?"

"Who'd suspect him? And why abandon that money in the caravan? And kill the goose that was laying the eggs. Oh no. The last thing to do at the moment is to have theories. Sambord's somewhere. Matthews is putting out a call and sooner or later he'll turn up. Find Sambord and we'll have a lot of answers. Meanwhile, it strikes me that City Investigations might do with a bit of investigating."

I didn't see what good I could do staying on in that house, but I didn't intend to say so. In the old days I might have been helping officially, but the Yard was under new management, so to speak, and those days had gone. All I could do now, to slake that incurable curiosity of mine and insert myself somehow into the case, was to keep my mouth shut and watch which way the wind blew.

"What about the bullet that killed Peplock?" No harm in that one question.

"A point two two," he said. "It's now with ballistics."

"Fired at what range?"

"About three feet. Caught him at a slight angle and downwards. Probably he was seated and the other one standing in front of the desk. Well try a reconstruction in the morning when we've pieced things together." He looked at his watch and I knew the axe was about to fall. "Don't think there's any need to keep you longer—"

The telephone went. Jewle nipped across the room. The only thing of any interest to me was his last sentence. "Yes, bring them along."

"A fantastic thing," he told me. "About a quarter-past seven last night a man was coming along the road here when he came across what he claims was a dead man. He went back about two hundred yards to his daughter's, where he'd been, to telephone the police. They said they'd send an ambulance and so on at once. One of their two cars was alerted but when it got there, there wasn't a sign of a man. Privately, of course, they thought it had been a drunk and he'd got up and walked off, but this man who found the supposed corpse wasn't happy about it, so he called at police headquarters just now to see if there was any more news. He works in town and he went straight there from the station. Somebody had the sense at last to think it a bit of a coincidence and that's why they rang. They're coming along now."

A car was drawing up. A couple of men came in: one a patrolman who hadn't found a body and the other the man who'd said he had. He was a prosperous-looking middle-aged man named Vingram. This was his story.

He was a senior cashier at a city bank: a widower who lived alone not far behind the Hare and Hounds. His wife had died a year ago and he had since made it a habit to spend Sunday afternoons with his married daughter and family at Rivercroft, a house farther along the road. He had a car but preferred to walk for the sake of the exercise, and he left the house for the homeward walk at about ten-past seven. It was when he got past River Cottage that he saw a man lying against the low hedge of one of the gardens. He had a good look at him and knew he was dead.

"Pardon me," Jewle said, "but what tests did you apply?"

Vingram smiled. "I was a warden in the city during the war. Also I'd had a course of instruction in Red Cross work. There wasn't any need to apply any tests, other than the obvious. The man was definitely dead, I'll stake my reputation on it. I saw plenty of dead during the war. I've helped to dig 'em out of ruins and even shelters, and you can't tell me. Superintendent, a man's still alive when I know he isn't."

"I don't question it," Jewle told him. "So the man was dead. What then?"

"I went as quickly as I could back to my daughter's and rang the police. I was told to go back and wait, which I did. When I got back there, the body had gone. Then a couple of police officers arrived—one of them this officer here—and they thought the man had only been a drunk. I didn't want to argue so I left it like that, but I thought about it a lot today and that's why I made enquiries just now."

"Glad you did," Jewle told him, and to the policeman, "And what about you? Tell us what you did when your car arrived."

The patrolman said there'd been nothing to do. Nobody was there. He and his colleague had scouted round but there was never a trace of the man Mr. Vingram had described.

"Did you disturb the body yourself?" Jewle asked Vingram. "No, sir. I know better than that."

"Would you be so good as to lie down on the carpet here in the same position as the body?"

Vingram got down. He drew his knees slightly up. The right arm was bent under him and the left across the face.

"Fine," Jewle said. "We're much obliged. Which way was the body headed?"

"Up the road, towards where I was coming from."

"You could see him clearly before you got to him?"

"No, Superintendent, no. The Lighting's none too good there and I was practically on him before I saw him."

"You heard or saw nothing else?"

"Nothing at all."

"Right." Jewle told him. "Now will you try to give us a description. Only facts. Nothing you might have deduced since. Just facts."

"Well, sir, he looked about my own age only much thinner. His hair was white—"

"You didn't see a hat?"

"No, sir, but he was wearing a dark overcoat. He was clean-shaven and there was just a faint smell of liquor about him. He was much more spare of build than me. That's about all I could actually see. Oh, and he had on dark trousers and black shoes."

"That's fine," Jewle told him. "Now let's adjourn to where you actually saw him. We'll have the car lights trained on the spot but not till I give the word."

It was about forty yards down the road, at a spot between two street lights: dim enough as Vingram had said. That whole road was far from well lighted. The body had been lying against the clipped privet hedge that separated a lawn from the road, much like the layout at River Cottage itself. Jewle made a couple of chalk marks where Vingram indicated, and that was that.

"No need to have the car lights on," Jewle said. "Anything else you can think of, Mr. Vingram, that might be helpful?"

There was nothing. Jewle held out his hand. "All there is to do, then, is to thank you. I take it, by the way, that you're a man of discretion?"

"Well, sir, I hope so."

"Then keep it to yourself, but you'll be glad to hear you may have been right after all. Bodies can be moved."

Vingram looked a happier man. Jewle went with him to the police car. I went past them to River Cottage.

"No need for you to wait any longer," Jewle told me when the car had moved off. "I'll have a good look round where that body was. There might be something. You never know."

"It was Sambord?"

"Everything fits. I'd bet fifty to one on it."

"Then who killed him? Peplock?"

Jewle chuckled. "If he did, then who killed Peplock? Only one certainty. A third person was involved."

He held out a hand. "Thanks for all you've done. I'll keep in touch. I haven't changed my mind about that client of yours."

"Neither have I," I told him. "Maybe I'll do a bit of work on her myself."

5
FIND THE CLIENT

As I slowed with lights full on at the T-head, I just caught a glimpse of that crime reporter, Rodey, walking briskly in the direction of River Cottage with a man who might have been a fellow reporter. They were laughing at something, so maybe Rodey was talking of the fast one he'd tried to pull on Jewle. My guess was that now they were getting at the head of the queue for Jewle's official hand-out.

I must have been thinking of that when I swung at last into the easy stretch of the arterial road, and somehow it made me think of something else. I'd assumed, and I thought Jewle had, that because the body—which meant Sambord's body—had been found with its head towards River Cottage, that was proof that he'd been going in that direction when he'd been killed. Now I realised it was no such proof at all. If he'd been, say, killed by a blow on the head, then he might have fallen either way, depending on the position of the man who'd struck him. On the other hand, if he *was* going towards River Cottage, then he couldn't have killed Peplock. And that, of course, brought the simple, logical question, that since he hadn't killed Peplock, who had? The simple answer, again, was the one supplied by Jewle—a third man, and if that wasn't a further complication, then I didn't know one when I saw it.

I gave it a rest and came back to it later on: the few moments or minutes between the first warmth of bed and dropping off to sleep, and it was then that something else struck me. *How* had Sambord been killed? Since Vingram had said nothing about it, there couldn't have been any blood. A further proof of that was that the patrolmen had found no trace of a body. Presumably, too, there'd been no sound of a shot. Brass's men had almost certainly questioned every house about that and about movements along the road just prior to Vingram's discovery.

Something else struck me, and I wasn't so conceited as to think it hadn't struck Jewle. Peplock's killer must have been fully acquainted with his Sunday habits and he also must have taken into account the fact that in a place like Ambourne on a December Sunday night, River Lane would be practically deserted. It was the one night when everybody would be indoors.

It was at that point that I dropped off to sleep. When I woke in the morning I found myself picking up the train of thought where I'd left it, only this time it was a question of A B C, with A for Peplock, B for Sambord and C for Jewle's third man. Did B kill A or A kill B long before he was killed himself? Did C kill A and then B? Was B there when C killed A and was that why C had also to kill B?

You see how hopeless that was? There was hardly a combination of those three letters that couldn't have been made to fit; and the only constant was that someone had killed both A and B. I shifted to something else, even more futile. What had happened to Sambord's body? Did his killer have a car handy? If so, wouldn't Vingram have heard it as he moved away or noticed the lights on so dark a night? And then a possible solution suddenly struck me. There was no need of mechanical transport. All Sambord's killer had to do, once Vingram had set off briskly back towards his daughter's house, was to pick up that none too heavy body, nip across the road and dump it in the river. It had been as easy as that.

Jewle rang me that morning when I was having breakfast. He was just returning to Ambourne and wondered if I'd had any ideas. As soon as I mentioned the river, I knew he'd had it in mind.

"Yes," he said, "but there was a lot of rain, as you know, and it's pretty fast-flowing. We've asked for a general lookout. Hopeless to try and drag. If the body ever was in there, it might have been carried miles away."

"Any idea how Sambord was killed?"

"Almost certainly a cracked skull. We found behind that hedge definite proof that a man crouched there, probably while Vingram was looking at the body."

"Any other news?"

"Only that Matthews has proof that the man who drove that Jaguar with Sambord in it was definitely Peplock. If it interests you, Peplock drove round in a wide circle and took his time over it, which seems to show that all he wanted Sambord for that morning was a conference. To make some kind of plans. Part might have been where and when to pick up Sambord on the Sunday morning."

"Wait a minute," I said. "Sambord must have been picked up between twelve and one. What was done with him after that? Surely he must have been with Peplock in the house up to near the time when Peplock was killed?"

"You've forgotten something," he told me. "Peplock wasn't alive after six o'clock at the latest, so where was Sambord from then till the time Vingram found him?"

It might have been a bit ruefully but I had to laugh.

"You're right," I said. "The more you think about it, the more of a muddle it gets."

"You're telling me," he told me, and that was about all before he rang off.

Too often in life we think of snappy answers and devastating quips, but only after the chance to produce them has gone. No sooner had Jewle rang off than I thought of something perfectly astounding. Jewle had wanted to know where Sambord was from the time Peplock was killed till the time he was killed himself, and now I knew that if I'd had just a couple or minutes more. I could have told him. Sambord had killed Peplock and then had to set to work methodically to search the house. That had taken him at least the hour or hour and a half till seven o'clock. As for the third man. he'd either witnessed the killing or come in later, or he might have been keeping the house under observation, but the fact remained, or so it seemed to me, that he'd then killed Sambord. Maybe there'd been something that both men wanted, and he'd taken whatever it was from the dead Sambord. All the same he must have had some uneasy moments when he saw Vingram approaching, and had had to nip behind that privet hedge.

Naturally, I told myself complacently, that didn't clear the whole thing up. The third man had to be found. Do that and you'd have all the answers. And since the problem wasn't mine, it was easy enough to shrug away all difficulties. Besides, if I was going to have any hand whatever in the case. I had problems of my own. Jewle didn't want me as an onlooker, so the only hope I had was to make little driblets of contributions. Just what they were to be I hadn't at the moment thought.

The papers had only a paragraph about the Ambourne murder and Sambord wasn't mentioned at all. On my way to the Agency I bought a *Record* to see what Rodey had made of it. He'd had little luck. There was a picture of River Cottage taken before Peplock had acquired it. and another as it had been at the murder date, and my guess was that he'd got them from the house agent who'd handled the property. The half-column was padded out with what Rodey had learned about Peplock's habits, plus anything which might be in any way relevant about Ambourne itself.

In the quiet of my Broad Street room I began looking for ideas, and naturally I began with the woman who'd been our client. It was in her that Jewle had been interested. Somehow or other I had to find her. Whether every detail of what she'd told me had been gospel truth I didn't know, but I was beginning to suspect it wasn't. The thing was to find her. Confidences cease to be respected in cases of murder, so when I found her I'd give her an option. Tell me the absolute truth or I'd have to turn her over to the police. What I needed was the name and whereabouts of that relative who'd had the interest in Sambord.

Ten minutes later I hadn't the least idea where to begin. The more I thought, the less I knew. Given ample time, of course, and the men to do the job, I might have checked if Mrs. Hugh Wilson had flown to Paris or taken a car by ferry across the Channel. It was then that l thought of something that literally gave me the cold shivers. In all probability she'd never gone to France at all!

I'd assumed that using the *New York Times* had been the easiest means of letting her know in France what she had wanted to know, but now it struck me that it was precisely the other way round. From the start, the lady had had me dangling on a bit of string. The paper hadn't been brought in to fit the occasion: the occasion had been manufactured to fit the paper.

What I now as good as knew was this. She wanted at all costs to conceal her name and address, but, if she did. then how could l tell her the result of the enquiry? The answer was found in two things: The *New York Times* and a fictitious tour in France. And I'd swallowed it, head, bones, fins and all. Mrs. Hugh Wilson was almost certainly not her name, and she'd never left England, and the relative whom she was trying to help was almost as certainly herself.

And where did that leave me? Out, far out. in the middle of nothing. All I knew about the client was what she looked like and how she spoke, and I doubted if even the great Sherlock himself could have traced her very far from that. Another minute or two and I'd given up the idea of tracing Mrs. Hugh Wilson and was looking around for something else on which to make a start. Jewle's third man was out of the question. All that remained was Sambord.

So I did some thinking about Sambord. There was no point in going to Wishington again. Granding must have told me all he knew and Matthews must have pumped him, the farm and the neighbourhood bone dry. All the same there did seem a couple of events in Sambord's life which it would do no harm to explore— his acquisition of Lambelli's act. and his marriage in England. If I could find, for instance, the wife who'd left him. She would be a first-class source of information.

I took my time about the cable to Bob McGuffie, head of McGuffie Investigations, our agents in New York. When it went it read like this:

INFORMATION URGENT VAUDEVILLE AND CIRCUS ARTIST ED. LAMBERT ALIAS LAMBELLI DIED FORTY- EIGHT STOP ALSO RICHARD SAMBORD ALIAS HERE

THE GREAT SAMBRINO STOP ALSO TERMS UNDER WHICH SAMBORD ACQUIRED ACT STOP

Finding out about the marriage was pretty easy. It was a brisk morning so I walked to Somerset House. Ten minutes after I'd paid the necessary fee, I had what I wanted.

The couple had been married at the Register Office, Holborn, on the 14th September, 1949. The bride was a Trude Layman, aged 19. Address, 7 Hyman Terrace, Lewisham. Parents, both deceased, were Samuel Layman and his wife Trude. Those, at the moment, seemed the essentials, with the addition of Sambord's address, which was given as Welland House, Holborn.

The taxi driver thought he knew where Welland House was. It turned out to be an antiquated block of office buildings. I had a look round and decided it was the building where Sambord had had his office, and where Trude Layman had been his secretary. In the old-fashioned vestibule I did some wondering about her address. On marrying Sambord she'd almost certainly left it for wherever it was that Sambord was actually living at the time. That office address he'd given was merely a residential one given as qualifying for the Holborn marriage.

I went back to the agency. Somehow I didn't feel like taking a chance in Lewisham. Eleven years is a pretty long time, and I doubted if she'd gone back there after she'd left Sambord. What I did was to ring the office of the Borough Surveyor. I said who I was and mentioned urgent enquiries about a Trude Layman who'd lived in 1949 at 7 Hyman Terrace.

My informant laughed. "Afraid you won't find that address now, sir. Part was pretty badly blitzed and the whole area was reconstructed in 1952 and onwards. It's all flats now, and offices."

"Would you be likely to have any information whatever about her?"

"Well," he said, "what was her age?"

"Nineteen."

"No good. then. She wouldn't even have appeared on the electoral roll."

So that was that. As far as I was concerned, Trude Sambord had disappeared into thin air. I was putting my notebook back in my pocket when I remembered something else. Granding had mentioned a rumour that when Trude left him, Sambord employed a detective agency to find her but had no luck. I wondered which agency he'd employed. Was it City Investigations, or would that be too much of a coincidence?

The trouble was that since Dorlish had seen me with Jewle at Ambourne, and since Jewle had had his own reasons for not announcing who I actually was, I couldn't very well call on City Investigations myself. Maybe, though, I could use Bertha. She could claim that she'd been a relative, so I went through to Bertha's room and who should come in but Hallows, our senior operative. He'd been working on a sabotage job at a factory in the suburbs.

"Didn't expect to see you," I said. "Anything gone wrong with the job?"

"Everything cleared up," he told me. "Reported in yesterday."

Hallows, like Bertha, grew up with the Broad Street Agency. As far as I'm concerned, he's as much friend as employee. If there's a better operative in town, I've never heard of him. He's also the only one of our people to whom I'd have given a complete and detailed account of the Peplock murder. Usually you tell so much and no more.

"A queer business," he said. "And you're thinking this Mrs. Sambord could throw some light on it."

"The only way I can think of to get any light on it. What about City Investigations? You know anything much?"

He'd known them pretty well when Harry Frimmer was alive. He'd heard nothing whatever since the business had changed hands.

"Tell you how I could find out a few things. You never ran up against Jack Ritcher?"

"Never heard of him."

"Well, he was Harry's senior man and I ran up against him the other day. He left when Harry sold out and got a job as a store detective with Montagu-Prince at Streatham. He might know something about the Sambord affair: that is if it was Harry who did it." He thought for a moment. "I might do worse than ring him up."

He went back to the reception room. It was ten minutes before he was back.

"Corn in Egypt," he told me. "It *was* City Investigations and it was Jack himself who did the job. He has a room at the store and he's coming here in his lunch hour. I told him there'd be a fiver in it for him."

Ritcher was arriving just before one. I went out for an early lunch and I couldn't help thinking there was more than a coincidence in City Investigations having handled that Sambord job. One of the new owners had been murdered and Sambord himself might have done it. There was also the queer fact that if the killing had arisen out of that 1949 enquiry, Sambord had killed a man who could have had nothing whatever to do with it. All the same it was the first real hand-out I'd acquired for Jewle.

It was just after one o'clock when Ritcher and Hallows came into my room. Ritcher was a burly, tough-looking man of about sixty. He didn't strike me as the stuff of which good operatives are made, but you never know.

"Yes, sir," he said. "I did that job just as Mr. Hallows told you. The boss called me into the office so as I could hear all that was said."

"One question before you go on," I said. "Were you perfectly happy yourself about the facts Mr. Sambord gave you? Did it strike you at the time that he was making a clean breast of things? Wasn't colouring things to suit his own case, for example, or keeping things back?"

"I can't really tell you," he said. "It was a long time ago, also . . . well, I don't know how you run your business, sir, but with us the client always had to be right. I must say he was a bit vague about the jewellery."

"Jewellery?"

"Yes, sir. When his wife left him she was supposed to've gone off with a diamond ring and some ear-rings and a diamond brooch. He was pretty well off and he'd been investing in jewellery—that's what he said. Far as I remember, he reckoned the whole lot were worth a thousand pounds."

"You don't think he was more anxious to recover the jewellery than he was to find his wife?"

"Begging your pardon, sir, but wouldn't the two go together?"

"You're right," I said. "But what did you actually do?"

"Went first to where she'd been living before the marriage but she hadn't gone back there. There wasn't any relatives Mr. Sambord knew of except a brother, and as far as I remember he was in America. An older brother I think he was, so after we'd made enquiries at all sorts of hotels and so on, the boss and I began to think she'd gone to America, too. I remember I wrote my usual report but I never clapped eyes on Mr. Sambord again, not personally."

"Let Mr. Travers see those photographs, Jack," Hallows said. "He has a couple of photographs, sir. One Sambord gave him and the other a wedding photograph which showed the wife. That was for the purpose of the assignment."

I had a look at them. One was exactly the same as Tom Holberg had shown me, a professional photograph of the kind that would be sent to fans. It was signed—*Yours, Sambrino*. The other showed a young and very pretty woman in a smart tweed costume holding Sambord's arm. I took out my glass and had a look at it more closely. The hair visible beneath the hat looked jet black.

"Might I borrow this one? I'll take good care of it."

"Keep it, sir," he told me. "It's no use to me. I didn't even know I had it till I was looking for the Sambrino one."

I thanked Ritcher, gave him the promised fiver and added a pound-note for the photograph. Hallows saw him out. When Hallows came back he was apologetic about my not getting my money's worth.

"You never know," I told him. "At least we've now got something tangible. This photograph shows there actually was a wife. As for finding her, I don't think it's worth trying. There's a job for you, though. You know where City Investigations are?"

He did.

"Right," I said. "I want you to present yourself there as a client. Ring them this afternoon and make an appointment for the morning. I want the assignment to be something they'll definitely be unable to accept, so you've got to do some thinking. What I really want you there for is to be able to give an impression of the place since I can't go myself. You can do that?"

"I'll think of something," he said. "The moment I have, I'll give them a ring."

As soon as he'd gone I rang the Yard and asked for Jewle. He was in. I asked if he was busy and he said he wasn't. Just a matter of ebb and flow.

"Then I'll come along," I told him. "Got something interesting for you."

"Such as what?"

I was too old a bird to rise to that.

It was half-past two when I went into Jewle's room. There was the usual inconsequential minute and then I reminded him about what he'd said about coincidences.

"That client of mine, Mrs. Wilson, wanted to know Sambord's whereabouts. I didn't want to have the Agency involved in anything shady, so I thought I'd try to prise her out and I found I hadn't a single thing even to make a start with."

I told him what I'd deduced: that her name wasn't Wilson, that she'd never left England and that the *New York Times* had merely helped to keep her strictly anonymous. I went on to say that since she was interested in Sambord I'd switched to Sambord. I'd hoped ultimately to find the wife who'd left him over ten years ago and to get from her any information that might throw light on Peplock's murder.

"All I found was at Somerset House, that her maiden name was Trude Layman and she was nineteen when she married Sambord. Then I remembered something else. Granding had told me that Sambord had asked a detective agency to find her, and I thought to myself what an extraordinary coincidence it would be if the agency he'd gone to was City Investigations. I got Bob Hallows to do some discreet inquiring and you know what he found out from one of their old operatives who'd retired when the agency changed hands?"

"Don't tell me. It *was* City Investigations."

"Dead right."

"Incredible!" he said. "Sambord goes to them to find his wife. I take it they couldn't. Ten years later a woman asks you to find Sambord. Then the man who's had that agency only a couple of years is murdered and Sambord's found dead close by."

"Add this," I said, "that the woman couldn't have been involved directly since she didn't know Sambord's whereabouts at the time he was in contact with Peplock."

He slowly lighted a cigarette. "It's a most unholy mix-up. And after I thought we were beginning to make progress."

"How d'you mean?"

"Well, we'd begun to tie one or two things in. We found a courting couple who were walking past River Cottage, and towards where Vingram found the body, at soon after seven o'clock. No body was there then, but as they were turning into Handley Road"—that was the one that led from the Hare and Hounds to River Road—"a man passed them turning into River Road, and a few feet behind him was another man, this one wearing crêpe-soled shoes. The first man answers somewhat to a description of Sambord. The second was tallish and had a muffler round his neck and mouth."

"Our third man?"

"Don't know," he said. "But we do know this. Peplock got to Ambourne at about a quarter-past one on Sunday and he parked Sambord at the Griffin: that's a smallish pub about a couple of hundred yards short of the Hare and Hounds. He asked the land-lord if he could find 'my friend here' some lunch and he warned him not to let him have more to drink than a pint.

"Peplock got to the Hare and Hounds just short of half-past. And now comes what's largely deduction. In the afternoon Sambord had a nap in a small lounge at the pub and read the Sunday papers after the landlord had brought him some tea at five o'clock. Everything had been paid for in advance by Peplock. Just before seven o'clock Sambord nipped into the bar and had a pint and he kept looking up at the dock. The bar overlooks the main road and Sambord went out. He came back looking a bit perturbed and asked the way to River Road and how far. Then he left.

"That's all strictly fact. The deductions are these. Peplock didn't want to be bored by Sambord's company for quite a few hours so he parked him at that pub, making sure that Sambord kept sober. What he'd said to Sambord was, 'I'll come for you in the car at seven o'clock. I've got to have you at my house not later than'—say—'a quarter-past seven.' That's why Sambord set off on foot. He was afraid of being late and he probably hoped to meet Peplock on the way. But Peplock was dead. From the actual times it seems certain that Sambord was killed, probably by the man who was seen behind him, just before he reached River Cottage."

It was sound enough deduction to me.

"What about that man who was following Sambord?" I said. "He must have been keeping him under observation for quite a time. Anything to be found out at the Griffin?"

"Matthews is sweating blood at it now," he told me. "But a Sunday's a bad day. No end of non-regulars drop in, and the landlord always has a stand-up lunch available. The devil of it is that this man's now our key link. He's just got to be found."

"You'll get a line on him," I said. "Which reminds me. There's something I didn't tell you."

He'd been just sufficiently despondent to need a bit of cheering up, so I told him about Jack Ritcher.

"This is the photograph of Sambord's wife."

He had a good look at it, then he looked at me. He was smiling a bit wryly.

"Well, at least we know now that he did have a wife."

"There's more to it than that," I told him. "I know that photograph was taken ten years ago, but you know who I'd be prepared to swear that woman now is? The one who called herself Mrs. Hugh Wilson."

6

EVENING IN THE PAST

As I told Jewle. I wasn't a hundred per cent sure. If a person's life or liberty depended on my evidence, then I wouldn't be prepared to swear that the woman in the photograph was the woman who had called herself Mrs. Hugh Wilson. That didn't say that I wasn't still sure in my own mind.

"Both had dark hair and both were tall for a woman," I said. "Faces don't alter all that much in ten years. And look how erect the Trude Sambord holds herself in the photograph. If I had to compare strength of character, I'd say she was worth ten of Sambord. Remember she found out something about him only a month or so later, and she straight away left him flat. Not a lot of women would have done that. Sambord was in the big money. He'd bought valuable jewellery; if not for her, for her use. I admit she took the jewellery, or maybe Sambord was lying. I'd say he always was a fluent liar, and he'd bought the jewellery for her."

"Let's admit all that," he said. "Work on the assumption that everything was as you say, and tell me why a woman who left her husband ten years ago, and apparently kept well out of his way, should suddenly want him found."

"When you know that, you'll have most of the answers," I told him. "I will point out this, and it's up to you to think it important or not so important. Assuming the woman who came to me was Trude Sambord, then she'd gone well up in the world in those ten years. Her parents couldn't have been all that affluent, and the secretarial job she took with Sambord might have seemed a bit glamorous, but it couldn't have paid all that much. Ten years later I put her down as some wealthy business executive—"

"Because she wanted you to think that."

"Maybe, maybe not. If so she spent a devil of a lot dressing for the part, and she had had the good taste to do it right. But poise, general manner, the aura of competence—you can't just assume those and get away with it; not with people like you and me."

"Which implies what?"

"It provides a theory," I said. "She'd acquired money and status in those ten years and her conscience suddenly troubled her. Sambord might have been telling the truth for once about the jewellery, and she wanted to make restitution, or she might simply have wanted to help him if he really needed help. I think it was more than that. Suppose she wanted to get married again."

"Yes," he said. "There might be something in that. She'd want to know if he were alive or dead. Or if he'd gone back to the States. And got a divorce there. There's just one little thing against that. You found Sambord for her. What ought to have been the next move? Surely to get in touch with him. But did she? Not that we know or even have any reason to suspect. Peplock couldn't have been working for her, too. He, as we know, had been in touch with Sambord before she knew where Sambord was."

"True enough," I said. "So what now?"

"If you'll let me, I'll have copies made of this photograph, then we'll get busy here trying to find Trude Sambord. It's rather a vague tie-in at the moment but it's worth following up."

I wouldn't call Jewle secretive because the word doesn't fit him. Let's say he knows just how much to divulge or keep to himself, and the way he does both so fits in with his natural manner that you take it for granted. Not that I had any cause to be dissatisfied with that call at the Yard. Jewle was going to throw wide the net for Trude Sambord. That should have pleased me, and yet, as my bus neared Broad Street, I knew I'd rather be doing that job myself. Mind you, I didn't think that if Jewle did find her, he'd keep her strictly incommunicado, but that didn't change what was becoming an urge to find her first.

The night brings counsel. I'd thought a lot about Trude Sambord before I fell asleep, and I woke, as I often did, with an idea. Trude's parents had been a Samuel and Trude Layman. Why not find out a bit more about them both in case it threw light on Trude herself?

Hallows was waiting for me when I got to the office. He'd seen Ritcher again and now had a good idea of what things had been like at City Investigations two years ago. And he had an appointment at Whitmore Court at eleven. Ostensibly he was wishing to find a fictitious man who'd been in partnership with a fictitious uncle in a prospecting business in Fairbanks, Alaska, around 1910. It was a good story but I wouldn't have taken the case unless I'd had a retainer of at least five hundred pounds. Hallows was going to admit that he had less than a hundred, and I doubted if City Investigations would do more than politely listen. Unless, of course, they weren't above a little sharp practice.

I paid a return visit to Somerset House in order to have a look at the marriage certificate of Samuel Layman. Trude's present age was about thirty but Ritcher had thought she'd had a brother who was living abroad. I'd thought a good deal about that and it seemed that since Trude Sambord hadn't given her husband more information about him, the two had ceased to correspond. Either that or Sambord just hadn't been interested.

I decided to ignore the brother and quoted the marriage date as the late twenties. I wasn't to be far out. The year was 1929. Trude Rubenstein, widow, had married Samuel Layman, a furrier of 21 Delmer Road. Whitechapel. She was thirty-two and he two years older. That didn't tell me much except to confirm that their daughter. Trude, had been born the year after the marriage, so I decided to explore further. Who exactly had been the Rubenstein who'd been the first husband? I had no dates to be sure of. so I took ten years off to allow for a marriage at just over twenty. That search took very much longer, and, when it was over, I was at a dead end. There was no record whatever of the marriage of a Trude Rubenstein. If she'd been genuinely a widow at the time of her marriage to Layman, and there was no reason to suspect otherwise, then that first marriage must have taken place abroad.

It had been a good try but you can't always be lucky. I dropped into a restaurant for a coffee and began hunting for other angles and, before I'd hardly stirred that coffee, I thought of something that should have struck me before. Mother and daughter were both Trudes and Trude isn't a common English name. There was something German or Austrian or even Swiss about it, so a Trude Something-or-other might have married in one of those three countries. Since her nationality at the Layman marriage had been British, it wasn't unreasonable to suppose that she and her husband had later come to Britain. And that he had become naturalised.

And there was the snag. I'd never had occasion to enquire into the bona fides of any naturalised person but I thought it might be a pretty tedious business, and I hadn't a lot of time to spare—not if I was going to find Trude Sambord before Jewle. I've a flibbertigibbet sort of mind that darts hither and yon, and it wasn't long before I thought of something else. By the time I'd finished a second cup, I had another avenue, as the politicians say, that it might be worth while to explore.

It had risen out of Trude the second, the daughter. Being secretary to the Great Sambrino struck me as a queer, specialised sort of job. Maybe there'd been a touch of glamour about it, but surely it'd been very much of a dead end. How had she got the job? Through an advertisement in *Variety*, or how? And why had she taken it? Could it possibly be that she'd been brought up in a music-hall or circus atmosphere?

I went back to Broad Street. Hallows was back already so I asked him to wait while I rang Tom Holberg. Ruth said he was extremely busy but could she help. Maybe she could, I said. All I wanted was information about a family of circus or/and music-hall artists named Rubenstein. One was named Trude, and they might be German in origin or Austrian or even Swiss.

"I've heard the name," she said, "but I'm not sure of the context. Do you know Carl Chapman's *British Circuses*?"

"Never heard of it."

"You should get it," she said. "It has an awful lot of information. There's a companion volume dealing with the music-hall. You in any hurry, by the way?"

"Well . . ." I began.

She laughed. "I know. Still, seeing it's you. Shall I ring you at the Agency?"

I told her she was an angel straight from heaven. She laughed again. In that case she might fly instead of giving me a ring.

Hallows didn't smile much when he told me City Investigations had made it gently clear they mightn't be able to handle his case.

"Mightn't?" I said.

"Well, they tried to get me on a string. If I was prepared to pay twenty pounds against costs, they'd get into touch with their American agents and start preliminary enquiries. It was just a racket. The way I put things, no one but a Johnny-On-The-Spot at the time could have enquired into anything."

It was a common enough racket among the less reputable agencies, especially the one-man concerns. Nothing would have been done except bank the twenty pounds and then create a situation likely to entice the client into paying still more.

"Whom did you actually talk to?"

"Dorlish," he said. "He's a pretty slick operator, that fellow. Business-like, persuasive, a good listener—the whole bag of tricks."

"But you didn't fall for it."

He smiled. "Said just a bit reluctantly that I'd think it over and see him again."

The place itself, he said, had smartened up tremendously since Frimmer's day. It was bang up to date. Dorlish's office might have been that of a bank vice-president, supervising a new important branch.

"You know the place?" he asked.

"No," I said. "I can't put a finger on it, but Frimmer was a man I didn't exactly like having dealings with."

"Well, it's in one of those little courts just off Chancery Lane. The ground floor with a nice little brass plate on the door. The only other storey's a wholesale toy business. There's a short corridor with what I thought was the staff room at the far end, just as it was in Ritcher's day. ENQUIRIES is just along the corridor and turned out to be the secretary-receptionist's room and waiting-room just like here, only more elaborate. The secretary's a smart-looking brunette. There was a room straight ahead with *Mr. G. Peplock* on the door." He smiled dryly. "Didn't get a chance to look inside. The one I was shown into after all the flummery about Mr. Dorlish being busy taking a transatlantic call, was marked *Mr. S. Dorlish*."

As we agreed, Peplock and Dorlish must have spent quite a lot in smartening up those premises, inside and out, and refurnishing, and we couldn't help wondering what return they were getting for their money. An agency that deals these days only with the general run of private cases, including divorces, has to have a lot of luck even to make ends meet. We'd be out of business inside a month if that kind of thing—and we never handle divorce business—was our sole income.

"If you take into account what Dorlish told you about Peplock," Hallows said, "Peplock might have acquired the business largely as a hobby. He must have had money. Look what you thought he'd spent over that place at Ambourne. Mind if I say something?"

"Say on," I told him.

"Well, don't take this amiss, but you do quite a lot of work here but you also have quite a lot of fun."

"True enough. But I'm lucky enough to make money at it. Also the whole thing's a fallacy. Ostensibly, I'm spending my own money over this Peplock murder. All I'm really doing is to take it out of one pocket and put it in another."

He laughed.

"That's all right if you can convince the tax authorities. But about this business. Anything else you want me to do?"

"Yes," I said. "I have a hunch that our Mr. Dorlish will stand investigation."

I'd already told him the little I'd learned from Jewle about Dorlish, and what I now wanted was to see what Dorlish did with himself after hours.

"Take things easy during the day." I said, "but try to find out if City Investigations have sources of income outside purely private cases. That's just a sideline, but pick up Dorlish when he leaves his office at night. Just keep tag on him till, say, about nine o'clock. Since he's already seen you, it'll need a bit of disguise, but that's up to you. That all right?"

It was a job, he said, after his own heart.

I was just about to leave the office that evening when Ruth gave me the promised ring.

"About the Rubensteins," she said. "I think I've got them for you, except—well, prepare yourself for a shock. They're dead."

"Doesn't make any difference." I told her. "All I'm doing is sort of reconstructing a family tree."

"Then I've got someone you might see. Got paper handy? It's a Victor Lang. Convey anything to you?"

"Never a thing."

"Well, he's the Lang of what used to be Lang's Imperial Circus. He retired just before the war. He's a very old man but I'm told he's still mentally alert, and he's living with a daughter at 15 Brownlow Avenue, Highgate."

"Victor Lang, living with a daughter at 15 Brownlow Avenue. Highgate. Anything else you think I ought to know?"

"You'll do better getting information direct." she said. "I do know that a team he used was the Rubensteins—Trude and Martin."

Five minutes later I was on my way, and a quarter of an hour later still, I was paying off the taxi-driver. The street was a pleasant backwater, quiet and clean. The plane trees that made it an avenue had already been lopped, but by summer there would once more be a green shade. The house I wanted was medium-sized and detached: the unobtrusive garage at the left, a later addition. The property looked well cared for.

A bosomy, grey-haired woman answered my ring. The hall light was on and she read my business card.

"I'm trying to find someone in connection with a legacy," I said, "and was told that Mr. Lang might help. The legatee is a Trude Sambord."

"Trude!" She looked almost startled. "She hasn't been heard of for years. A legacy, you say."

I was skating on very thin ice. "Yes," I said. "I understand it's from a distant relation abroad."

"Vienna?"

"How'd you guess?" I said.

"Well, Trude's people came originally from near Vienna. But come in. Wait in here for just a minute and I'll speak to my father."

It was an old-fashioned sitting-room or parlour that at once recalled my youth. There was a cluttering of Victorian furniture and knick-knacks. Photographs, mostly framed, were everywhere, but before I could do more than glance at the half-dozen on the mantelpiece, the lady was back.

"Father will see you," she told me. "My name's Foster, by the way. Father's eighty-seven, you know, so will you try to make it as brief as you can? Anything about old times makes him excited and then he sleeps badly."

We crossed the hall to a door that opened into a dining-room. That sitting-room had been cold, but this room was uncomfortably warm. The table had been pushed back to afford a clear view of a television screen. Two cats were asleep on a rug before the open fire, and the smell of them and tobacco smoke was faintly in the room.

Lang was in a wheel-chair and he swivelled it slightly round to get a good look at me. I'd have taken him for far less than eighty-seven. His eyes were alert and only the thin hands and the face showed the tincture of age. I held out a hand.

"Mr. Lang? Glad to have met you, sir."

His grasp wasn't very firm. He peered through his glasses at my card.

"A Mr. Travers, isn't it? And you've come to talk about Trude. Ellen says she's comes into some money."

It was a slow, careful sort of voice. Now and again his dentures would shift and he'd have a momentary trouble with his sibilants.

"Don't know who should leave her any money unless it was that brother of hers."

"She had a brother?"

"Oh, yes," he said. "He was almost grown-up when she wasn't more than a child. That was when he went away. He never could get on with Sam Layman."

When I thought later about that interview, I knew he'd been as much in the past as in that room. He'd rambled from a point and it'd been hard to bring him back. There'd been, for instance, my first mention of Sambord.

"Never did like him. 'Mother.' I said, 'he's a rotter.' I know what men are. I've seen 'em; all sorts and conditions, as they say, but there you are: she was all on Trude's side. 'You women all stick together and that's where it gets you.' I said. If she'd listened to me . . ."

In his time, too, he must have been something of a martinet: now, like Giants Pope and Pagan, his teeth had gone. The daughter, Ellen, just ignored him when he checked her tartly for some interruption. Now and again she'd catch my eye and give me a quiet smile or a nod.

Perhaps I'd better condense the whole thing into my own version of what I learned. Lang's Imperial Circus dated from mid-Victorian times. In the era of Victor Lang's father it had definitely been honoured by various crowned heads of Europe. The Langs had been some of the first to use continental acts, and one that had been brought over by Victor was the Rubensteins. Trude and Martin, gymnasts. Lang mentioned them with affection. They stayed with him for some years and Martin later became naturalised. It seemed to have been a very personal loss when Martin was killed in a train accident in 1928. Trude stayed on for a time as book-keeper and then she married Sam Layman. Lang spoke of it as a come-down. Later the Laymans were to be killed in a London blitz, leaving behind the daughter, Trude.

I gathered that the mother had spoiled her son Martin, which had led to bad blood when she married Layman. Martin had ultimately run away, and Layman had accused him of taking money. Be that as it might, the mother had also had special plans for Trude. She'd been very clever, Lang said, and had done well at her school: a good school, he said, that must have cost the mother more than she could afford. When the Laymans had been killed. Trude had gone to a sister of Sam's in Cricklewood. but she hadn't liked it there.

"You knew young Trude well?"

"The way he's always talking about her, you'd think she was his granddaughter." Ellen said.

"You keep quiet, Ellen." he told her. "This gentleman and me are doing the talking."

Lang himself had retired by then and his wife didn't die till quite a few years later. Trude, it was easy to see, had indeed been almost a grandchild. During her holidays she was always in and out of the Highgate house. Always the little lady, Lang said, and the funny thing was that she always had a secret hankering for the circus. That had been her mother coming out in her.

What she did do when she finally left school was to go to a secretarial college, her idea being to get a job as a secretary to one of the big circuses. What she actually did was to work for some big firm or other in Cricklewood, and as soon as she got that job she left her aunt and shared a room with another girl. Later still she got that job with Sambord and moved to a place of her own at Lewisham.

How she got that job he didn't know. It was plain that he hated even to mention it. Trude could have had anything, so maybe she'd regarded that job as a kind of gateway to circus life. The Langs didn't see much of her for a time, and then she suddenly announced that she was bringing Sambord to see them.

Lang's dislike of Sambord had apparently been so plain, and Trude had so taken umbrage at the advice he'd given her, that she'd left in something of a rage. A week or two later the news of the marriage came as a shock and a very deep hurt. The Langs hadn't been invited to the wedding. And from that day to this, never a word had been heard of her or from her.

"You shouldn't have interfered, Father."

The old man glared. "You keep out of this, Ellen. You know nothing except what you were told. And I was right, wasn't I? Look what happened to that Sambord. Ashamed, that's what she was. Ashamed to own up that she'd been wrong and I'd been right."

I asked if he could make a guess at what had happened to her. He told me he neither knew nor cared. Then, to disprove it, he was telling me what a beauty she'd grown into and how she could have made anything she liked of herself. It was then that the daughter made a quick sign to me and I said goodbye to old Victor Lang.

She went with me into the hall. I asked her if she'd any photographs of Trude, but all she knew of were one or two when Trude was a child. I did see a professional take of the two Rubensteins. The mother was a tall, powerful-looking woman.

The father was tallish, quite handsome and beautifully muscled. The photograph was autographed: "To Victor, from Martin and Trude."

"You knew young Trude yourself?"

"Oh, yes," she said. "Until my husband died. I was often here!"

"You shared your father's opinion of her?"

She smiled. "Well, in some ways. yes. She was really handsome. And very clever."

"But—?"

"Well, I thought she grew up into a bit of a madam. She'd made up her mind to be really somebody, not that it was altogether her fault. It was that fool of a mother and the way she was brought up."

I walked down the hill to a bus-stop. When I got to the flat I still couldn't quite balance that evening in a mental ledger. One thing only was now on the credit side. I no longer had any doubts about Mrs. Hugh Wilson. Everything I'd learned about Trude Layman made those two women one and the same.

On the debit side was the fact that I was no nearer finding Trude than I'd been before I'd left for Highgate. Maybe a kind of second-hand, circus glamour that still coloured that half-hour with old Victor Lang made me not too worried about that. Maybe something I'd heard would suddenly start some new train of thought. That's how it often is. You listen for the vital and it just isn't there. Then, later, something trivial turns out to have been vital, and you wonder why you didn't recognise it for what it really was.

On the indeterminate side of that ledger was the fact that I now had a pretty clear picture of the Trude Sambord who'd suddenly left her husband and disappeared. I thought, from what both Lang and his daughter had told me, that I knew the reason why. Also I had another snippet to hand to Jewle.

After the meal I had a look through the evening papers. A new sensation—two children who'd disappeared—was front-page news, but in another column I did find something about the Peplock murder. In connection with that killing, the police were anxious to trace . . .

There followed a description of Sambord, down, you might say, to the last wart and the last button. I wondered what Jewle was up to. In the morning I'd do my best to find out.

7

THE LADY FOUND

"JUST a matter of having more than one string to the bow," Jewle told me. "The obvious isn't always right, you know. It's purely supposition that Sambord was dumped in that river."

"Maybe you're right," I said. "Anything else turned up?"

"Early yet." He gave me one of his dry smiles. "You know us. No brain-waves. No short cuts. Just slogging quietly away."

"Nothing whatever about that third man?"

"Don't know," he said. "There's something Matthews is down there trying to follow up. On that Sunday at about half-past five a constable on the beat was turning into Handley Road from River Road when a motorist cut the corner very sharply. The constable says that if a pedestrian had been stepping off the kerb on his own side of the road, he'd have been knocked down, so he hollered to the driver to stop, but he didn't. He even extinguished his lights for a moment or two and accelerated, and all the constable got of the car number was a double three at the end. No use chasing the car. River Road leads right back to the main road just short of the town. And there are all sorts of side roads."

"The make of car?"

"A black saloon. American type. Bulldog front and tail fins."

He brought the conversation back to my call on Victor Lang. Would there be any point in making another call himself. I said there wouldn't be. I didn't set myself up as infallible, but the fact was that Lang and his daughter Ellen Foster knew nothing whatever about Trude Sambord since the time, ten years ago, when she'd disappeared. The only difference that call had made was that now I'd be prepared to swear in any court of law that my Mrs. Hugh Wilson and Trude Sambord were the same person.

It had been an early trip to the Yard. Jewle was going to Ambourne himself and I went down with him to his car. It was just after ten o'clock when I got back to the office, and it was just about half-past when Bertha said a Mr. Rodey would like to see me. I told her to show him in.

Rodey was wearing an overcoat instead of the battered waterproof, and he didn't favour me with that ironic smile of his. He was altogether a much more sober person. I got up from behind the desk as he came in and held out my hand.

"Sorry to bother you, sir, but could I have just a minute or two of your time?"

"Why not?" I said, and waved him to a chair. "You'd like coffee? I'm just having some myself."

I passed the cigarette box but he didn't smoke. Bertha brought coffee and went back to her room.

"Now what can I do for you?" I said.

"Well, it's rather tricky," he said. "People like me, Mr. Travers, can't make bricks without straw. You've got to have both. All I'm pretty heavy on at the moment is straw. No clay." He smiled: "Could be the other way about."

I smiled, too. "Let's leave the Book of Exodus and get down to facts. You're thinking of the Peplock case?"

"Exactly. All I get from the Yard is a handout. A paragraph that just won't stand padding. My editor's getting a bit impatient. That's why I thought of you. You were down there even before the story broke, so I wondered if there was anything you could hand on. I'd guarantee no mention whatever of your name. Or your agency."

"Depends what you want to know. Suppose you make a start."

"Very well, sir. Why were you down there at all?"

"Confidentially, I was there inadvertently. It so happened that Peplock knew someone for whom we'd done a job and he'd given Peplock one of our cards, and it was found on Peplock's body. I should add that it's now been all cleared up but naturally Superintendent Jewle wanted to ask me some questions."

"I see," he said slowly. "But doesn't that look to you as if Peplock took that card because he knew he might be wanting the services of someone like you himself?"

I had to laugh. "My dear fellow! Peplock was an enquiry agent himself."

"All the same," he persisted, "he might have wanted to keep something from that partner of his—Dorlish."

"You're making a mystery out of nothing," I told him. "The man who gave Peplock that card was enthusiastic about what we'd done. He virtually had to force that card on Peplock."

"Ah well," he said. "And there's nothing else you know that might be useful?"

"Never a thing. I'm in a worse position than even you—if I did want to know anything. I'm not in a position to go to the Yard like you fellows and ask for a handout."

Bertha brings in a pot, not a mere cup, when I have a caller. I filled Rodey's cup again.

"Thanks," he said. "Looks as if I'll have to scrounge elsewhere."

I asked him about that missing children case. Wasn't there a good story in that?

"Played out at the moment," he said. "It's more or less a dead end." The ironic smile came for the first time. "All the heart strings torn. It's back where I started. Bricks without straw."

"You a married man?"

"Oh, yes," he said. "Not very happy these days, not after that *News Chronicle* and *Star* business. No use telling your wife the *Record* isn't likely to go the same way. You married?"

"I certainly am."

"Then you'll know what women are like," he said.

"Any children?"

"Just the one boy," he told me, and his face suddenly softened. "Went down with polio last year. The worst type but he's slowly getting back the use of his limbs. We were able to get him into a special clinic in Switzerland. My wife's going to see him this week-end."

"I'm sorry," I said. "It's tough luck. On the boy and you both. If there's anything I can do at any time . . ."

"Good of you," he said, and began getting to his feet. "But he can't be getting better treatment than he is now."

"Why all the hurry?" I said. "Have some more coffee. All sorts of things I wanted to ask you."

I poured him another cup. "Didn't someone tell me you spent a considerable time in the States?"

"Well, yes," he said. "You know how it is. Tried all sorts of jobs: in a little detective agency and then a bigger one. Didn't care much for the life, so switched to free-lance writing. It didn't add up to much so I came back here."

"You didn't absorb much accent."

He smiled. "You just acquire it. Comes as a matter of course and then you get back here and it goes—most of it."

We chatted for a few minutes about American agencies and then he once more rose to go.

"Thank you, sir, for letting me use your time. I'm sorry about mentioning my private affairs. It must have sounded as if I was trying to drum up a bit of sympathy."

"Not a bit," I told him. "It's the last thing I'd have thought. And thank you for our little chat. If I get hold of something I can pass on without prejudice, I'll certainly do so."

I saw him out myself, and as I came back to the room I couldn't help thinking how verdicts that are purely transitory can change. An hour before, I'd have said that Rodey was brash, slick and none too particular: all of which, I had to admit, didn't make a man a bad journalist. Far from it. Now I'd changed my mind. Like Jewle, I had a sneaking liking for him. He'd put his cards on the table, face up, and hadn't tried to pull a fast one as he had so amusedly with Jewle. Also I *had* been sorry about that boy of his. Maybe I don't make any sort of a hand about being hard-boiled. Maybe I'm like a good many others—a sucker for a sob story—but I was pretty sure that he hadn't even dreamed of working on my feelings. One thing I did have to admit: I'd been a bit flattered perhaps by the deference he'd shown me, though there wasn't all that difference in our ages. In this day and age, as they say, it's nice to run across good manners with no trace of servility.

I had an appointment in the suburbs that afternoon and I drove my car. It was after five o'clock when I got back and, by the time I'd talked to Norris, it was almost half-past. I wasn't in any particular hurry to leave, so I thought I'd brew myself some tea and try to work once more on Trude Sambord: this time in the light of what I'd learned twenty-four hours ago at Highgate.

I was just about half way through my first cup when the telephone rang.

"That you, sir?" It was Hallows and the tone was urgent.

"Yes," I said.

"You don't happen to have your car?"

"I do. Why?"

"You'd better get along here, sir. I'll be looking out for you in Chancery Lane. Turn into the side street. It's on your left."

He rang off. As I grabbed my hat and gulped down the rest of the tea, I realised he must have been speaking from somewhere near his observation point at City Investigations. I was putting on my overcoat as I went through the door. Another car had parked near my own and it took a maddening couple of minutes to inch mine out.

It was as bad a time as any for traffic. There was a hold-up at the end of Fleet Street and almost five minutes went by before I could make the right turn. I had to keep waving on the traffic behind me till about half way along the Lane I saw Hallows.

I stopped the car just inside the short passage that led to Whitmore Court and he nipped in beside me. He told me to drive through and keep to the left. A few yards on he told me to stop, and I drew the car close in at the kerb.

"She can't have gone," he said. "There's only one way out. Mind if I get in the back while I tell you about it and then I can keep my eyes on the place."

This is what he told me. He'd come on duty just before half-past five. A minute or two later the secretary-receptionist had left and only a dim light was left on in the inside above the door. A few minutes later a woman had suddenly appeared in the Court and she was looking for something, and she'd passed so close that he'd had a good look at her.

"According to that description you gave me of that Mrs. Wilson. I'd almost swear it was her. She went on, round there by the light, and then she had a look at that plate on the door there, and then she went in. As far as I know, she's in there now."

If it really was the woman we wanted, then no wonder he'd sprinted for the nearest telephone. That Court was far from well lighted but I was peering through my window at what I could discern of the premises that housed City Investigations.

"Who's likely to be there?"

"Probably only Dorlish. Might be an operative on night duty in the staff room: if so I didn't see him go in."

"It's amazing." I said. "What the devil can she want with Dorlish?"

"Probably wants to use him. Pulling that same stunt as she did with you. Didn't want to use the same firm twice."

He might have been right. Sambord was dead but she didn't know it. All that had been announced was what had appeared the previous night, that the police were anxious to get into touch with him. And that made him still alive.

"Something's badly wrong," I said. "Let's look at it logically, step by step. I found Sambord for her. All right. What should she have done? Got into touch with him. He was still where I told her he was. Perhaps she did, personally or through an intermediary. We're not sure Sambord's money hidden in the caravan came from Peplock. Perhaps it came from her. You're with me so far?"

He said he was.

"Right. We move on to City Investigations. Mrs. Wilson reads the papers, so she must have read about the Peplock murder and that he virtually *was* City Investigations. In that case there must be some special reason if she wants them to find the missing Sambord for her. Am I right in suggesting that she knows there's some connection between Sambord and Peplock?"

"Damned if I know." he said. "The whole thing's got me tied up in knots. What I do know is what you said about coincidences. Too many of them. That woman has to be up to the ears in what happened down at Ambourne."

I got my pipe going. Hallows rarely smokes but we both sat looking across the dimly lighted Court. It was really more of a Square in miniature. Now and again someone would come in from Chancery Lane and enter one of the few buildings, and two or three people had gone out. But nothing had stirred at City Investigations. The only sign of life was the dim light through the fanlight above the door.

Twenty minutes had gone and then there was a movement. We didn't see the door open or close: just the sudden movement, and then the knowledge that the woman must have come through that one door. I moved the car gently on and round. At the T-head there was a doubt which way she'd turn, but she went left towards Holborn. Traffic was being held up at the Fleet Street end and we had the left side of the street to ourselves and could dawdle. We kept her just in view till the sound of traffic behind us made us move on.

"Slow a bit and I'll nip out," Hallows said. "Looks to me as if she's making for Chancery Lane Station."

As I passed the woman who was walking quickly along the pavement, I knew for a certainty who she was. There was a hold-up at the end of the Lane and she overtook me, and when I was able to turn left, she'd gone from my sight. I didn't even see Hallows.

I just caught sight of her as I neared the Underground Station and then I was looking for a place to park. There wasn't one handy enough so I kept the car moving. Everything now depended on Hallows.

I drove the car to my garage and went home. I rang the Agency and asked for any call from Hallows to be put through to my private number, and after that there was nothing to do but to wait. Bernice was out for the evening, so I switched on the fire, got myself a bottle of beer and tried to concentrate on the evening papers. As far as I could see, there was never a word about the Peplock case.

It was not until half an hour later that Hallows rang.

"Everything okay," he told me. "I know who she is and where she lives."

"Where're you speaking from?"

"A telephone box at Hampstead Tube Station."

"Right," I said. "Shouldn't take you long to get here. I'll have a meal ready."

This is why I rang Jewle that night at his private address, The woman had taken the Underground as Hallows had guessed, and he'd followed her to Hampstead. She'd looked around for a taxi but there hadn't been one, so she'd walked. It was only about half-a-mile in any case, and she'd ended up at a handsome block of flats called Waterford Gardens. Hallows put the flats in the seven-fifty-a-year class at least.

He'd given her about two minutes' start, then he'd gone in. At the desk he said he was looking for a Mrs. So-and-So. The clerk on duty said no such person lived there. Hallows said the lady who had just come in had looked like her. The clerk said he'd been mistaken. That was Mrs. Hayhill. For the sake of appearances Hallows asked if it would be in order to wait, and it was. Hallows sat in one of the easy chairs in the handsome vestibule, kept looking at his watch, and finally left.

I wouldn't tell Jewle what I wanted the early morning appointment for but he said he'd be available from half-past eight onwards. I said I'd be with him at nine sharp, and I was. What I was going to ask him to do was more than tricky. And I'd have to lay down certain conditions, and you just can't very well do that with anyone of the standing of Jewle.

Matthews was there, too, when I walked in that morning. A friendly word or two and I was waved to a chair.

"All right," Jewle said, but not too seriously, "start talking."

"Only too glad to," I told him. "I've found Trude Sambord for you."

"You have!" His eyes popped a bit. "How'd you do that?"

Matthews cut in. "Don't say you've been keeping her in cold storage?"

"Nothing like that," I told him. "You ought to know me better. In any case I can claim that she's a client."

"Not in a murder case you can't."

That was Matthews again. Jewle waved at him for quiet.

"Tell us about it."

I told him we were looking for something quite different and we'd picked up her trail quite by chance.

"This is what I'd like you to do," I said. "You can't force me to tell you who she is and where she is, or if you do, I can easily tell you anything that fits certain aspects of the case and you won't be able to prove just how much of it is worth the while. You agree to what I'm going to propose, and I'll put every single card on the table."

"And what do you propose?"

"That I call on the lady before she's likely to go out: say when I leave here, and that either you or Matthews goes with me, posing as my partner at the Agency. Also I'm perfectly willing for you people to decide what course the conversation with the lady takes."

Jewle actually laughed. "Why not? What did you make all the mystery about? Matthews will go. Just give him time to posh himself up a bit. And now what's the whole story?"

I told them. Neither said a word till I'd finished. Then Jewle gave a wry shake of the head.

"I don't know but this gets a more fantastic business than ever. It's like one of those puzzles there used to be when I was a boy: a whole lot of rings you had to detach and you never saw how the devil it could be done, not if you didn't happen to hit on the knack of it. What was she seeing Dorlish about? As you said, she'd known where Sambord was. She can't have known he's dead."

"Peplock's dead and Dorlish was his partner," Matthews said. "Strikes me the quicker we get that woman to talk, the quicker we'll be getting places. And since I'm going with you, Mr. Travers, how are you proposing to tackle her?"

"More in sorrow than in anger," I told him. "Give me a moment to light my pipe and we'll put together a few ideas."

The clock above the ornate desk at Waterford Gardens showed exactly a quarter-past ten. The number of the apartment was five. We'd unearthed that at the Yard by getting a policewoman to ask if Mrs. Hayhill was still at Waterford Gardens.

Matthews and I went straight on past the desk and the newsstand, and up a short flight of stairs to a heavily carpeted corridor. We turned right at the far end of another corridor. Apartment No. 5 was the first on the left, which meant that it overlooked the car park. I looked at Matthews. He shrugged his shoulders. I pushed the bell.

I didn't have to ring a second time. The door opened almost at once and there was the lady. She stared. The whole of her seemed to tremble at the sight of me.

"Good-morning, Mrs. Wilson," I said. "I and my partner here would like to have a word with you. May we come in?"

She still couldn't speak, but she drew back. We went through the door. She stayed there for a moment after she'd closed it and then she pulled herself together. She even managed to smile.

"I'm so sorry," she said, "but you were the last person I expected to see. It's Mr. Travers, isn't it?"

"Glad you remembered. This is Mr. Matthews, one of my partners."

"Won't you sit down? And if you'll excuse me just a moment."

She disappeared through a door to the far right. Matthews and I had a look round. That lounge room was beautifully furnished: deep piled carpet; deep, loose-covered chairs and double settee; fireplace with a reproduction Georgian break-front bookcase, modern Swedish coffee table, and what looked like genuine eighteenth-century prints on the walls. A pink telephone set was on one of the side tables, but my guess was that she was now telephoning heaven knows whom from another room.

If she was it wasn't taking her long. Hardly before we'd taken in that room, she was back. Now she was absolutely herself again. I doubted if I'd ever seen a more attractive-looking woman, and the dark red jumper and the black skirt went wonderfully with the jet black hair. The voice was almost gay.

"Can I get you both some coffee?"

"Thanks," I said, "but we're in rather a hurry. We're also a bit puzzled. I mean, you came to us as a Mrs. Hugh Wilson, and now it turns out that you're a Mrs. Hayhill."

"Very simple," she said calmly. "Does everyone want to give her real name? Besides, I was only dealing with a firm. Did it really matter?"

"Only to this extent," I said, "that it cost a lot in time and trouble to trace you here."

Her head went slightly sideways and there was just the faintest smile.

"Trace me? But why?"

"Well, I'll be blunt," I said, and looked questioningly at Matthews. "We think you ought to know what's happened. You asked us to find a Richard Sambord, and we did. You've seen anything about him in the papers?"

"Should I?"

"Look," I said, "don't temporise. It's far too serious for that. Did you or did you not?"

She tittered slightly. "This is all very mysterious but say I did. There was something about the police wanting to interview him in connection with the death of some man or other."

"Exactly," I said. "A man named Peplock. But what we can tell you in confidence is that Sambord is dead, too. Probably murdered."

She moistened her lips. She stared. I think if she'd had just a fraction of a second's more time, she'd have thrown a faint. She looked away, moistening her lips again.

8

THE PHILANTHROPIST

MIND you, I wasn't dead sure at the time, but later I knew she was realising that her cards were being played the wrong way. There was no personal interest, she'd told me, in Sambord. Everything was being done on behalf of a relative.

"But this is dreadful," she said. "I just can't believe it."

"From our point of view it's worse than that," Matthews told her. He took a chance and drew the longbow slightly. "We aren't prepared to be driven out of business for concealing evidence or shielding a probable witness, so you'd better tell us the name of that relative who wanted to get into touch with Sambord. The one for whom you were acting."

"Oh, but I couldn't do that. I promised I wouldn't say a word."

"I see. And what did you actually do when you read our message in the newspaper?"

"I checked it. I found the telephone number of that farm and gave them a ring. Mr. Granding's secretary answered. She seemed very suspicious at first and then she admitted that Mr. Sambord was staying there. After that I told my cousin and washed my hands of the whole thing."

"But you were touring France?"

"Oh, I came home specially. I had to see my cousin in any case before he left for America."

Matthews gave me a questioning look. I shook a sad head.

"I'm afraid, Mrs. Hayhill, we'll have to report all this to Scotland Yard. Any promise of ours about secrecy isn't valid when there's murder involved. I expect you'll be hearing from them at once."

She was really scared. "Must you do that? Listen, I'm prepared to pay." She began opening her handbag. "I'll pay anything."

"That'd only make things far worse," I said. "We've been very lenient with you, you know. Even up to this very last minute you've told us all sorts of untruths. I doubt if you've told us a single word of truth since we entered this room." I held up a hand. "Don't get indignant. We're enquiry agents, Mrs. Hayhill, so when it became necessary to protect our own interests, we did a whole lot of enquiring."

We'd given her enough rope. The time had come for the truth. She was scared but she still had a grip on herself.

I turned to Matthews. "Shall I tell her or you?"

"You did most of the work," he said, so I told her. I smacked her clean in the eye by addressing her as Mrs. Sambord. I told her her whole history. Whether the tears were real I didn't know, but before I'd finished she was blubbering into a cushion.

We waited till she'd recovered. We'd plenty of time.

"Let's start again," I said. "Anything but the absolute truth and we ring Scotland Yard. And don't forget there're things we know that we haven't even told you. Let's begin with Sambord. Why did you leave him?"

The poise, the arrogance of voice had gone. Now she was playing the penitent. "Because he was married already."

"How did you find out?"

"A woman came to the office to see him and I heard them talking. There wasn't any doubt about it. I left the office before he came into my room and went to the hotel and packed and left."

"You knew who the woman was?"

"No, but she was American. I knew that by her voice."

"We'll accept that—for the moment. Later you married again— someone called Hayhill. Who is he?"

"His name is Frank Hayhill. He's a wealthy philanthropist. He's head of a Refugee Society and working over here on behalf of refugees."

"When did you marry him?"

"Eight years ago. When I left Sambord I got a job as secretary at the Belfort Hotel, Southampton, and I met him there. I never told him about the other marriage."

"I see. And why did you decide after all these years to get into touch with Sambord again?"

Some of her confidence had come back. So far I'd believed her. About what was to come I wasn't to be so sure.

"I couldn't help wondering about him. Whether he was dead or not. Also he mightn't have been in—well, good circumstances, so I was going to send him some money. Anonymously, of course."

I thought she was due for a little encouragement. "You did ring Mr. Granding. Mr. Matthews verified that. You actually spoke to his secretary and she told you Sambord wasn't too well off. Did you send him money?"

"No. I got a bit afraid. I thought something might come out. And I daren't risk injuring my husband's reputation. He's doing important work. I never told him about Sambord."

"And so?"

"Well, I just kept putting it off and then I read in the newspaper about the police wanting to get into touch with Sambord and that scared me still more. Then yesterday I decided to employ another agency to find out why the police wanted him."

"City Investigations?"

She stared. "You knew?"

I reminded her that we'd told her we'd known a lot more than we'd divulged. And that was where I should have kept my big mouth shut. She'd spiked one of our big guns. If we knew such a lot, then she'd guessed we might know about that night call on Dorlish. When she'd left us after we'd just arrived, she'd probably given Dorlish a quick ring.

I glanced at my watch. "You'd better get back to the office," I told Matthews. "In case anything's turned up. I'll be along in a few minutes."

He said goodbye and left.

"Now I come to think," I said. "I don't think there's a lot more to ask you, Mrs. Hayhill. Where's your husband now, by the way?"

"Actually he's away for a day or two. He lectures, you know, and shows films of displaced persons and refugees. Tonight he's in Edgeford."

"And where did you live in Canada?"

"Various cities. Mostly in Montreal, but we always preferred hotels to keeping a regular apartment."

"And you've been back here how long?"

"About two years. My husband knew the Refugee Year was coming and he thought he'd do better work here. It's nearer to Europe you know."

I had to hang on a bit longer to give Matthews more time. A little upbraiding wouldn't do any harm. I even quoted that tangled web piece. Travers, the moralist. I sounded so convincing, even to myself, and she was so abjectly sorry for the trouble she'd given me, that a tiny bit of pity for her was creeping in unaware. Or was it that the lady was what she was?

Not that there was any great danger of my becoming a Samson to her Delilah: all the same I knew it was time to leave.

"For the moment," I told her, "we'll leave things as they are. One thing, though, we must insist on. If you have anything new at any time concerned in any way with what we've been talking about, you're to get into touch with us at once. You agree to that?"

"I do. I really do. And I think you're being very generous considering the way I behaved. And now you must let me pay you."

I shook my head.

"Couldn't dream of it. Just one of those things."

"That's very generous of you. You're married yourself?"

We were now at the door. I was wondering just what was coming.

"Yes," I said.

"Oh." She gave a little tinkle of a laugh. "I was only wondering if you'd care to have lunch with me some time. It'll be rather lonely while my husband's away."

"That'd be delightful. Perhaps you'll let me give you a ring."

She was so close that I actually jolted her as I opened the door.

I went back to the car, drove round the block and picked up Matthews as arranged. We sat on for a minute or two comparing notes. On the whole we'd done well enough and everything had proceeded much as arranged—all except that call of hers on Dorlish. That had been planned as one of our bombshells. It had ended as a very damp squib.

Matthews had left early because we'd brought a man along, just in case. From now on the lady would have someone on her tail.

"Might as well call your own man off," he told me as he moved the car on. "We'll keep Dorlish under observation from now on."

We went back to the Yard. Jewle had a question when he'd heard the report.

"Anything unusual beginning to strike you about all this?"

"Heaps of things," I said. "When she'd verified where Sambord was, why should she put off sending him money? All she had to do was to send anything she liked by registered post. Also why go to Dorlish of all people? And after normal hours. Hallows saw the secretary leave, and our guess is that Dorlish was in there alone."

"Yes," he said. "I don't want to hurt your feelings, but she was still having you two on a piece of string. Not that you didn't learn a whole lot."

He gave himself a little congratulatory nod.

"I think the knots are beginning to get untied a bit. Dorlish, Peplock, Sambord, the lady. Which reminds me of what I was going to say. Doesn't it strike you we're getting too many Canadians? Peplock was one and so is this Hayhill. Maybe nothing in it, of course."

I asked him if he'd got any sort of a line on Peplock and Canada.

"We sent his prints over," he said, "but we haven't got anything yet. Also a photograph. Vancouver, where he was supposed to have operated, knew nothing."

"And Dorlish?"

"He was given the option of resigning, or else. We think there was something like a minor Brighton case up there in Mainford, but I doubt if we'll ever really know. Those provincial forces can clam up when they like. Don't like any slur on their own efficiency." He went off at a tangent. "What's this Hayhill's full name?"

"Frank," Matthews told him. "Frank Hayhill. I managed to verify it back there."

Jewle pushed the buzzer and picked up the receiver. He gave instructions for an urgent message to Edgeford. That isn't its real name, by the way. It's a famous spa. At any rate, as I said, Jewle wanted information. A Frank Hayhill was lecturing at Edgeford that night, probably to the local refugee organisation. What was wanted was a full description of his car, if, that is, he'd arrived by car.

"That car at Ambourne that cut the corner too fast?" I said.

"That's about it," he said. "Can't afford to miss a trick." He looked up at the clock. "A bit late for coffee, or isn't it?"

I said I'd like a cup. I wanted to stay on as long as I could. Jewle said he wouldn't mind another cup himself, so three cups came in. As I took the first sip of mine, I had an idea.

"I'm not trying to pull a fast one but I'd like a look at this Hayhill in action. Plenty of time to get down there by train." Jewle set his cup back in the saucer. He gave me a queer look. "Just why should you be so interested? You're no longer involved."

Matthews, of all people, came to the rescue. "If he wants to go, we can't stop him. I think it might be a good idea. Besides, you know Mr. Travers. He's like that camel that wanted to get in the tent."

"Don't see the point," Jewle told him, and then I saw something like a twinkle in his eye. "But as you say, if he wants a trip down there at his own expense, that's no business of ours."

"Mighty generous of you," I told him. "Could I trespass on your kindness a little further and ask you to look up trains?"

He reached for the Bradshaw. There was a train, he said, at two that afternoon. And if the meeting didn't last too long, a return to town at nine-thirty.

As I went through the railway station barrier I felt a touch on my arm. It was Matthews, and we went through together.

"Nice of you to see me off," I said. "But where're the flowers?"

He laughed. "Still one for a joke. But, as a matter of fact, the Old Man thought you'd like a bit of company." He showed me his ticket. "You see? First-class and everything."

"And suppose I'm second?"

"With the income-tax what it is? Don't make me laugh."

We had a first-class compartment to ourselves. He'd come provided with a pack of cards, so we played rummy most of the way and he took about six shillings of my money. In return he stood me tea.

We went straight to police headquarters. A message had already been sent to Jewle. Hayhill was staying for the night at the Majestic and he'd booked in at just after midday. His car was an almost new 1959 Humber saloon: licence number LX 1009. His lecture was being given to the local refugee society and friends in the large annexe to one of the local halls: time, seven o'clock.

We had a wash and brush-up and asked about an unobtrusive place for an early dinner. Just before seven o'clock we were seated at the back of that lecture hall. On the platform was a table and two chairs and behind that a large white screen. The room wasn't all that small but there weren't a lot of empty seats. The audience was roughly about a couple of hundred, women for the most part, and fairly elderly women at that. Up in the front were a couple of clergymen.

There was nothing theatrical about Hayhill's entry: the lights merely came full on as two men came from the right towards the table. One, a lean elderly man, was the chairman, an Alderman Price. Hayhill, a man of medium height and build, was probably in the late forties. His horn-rims, larger even than my own. and the dark suit, gave him a studious look. His manner was quiet and, on the very few occasions when he raised his voice, you were aware only of a deep conviction.

When the polite applause had died down, the chairman introduced what he called the guest of the evening. The audience, he said, had seen something of the great work to which he had now dedicated his life, through a television film, and now they were being given the opportunity and privilege of seeing him in person.

There was quite a burst of applause when Hayhill rose to speak. His manner was quiet. His voice was cultured and resonant, with just enough accent to give his English a bite. It was what I'd call a friendly voice. Before he'd been speaking long, most of that audience must have been thinking that they were listening to a man whom it was good to know.

He apologised for beginning on a personal note. He had been born, not with a gold spoon in his mouth but certainly with a solid silver one, and later he'd prospered in business: so much so that ten years ago, still as a young man, he'd retired. He'd bought a ranch and bred horses; he'd hunted and fished and done all the things he liked. Then, as her only son, he'd accompanied his mother on a trip to the Holy Land, and while there had been given the opportunity of visiting the Gaza Strip. What he saw there was to change his whole life.

"In a few moments, ladies and gentlemen, you'll be seeing something of what I saw that day. God forbid that I should expect it to change your lives. All I ask is that these films you are about to see will make you more intensely aware of who is your brother.

Our Lord called them the least of these. My brethren. I hope, in that sense, they'll become your brethren too."

There were four films, three of them in colour, and each was prefaced by comments. The first, about Arab refugees, was harrowing enough: parents in wretched huts or make-shift tents and children looking at you with hopeless eyes. The second showed refugee camps in Austria. The third showed three remaining European camps for displaced persons, and contrasted one such camp with one that had been built with funds from the Hayhill organisation. It also included other work: a transit camp in full operation for both refugees and displaced persons.

The fourth film, Hayhill said, was short and, in a way, personal. It showed a squalid camp for displaced persons somewhere in Europe. The camera moved to a room and a pallet and the thin tuberculous face of a man. The wife—under thirty but haggard as if more than twice that age—was standing by that wretched bed. Two children were holding her ragged skirts: a small girl and a boy of eleven. The eyes of the boy were intensely dark and they looked out at you from all the sorrows of the world.

The short film ended and the lights went on.

"The film you have seen," Hayhill said quietly, "was almost the first I took. The girl died about a month later and the father about the same time. Both might have been saved if only some of us had cared a bit sooner and a bit more. You'll pardon my going off at what seems like a tangent, but I don't suppose any of you have given any thought to the man in the projection room this evening. Why should you? He was paid to do a job and you took him for granted. But I'd like you to see him."

A young man appeared from behind the screen. He moved to the front of the platform and bowed. There was a curiously perfunctory applause as if people didn't know what it was all about.

"May I present to you Harry Mitchell," Hayhill said. "Once he was Hari Mitzov, the boy you saw in that last film."

The applause was suddenly deafening. The young man bowed again and left.

"Forgive me, ladies and gentlemen," Hayhill said, "for what must have seemed something far too personal. It does show what we've been able to achieve in the matter of rehabilitation. And now for my final words. World Refugee Year may be over, but an enormous deal remains to be done. Great Britain's contribution to the International Fund was magnificent, but don't let the fountains of charity dry up. We could have shown you pictures of Hong Kong. South Korea and even India. Millions are still living on the verge of starvation, and, what is perhaps even worse, without hope. We want to give them hope. We want to restore their dignity. To do that we must feed and clothe.

"This evening's expenses have been most generously borne by your society here. What I say to you, then, is go home and think, in the quietness and comfort and security of that home, about what you have seen this evening. Take out your chequebook or your wallet and do what you can for these your brethren. This is the address."

It was flashed on the screen: first that of the local society and then the other—

THE GOOD SAMARITANS
103 Gardener Road,
Highbury, N5

That was virtually all. Alderman Price moved the usual vote of thanks which was carried by acclamation. He also added that any contributor could earmark his contribution for any special object if he thought fit, and such instructions, wherever possible, would be scrupulously carried out.

Hayhill was surrounded by quite a small crowd of questioners when he came down from the platform. Matthews and I were handy for the door. I'd looked at my watch and we had almost half an hour before our train left. Matthews said we might as well go straight to the station and get ourselves a drink and a snack. It was only five minutes' walk.

"Well, what'd you think of him?" he said. "What is he? What he makes himself out to be, or a charlatan?"

"Don't know," I said. "If I was betting, I'd say he was a deeply and not too pretentiously religious man."

"A genuine Christian?"

"If you like."

"Well, that's where you're wrong." he said. "Religious people are ten a penny but how many real Christians have you come across?"

"Depends upon what criteria one uses."

"All right," he said. "Let's take the Sermon on the Mount. If you have two coats, give one away. Turn the other cheek. Take no money in your purse. Take no thought for the morrow, and all that."

"Very well," I said. "Let's accept those standards. Who says Hayhill doesn't live up to them in what he's doing."

"You're dodging the issue," he told me. "Leave out what he's supposed to be doing and take the man himself. Is he living by the Sermon on the Mount?"

"Don't know," I said. "But as you seem to have suddenly become a kind of Judgment Day juror, not to say an authority on Holy Writ, let me remind you that we're also told that the labourer is worthy of his hire."

"All right, I'll meet you on your own ground. When you get home tonight and think of those films and the dirt and disease and the half-starved kids and the rest of it, will you feel quite so pleased about yourself as you did, say, when you were having breakfast this morning?"

"Maybe not," I said. "I might even do something about it."

"Quite. And what about Hayhill? He's spent this evening showing us all the misery in the world. How will he feel in a few minutes when he has a late dinner in that posh hotel where he's staying? How will he feel when he gets home again to his seven-hundred-and-fifty-a-year flat? Will he make his wife go and sell that mink coat you mentioned?"

"You're a cynic," I said, and by then we were at the station restaurant. And yet, as I ate a sandwich and drank the incredibly bad coffee, I couldn't help feeling he was right.

9

THE GOOD SAMARITANS

AT BREAKFAST I asked Bernice if she knew anything about an organisation calling itself The Good Samaritans. Apparently it had been interviewed by television.

She said she'd seen the programme. It had been part of one of those feature programmes put out on an occasional afternoon. As far as she remembered, it had been about work being done for refugees and displaced persons.

"You remember the man in charge of it? A Canadian named Hayhill?"

"I don't remember any Canadian," she said. "I'm almost sure it was a clergyman who was supposed to be the one in charge. I do know that a great feature was made of the fact that all their staff were either refugees or displaced persons. I think they were all youngish women. Why do you ask?"

I told her it was somewhat in the line of business. In our home, unless it's very necessary, we keep business well outside the door. All the same I didn't see why I shouldn't tell her about the previous night. I even wound up with that little discussion between Matthews and myself on the way to the station. Bernice is the one in our apartment who has the better fund of good, sound common-sense.

"You can't apply the Sermon on the Mount to us," she said. "What was good for two thousand years ago needn't necessarily be good now. Besides, if this Hayhill is a wealthy man, why shouldn't he live like one? I mean he could give away an awful lot and still have plenty left. What was Inspector Matthews grumbling about? He couldn't surely expect anyone nowadays to sell all he had and give to the poor?"

I left it like that. Before the day was out I was proposing to learn quite a lot more about Hayhill. And then Bernice had to have the last word.

"Isn't there a fraud squad or something like that at Scotland Yard? I mean, if this Hayhill was a fraud, wouldn't they have had suspicions?"

I said I had an absolutely open mind. I did add that a really clever fraud would take a very long time to detect and expose. And there we left it. For my own part I still didn't quite think that Hayhill was rooking the great British public. Admittedly there'd been one or two times when I'd rather winced at some of the things he'd said, but that didn't make me too sensitive a plant or Hayhill a rogue.

When I got to the office, Norris handed me a cable from Bob McGuffie.

EDWARD LAMBERT BORN BROOKLYN CREATED ACT STOP RICHARD SAMBORD ASSISTANT AND UNDERSTUDY STOP LAMBERT MARRIED GRACIE KAHN NINETEEN THIRTY-FIVE STOP PROBABLY MARRIED SAMBORD FORTY-EIGHT ON LAMBERT'S DEATH THEREBY GIVING HIM CONTROL OF ACT STOP GRACIE DIVORCED SAMBORD NEVADA FORTY-NINE STOP REMARRIED NOW LIVING HARRISBURG STOP LETTER FOLLOWS STOP

I had to read that cable a couple of times to find out just how much in the way of information it was worth, and what I decided was that it hadn't done me any particular good. On the other hand it had backed Trude's story. Or had it?

In my room I tried to set out the pros and cons. As I now worked things out, Gracie Khan had been much younger than Lambert. Whether she and the handsome Sambord had been having an affair before Lambert died or whether the marriage to Sambord had been one of convenience to both parties, I didn't know, but what was almost certain was that Sambord had brought the act to England to try it out, and had left his wife behind.

Equally certain was the fact that it was Gracie whom Trude had seen and overheard that day in the Welland House office. And that seemed to make the rest of her story absolutely true. Only one thing was wrong. Why had Trude been so dead sure?

Why had she gone on taking things for granted when, if she'd taken the trouble to have enquiries made by some responsible firm, she'd have known as much as I'd just learned. And that led up to the one important question: Why had she let eight years go by since marrying Hayhill before she did make enquiries about Sambord? Surely she ought to have done it prior to her marriage. And after all, had Hayhill been so unworldly and self-righteous that he couldn't have been told about that marriage that hadn't been a marriage at all? And again, unless Hayhill had been an utter fool, or Trude much more clever than most, he must have known that he hadn't married a virgin. And that brought another question. Had Trude admitted a previous marriage, but not to Sambord? Had she said that the whole thing had been so painful that she never wished to speak of it again?

As far as I was concerned, that attempt to get at the truth was becoming hopeless. It was like driving along a road with no direction posts, and every short while a road that forked slightly to right or left so that you didn't know which was the original main road and which was not. I gave it all up. Maybe after I'd had a look at the Good Samaritans I might unearth some new ideas.

I took a taxi. It's no use keeping a dog and barking yourself, so it was for the driver to find 103 Gardener Road. It turned out to be a smallish detached house that had been wholly taken over by the organisation.

I paid off the taxi and walked along the short path to the front door. By the side was a white plate, lettered in black.

OFFICE OF
THE GOOD SAMARITANS
Please come in.

I accepted the invitation. In the small entrance hall was an enquiry room. To the young woman in charge who was almost certainly English, I gave a card which told her I was a free-lance journalist named P. L. French. She was a very pleasant, well-spoken young woman. She asked me whom I would like to see.

"Anybody who can give me the necessary information. I've written one or two articles on work for refugees and displaced persons, and a friend, who's a great admirer of your Mr. Hayhill, suggested you people might be willing to help."

"I'm sure we would," she told me. "Mr. Hayhill isn't available at the moment. And he doesn't like giving interviews. He's very self-effacing, you know. There *are* people who don't seem to believe that he's always avoiding personal publicity, but I do assure you that it's true."

"I'm sure it is. But who else can I see?"

She smiled charmingly. "Mr. Carnwell. The Reverend Herbert Carnwell. He's our secretary. If you'll wait outside just a moment, I'll give him a ring."

A couple of minutes and she was telling me, just as smilingly, to go upstairs and take the first door on the right. I went up. Both on the ground floor and then on the landing there'd been the clacking of typewriters. No 103 was a busy place. I was rather like a worm that's sneaked its way into an ant-hill.

The quite large room—a former bedroom—had been made into a well-fitted but strictly business-like office. The man who rose from behind the table to greet me was one of the most striking I'd ever seen. He was as tall as I was and even more spare in build. His white hair was swept across his high-domed head but failed to hide the baldness. The deeply sunk eyes were uncannily dark and dominated the thin, ascetic face. El Greco would have loved him. He glanced at the card I gave him.

"Glad to see you, Mr. French."

The smile transformed the face. Maybe Latimer had looked like that when he'd told Master Ridley to be of good cheer. The huge bony hand enveloped my own.

"Do sit down," he told me. The voice was very English with undertones of Oxford. "You'd like to join me in a cup of tea?"

I said I'd be very pleased and, while we waited, I went over my spiel again. He welcomed the idea of an article, provided, as he said smilingly, I'd be so good as to let him see the proofs. He also handed me that line about Hayhill and self-effacement.

A quite pretty girl brought in the tea. Her name was Elena. He told me that her parents had been killed at the Austrian frontier but she'd managed to get across.

"Practically all our employees here are unfortunates whom we've been able to rescue," he said. "Unhappily now the British quotas are virtually filled. But there's still a bright side. America's a great magnet for down-trodden Europe. It's chiefly a matter of finding guarantees or guarantors."

"A pretty intricate business?"

"Yes, indeed. And often an expensive one. We often have to shut a blind eye to bribery to get these unfortunate people out of a country. Still, as I often say, it's the Lord's doing and it's marvellous in our eyes."

I asked him about himself. I didn't know that Cambridge had his particular undertones, but we were both gratified to learn that we'd been at that same university. After a short period in the East End of London, he'd taken up missionary work and had spent all his life, until his retirement through ill-health two years ago, in Assam and Burma.

Back in England he'd met Frank Hayhill and had been enormously impressed by the earnestness, energy and faith of the man, and he'd offered to help in any capacity. It had been something of a miracle. From the comparative invalid of two years before, he'd become the man I now saw.

Hayhill, he told me, was the supreme organiser: the dedicated man to whom time, money and energy were merely trifles compared with the great work of human redemption.

"He's married?"

"Oh, yes," he said. "Mrs. Hayhill's a charming woman. She was actually helping him here before I was able to take over. She hasn't her husband's reserves of energy, you know."

He got to his feet again as he asked me what I'd like to see. If it was all the same to him, I said, I'd like to see anything and everything. He waved at the array of filing cabinets.

"That's where we keep documented histories of all our cases. The more material side is always handled by Mr. Hayhill himself, but I'm afraid I can't show you his room. He lectures, you know, and shows films of our work. Last evening he was in Edgeford and tomorrow he's in Harrogate." He pursed his thin lips. "Now what shall we see first. This floor, perhaps, now we're here."

Two other bedrooms had been knocked into one. Eight women, mostly young, were working there, with a middle-aged English-woman as supervisor. They were of various European nationalities and each was what I'll call a product of the organisation. Carnwell introduced me to each one and I ceremoniously shook hands. The job there was the compiling of mailing lists and I noticed that most of the desks were provided with telephone directories.

Downstairs there was a small canteen-kitchen where another elderly woman was working. In what had been the dining-room, more young women, with a supervisor, were handling the mail and tabulating receipts. In the former drawing-room still more were preparing receipts and printed letters of acknowledgement.

The tour had lasted about a quarter of an hour. No sooner were we back in Carnwell's room than his telephone went.

"So sorry," he said, "but that was a reminder that I have a meeting. I'd have liked to show you our annexe." He looked up at the clock. "You can see it from here."

At the end of the long garden was what looked like a prefabri-cated house. That, he said, was where they were always editing new film. He looked at the clock again and brought out a packet of literature from a drawer of his desk. It had a rubber band round it and I guessed there were plenty more like it in that drawer ready to be handed to visitors.

"Now I must be going," he told me, and held out his hand. I took it warily, thanked him, and promised again to send him proofs of what I wrote. I wasn't sorry to be getting away. The movement of his Adam's apple against the high clerical collar had been fascinating me.

I didn't go far away: just to a convenient corner from which I could watch. I was pretty certain there was nothing of the fake about the Reverend Herbert Carnwell, and there wasn't any about that meeting of his. Luckily for me he took the opposite direction. He was now wearing an overcoat and carrying an umbrella, and his step was almost jaunty as he walked towards the bus-stop.

And there went, I thought, a man who considered himself doubly lucky. It isn't all of us to whom life can offer at best part of seventy a new life through a new mission.

When the coast was clear I walked to Highbury Station. In the train I had a look at that bundle of literature Carnwell had given me. I suppose one could call it impressive. There was a list of patrons occupying best part of a brochure page, but I had a knowledge of only a very few of them. Two were Left-wing cranks. There was a pacifist peer and a female do-gooder whose main aim in life was the publicity through which she probably hoped to become a Dame.

What I'd just seen was only the machine that manufactured the fuel that kept the whole thing going. The actual work was, of course, largely done abroad. Practically all the photographs were stills from the films I'd seen: there were also quite a number of documented cases and laudatory letters from those whom the organisation had helped. Most of those letters had been written from America.

When I got back to the office I rang Matthews. He wasn't available, but I did get Jewle. I told him where I'd been that morning and wondered if he'd like to hear my impressions. He said he was up to the ears in work but thought he could get away for a few minutes.

"What about a scratch lunch at the Golden Eagle? That's handy enough to here."

I told him I'd meet him there at twelve-thirty. I like the Golden Eagle. It's in Hatcher Lane at the back of Victoria Street: and so far it isn't too well known. It was Jewle who'd first introduced me to it and I'd had a meal or two there since.

We filled our plates at the lunch counter, waited a minute or two for a table and made our way between the potted palms and past the huge goldfish bowl to the far corner. While we'd waited I'd asked him what he'd thought of Matthews's report. He'd been non-committal. When we were seated he took up the subject again.

"All these charitable organisations except the very old established ones are always under review," he told me, "not that it'll do any harm to focus our own particular attentions for a time on

Hayhill. You know Matthews. He's always posing as a cynic. I'm one too. You end up that way in a job like mine, so when I hear of someone giving something away, I wonder about a quid pro quo; and when anyone like Hayhill works himself into a sweat, I have a sneaking idea it isn't all just for love."

"Maybe it's not a bad point of view. Where *is* Matthews, by the way?"

He didn't answer for a moment "Well. I don't see why you shouldn't know. He's doing a job at Harrogate where Hayhill's appearing tomorrow night. Between ourselves we'd like a photograph, and some prints."

I began telling him about my morning: to begin with, just a general picture of the machine at work. I added that as a result of what I'd seen and heard, I was beginning to have considerable doubts.

"It's a smooth-running organisation," I said. "What I'm giving you are merely impressions, and they may be wrong. For instance, I wondered, from the attention that was being given them, whether those girls and young women weren't some kind of front. A sort of proof, always on tap, to convince callers like me. Carnwell himself is genuine—I'd swear to that—but I'm equally sure he fronts for Hayhill without being aware of it. He's a credulous, intensely well-meaning sort of soul."

"The place smelt of money?"

"Not a bit of it. Just quietly business-like. The way it all works is possibly this. Hayhill is supposed to hate publicity so everything about him is hush-hush. He keeps very much in the background. He makes those periodical tours to get more patrons for his list and to whip up business through the personal touch. I gathered that he alone handles the cash side of the thing. The way the money comes in is chiefly through appeals and literature sent by means of a mailing list, and this list is being extended and new sources tapped every day. After all, you can send a thousand for under ten pounds. I'd say that between tours Hayhill sees the figures and allocates the money. Some people there may make a guess at what comes in, but he's the only one who knows what goes out."

I gave him the literature Carnwell had handed me. He said he'd certainly look through it.

"Any other ideas?"

I remembered something else and gave him a copy I'd typed of Bob McGuffie's cable.

"Another interesting thing about our Trude is that she worked for a time as secretary till they had the good luck to run across Carnwell. He must have come straight from heaven. From what he told me I gathered that the excuse given for her retirement was ill-health. The real reason might have been that the name of Hayhill was cropping up too much."

"Let's hope Matthews gets hold of what we want," he said. "It could be that Hayhill's keeping in the background in order to support the claim of disinterestedness. Or it might be that he doesn't want his face to be too well-known. Or publicity finding its way to Canada, where he comes from. He's running a risk when he goes on tour, of course, but not all that much." He looked away reflectively. "Wonder if he really needs those big horn-rims he wears?"

The meal had come to an end. We walked back past the goldfish, through the potted palms to the desk. Jewle insisted on paying the bill. I walked with him back to the Yard. There was only one other idea about the Good Samaritans that occurred to me.

It was about those women employed by Hayhill, ostensibly as a visible and living proof of what rehabilitation could do. Wouldn't it, I said, be easier to gull them, say, than English women? Wouldn't it be harder to get information from them? My impression had been that each had been trained for one particular job and no more. They were pieces in a puzzle and only Hayhill knew the whole picture.

"Might be a lot in that," he said. Then he smiled wryly. "It's a funny thing about the Law: I mean the kind of spiral you always get. Our legislators uncover some loophole or other and get to work closing it; then the crooks get together and find a new loophole and so it goes on. You know what I thought when I first heard about the World Refugee Year or whatever they call it? In my mind's eye

I saw all the wise guys and wide boys and the big fellers rubbing their hands together. You know. 'What's in it for us?'"

"Where the carcase is, there will the eagles be gathered together."

"Sooner than that," he said. "Long before the victim even knows he's unwell."

I left him at the corner of Northumberland Avenue. He said he'd enjoyed the meal and we'd certainly have to have another, and if anything turned up about things in general, he'd let me know.

In every way it had been a stimulating morning and my brain was still busy when I got back to the agency. I'd enjoyed that short hour with Jewle and it was while I was thinking about it that I had a sudden idea. It was a queer association of ideas.

I just happened to think of that large goldfish bowl as one went into the luncheon room from the bar. I suppose the bowl made me think of that far-off night when I'd seen Sambord, and all at once I knew just why Jewle had asked for information about Sambord: why he thought, in fact, that Sambord might be still alive. Sambord had an extraordinary ability to hold his breath. When Vingram had bent over him, he had simply held his breath and shammed dead. Maybe he thought Vingram was the one who'd struck him down. Then, of course, as soon as Vingram moved off, he'd got to his feet and disappeared.

But did that explain why Sambord had never come back? Not unless he had a whole lot to conceal. Was it in the earlier evening that he had sneaked out of the Griffin and killed Peplock? And had he returned later because there was still something he hadn't found? I couldn't know, but it was a theory that was more than feasible.

I thought for a minute, then my hand went towards the buzzer. But I didn't press the key. I smiled a bit foolishly at what I'd been about to do—to tell Jewle I knew why he'd acted in a certain way. I think I even blushed at the sheer egotism of it, and it was probably because of that that I went into Norris's room. I knew he had something to which he wanted me to attend.

I did that job, and when Bertha brought in tea I began, of course, thinking of that complicated case again. My hand went to the buzzer again and this time I did press the key. It was Trude Hayhill I wanted, and she happened to be in.

"So sorry I haven't been able to get into touch with you," I told her, "but, believe me, I've had hardly a minute to spare."

"You're not still suspicious of poor me?"

"That's all cleared up," I told her airily. "What I just realised was that there was something we'd got hold of that you mightn't possibly know. It's about—shall we say—a Mr. S. Did you know that when his wife left him he went to enquiry agents to have her found?"

The line went silent.

"You there?"

"Sorry," she told me. "It was the shock of it. I mean I never dreamt he'd have the nerve to do such a thing."

"And he told them you'd taken some valuable jewellery of his."

"Taken it? What there was, was mine."

"I'm sure it was. Still, I thought you'd like to know."

"You don't happen to know what firm it was that he went to?"

"Frankly, no. It was a long time ago. Oh, and something else you might like to know. That American wife of his divorced him in the States in 1949."

That was when a strange thing happened. It was what she said: a queer, half-strangled, drawn-out, "Oh, n-o-o-h!" There was pain in it, or misery. I heard her receiver replaced and I knew it must have been involuntarily.

I sat there wondering what to make of it all. I could still hear that moan of hers when I'd told her about Grace Sambord's divorce, and the click of the receiver as she'd hung up. In a way it was incredible. By every rule she ought to have whooped for joy. That divorce had proved that what she'd told Matthews and myself had been true.

Somehow it haunted me. I went to bed with it and when I woke in the morning it was still there. And there was then another question. Why had she been anxious to know the name of the enquiry firm to whom Sambord had gone? And what would have been the reaction if I'd told her the firm was City Investigations?

10

TWO OLD FRIENDS

IT WAS just before two the next afternoon when I had a surprise call from Jewle.

"You busy for the next hour or so?"

"Not all that busy. Why?"

"A couple of old friends here I'd like you to meet."

"Really! Who are they?"

"Let's make it a surprise. See you shortly then?"

"I'll be there," I told him.

Naturally I kept wondering about that surprise. It couldn't be my old friend Ex-Chief Superintendent Wharton. George and I had had lunch together only a few days before, so I began thinking back to those I'd worked with in the old days, and for the life of me I couldn't recall a single one whom Jewle would be particularly anxious for me to see. By the time I'd reached the Yard, I'd gone most of the way through the provincial police forces with whom I'd had contact, and already I'd recalled quite a few whom I wouldn't mind seeing once more.

But it was strange, I thought, that Jewle should have some one on the look out for me. I was asked to wait. A couple of minutes and Jewle came down.

"Glad you could come," he said. "And I ought to apologise. I'm afraid I played rather a macabre joke on you."

"Such as what?"

As we headed for that chill refrigeration room I guessed what he'd meant by macabre. The attendant slid out the tray and Jewle drew back the sheet.

"Expect you know him."

I knew him. But I didn't look long. I may have told you before, but I'm really not the hard-boiled type. To people like Jewle and his back-room boys, a body is just something for identification, examination and possibly dissection. The greater the mess, the more to be learned. I've never schooled myself to see it like that, and there was about Sambord's body something so immediately repulsive that I looked away almost at once.

"Not a pretty sight," Jewle said, and whipped the sheet back again.

"Might as well keep him out," he told the attendant. "He'll be wanted straight away."

"You know how long he's been in the water," he said, as we went towards the lift. "Lucky, in a way, he could be identified at all. We did have his prints, of course. That trouble he was in some years ago."

"I thought it took eight days for a body to come up. Or is that an old wives' tale?"

"Not when it gets jammed in a sluice," he said. "I heard about it this morning, so I had him brought here. From where he was found, I guessed who he was. The clothes were right, too."

"And who's this other friend I'm supposed to meet?" I asked him amusedly. "Is he a corpse too?"

"Nice of you to take it this way," he said. "You might have wanted a last look at him for all I knew, so I just took a chance. The one I wanted you to see was Granding. I got him along straight away. Thought the three of us might do worse than have a conference."

He caught my quick look of alarm. "Nothing to worry about. I took the liberty of telling him who you were and gave him a rough idea why you went to Wishington that morning. I think he was quite impressed."

Granding's handshake was certainly cordial enough. We agreed it had been a bad business about Sambord.

"Sorry this had to happen to him but—well, he was getting more than I could stand. I suppose I oughtn't to say it, but in a way it's a relief. And for him, too. He always was his own enemy."

"Mr. Granding's in no great hurry, so I thought we three might have a private talk," Jewle said. "You're a man of the world, Mr. Granding, so I take it you know that whatever we talk about is strictly confidential. Nothing's to be said outside. Nothing to reporters except what I'll tell you later."

"If you say so, sir."

"That's all right then. Let's make ourselves comfortable. Cigarette, Mr. Granding?"

He smoked a pipe. I got mine going. Jewle came round from behind the desk and in a couple of minutes it was really cosy.

"You begin. Mr. Granding. Tell us all the things that made you sure Sambord was up to something before he finally disappeared."

Granding had to do quite a bit of thinking. Most of what he said I'd heard before, the principal thing being, in my estimation, the change in attitude of Sambord himself. He'd become objectionably cocksure. He'd spoken in an offensively condescending way to me of the man who'd literally yanked him out of the gutter. He'd thrown out hints that soon he would be The Great Sambrino again, and he'd gone so far as to make surreptitious enquiries about the modern cost of apparatus for his act.

Someone, we agreed, must have been encouraging that preposterous attitude and working cleverly on his gullibility. That someone had wanted to use him for some purpose or other and had advanced him money on account—the money that'd been found in the caravan.

"Still bearing in mind the importance of the confidential nature of what's being said here," Jewle told him, "I'm going to let you know what no one knows except us here at the Yard. The man responsible for all this was a man named Peplock. You heard about him from Inspector Matthews. The logical thing to assume is that Peplock used Sambord for some particular purpose and then killed him, or had him killed because he knew too much."

Granding stared. "He was killed?"

"From what we've discovered since, there isn't a doubt of it."

"Poor devil. A hell of a mess he got himself into, then."

"He did," Jewle said. "And our job is to find all those responsible for it. Peplock was only part of some scheme or other. So tell us. Can you think of anything else? Any other hints Sambord threw out? Any person seen loitering round your farm? Any person who might have asked, say, to look round?"

Granding could think of no one. Then he smiled a bit self-consciously. He didn't want us to think he'd been withholding evidence: well, not exactly evidence, but Inspector Matthews had asked him to report anything unusual. There'd been something but Granding just hadn't thought it all that important.

"Well, tell us about it now," Jewle said, and smiled. "What isn't important to you, may be to us."

It was a man on a motor-bike. Granding said. His secretary had had to go out one morning—on the Saturday before the Sunday when Sambord disappeared—and when she came back she saw a man sitting on a motor-bike near the gate. The bike was very near the hedge and the man was looking through a gap towards the farm. He didn't look at all alarmed when he saw her and he'd wanted to know if a Mr. Somebody-or-Other lived there and she said she'd never heard of him. and then the man had ridden away. It'd taken only a moment or so and she'd have thought nothing of it if she hadn't mentioned the matter very much later when she remembered something peculiar about the man. You didn't often see beatniks in Wishington. If that's what he was. He'd certainly had a beard.

"Might be nothing in it." Jewle said, and I couldn't help wondering why he was more or less laughing it off. "No other information about the man? Height? Build?"

Granding didn't know and he didn't think his secretary would know.

"Mind if I ring her now? Might as well get this cleared up."

I couldn't gather much from what was being said.

"As you said, she doesn't remember a great deal," he told us as soon as he came back from the desk. "He was pretty well wrapped up. for one thing. She just has the impression that he was tall. And he spoke in a high sort of voice."

"I did ask George Farmer—he's the landlord of the Waggoners—if he'd been in there, but he hadn't. I reckon that's what made me think it wasn't important."

"It almost certainly wasn't." Jewle told him. "But to get back to Sambord. When we went through his pockets this morning we found two five-pound notes. You remember the money found in the caravan? Well, this must have been a bit more paid on account of services that were going to be rendered. So tell us something. This man Peplock couldn't have been one of a syndicate, say.

who really thought Sambord could get back on the halls again? If he'd really been able to get right back to what he was in the old days, then there might have been quite a lot of money to be made out of him."

Granding snorted. "Never a hope, sir. He could no more have done that act than I could start walking up there on that ceiling. Isn't that right, Mr. Travers?"

I said it was. After that we talked for a few more minutes and got nowhere and then Jewle made a move.

"No relatives whatever?"

"Not that I know of," Granding said. "There was that wife of his who left him shortly after they were married, but where she is now I reckon no one knows. Might even be dead."

"And you still think you'd like to be responsible for the burial?"

"Yes, sir, if it's all the same to you. It sort of clears up the accounts, if you know what I mean."

I shook hands and said what a pleasure it had been to see him again, then he and Jewle went out.

It was a good ten minutes before Jewle came back.

"Might as well have some tea," he told me. "You're in no hurry?"

"My time's my own."

I'd no idea how quickly that afternoon had gone. It was much nearer four o'clock than three. Before I could say so, tea came in. I drew my chair up to the desk.

"How do you think Sambord died?" he asked, as he filled my cup.

I owned up that I hadn't really thought of it. Maybe I'd taken it for granted that he'd been drowned.

"That's curious," he said. "I'd have thought he was dead before he was dumped in that river."

I told him I'd an open mind, but now I came to think things over, I was still pretty sure he'd died of drowning.

"How do you arrive at that?"

I reminded him of Sambord's act. If someone had really convinced him that he could do that act of his again, then he must have done some testing to find out if he could really hold his breath again. Otherwise he wouldn't have been so cocksure. Jewle looked so surprised that I had to laugh.

"Still got a few brains left," I said.

"It wasn't that," he told me. "Just that you and I may have reached the same conclusions in different ways. But go on."

I said Sambord had been struck down but not knocked unconscious, even if he had been a bit fuddled for a minute. When Vingram had bent over him he'd thought it was the assailant and every instinct had told him to sham dead. As soon as Vingram had moved off, he got to his feet again and then he'd been struck down a second time. And dumped in that river. Since the first blow hadn't actually knocked him out cold, there was no reason to think the second had either. But Sambord had been sufficiently unconscious for drowning to ensue.

"Well, he *was* drowned," he said. "I've just heard so. Everything's just what we thought it was, except that I did have the idea that since he was such a good swimmer, he might have foxed his assailant and got himself ashore. Apparently he didn't."

"Any sign of those blows on the head?"

"Oh, yes. And one of them just drew blood. Must have been the second one."

"So what now?" I asked hopefully.

All I got was his usual smile.

"Now we just take it easy. Another cup of tea?"

I had a second cup and a second cake. My time was my own, and if he was waiting for something else to come in, and to surprise me with, then I was perfectly happy. So we just took our time. He began talking about the old days once we'd got our pipes going. It was about half-past four when the buzzer went. A word or two and he said he'd be down right away.

This time it was a quarter of an hour before he was back.

"Don't think I'm trying to produce rabbits out of the hat," he said, "but I've been waiting to have something tested. I didn't tell you, but when Sambord was brought in here this morning he had a gun in his pocket. It didn't take long to find the prints on it were his. Now ballistics say it's the gun used on Peplock. There isn't a shadow of doubt about it."

I let out a low whistle.

"Does that knock a lot of ideas all cockeyed?"

"What ideas?"

Something was telling me not to open my mouth too wide. "Well, Peplock died not later than six. Sambord was dumped in that river an hour and a quarter later, so why should Sambord be hanging around and why hadn't he disposed of the gun? If it was really he who shot Peplock."

"He could have," he said. "The landlord of that place where Peplock had parked him didn't have him under observation all the time. Far from it. All that business that subsequently followed could have been an act. Sambord might have slipped out and killed Peplock and later put on that act as an alibi. Guessing's no real good but I could suggest a reason or two why Sambord was going back to River Cottage when he was killed. You could, too."

"Maybe," I said, "but not why he was still carrying that gun. He ought to have thrown it in the river long before."

"Yes," he said. "You think that gun was planted on him just before he was dumped in the river. I do, too. I can't see any other way to fit things in."

He leaned forward, head in hands. A moment or two and he'd made up his mind to something.

"Let's look at it just once more. We've not got the alternatives. Sambord killed Peplock or he didn't. Let's start off by assuming he did. Where's the flaw?"

"Apparent absence of motive," I said. "Everything we've run up against so far tells us that Peplock wasn't doing Sambord any harm whatever: he was stringing him along and paying him for it. If Sambord was going to realise that ambition of his, the last one he'd want to kill was Peplock. As you said the other day, he was the goose with the golden eggs."

"Don't think it was quite so easy. Peplock might have displayed a wad of money. Sambord might have thought there was no point in working for it when he could take the short cut and help himself."

"It's feasible," I said. "In that case, where did Sambord get the gun? That means a wholly new enquiry. What about the other theory?"

"That brings in our old enemy, the third man."

"Very well," I said. "Let's bring him in. Was he the man that couple of sweethearts saw just behind Sambord that night? The tallish man wearing rubber-soled shoes?"

"Just as vague as everything else," he said. "Only one thing in favour of it and that's the timing. It fits in with the time Sambord actually left the Griffin to go to River Road. As for the rest, you can't rely on their identification of the man in front as Sambord. If it'd been you, say, who'd been there, your identification would have been accepted. You knew him. They didn't. For the rest, no end of people wear rubber-soled shoes. And another thing—"

"Wait a minute," I said. "Sambord *was* struck down from behind. His attacker did nip behind a hedge when he caught sight of Vingram in the distance. For my money, that makes the story more than reasonably credible."

"Right," he said. "Assume that and you come up against the really big question. The idea now is that the third man killed Peplock. He took the gun away with him. What happened from then till he made contact with Sambord? And why Sambord? How'd he know where to find Sambord?"

"Listen," I told him, "and don't bring in that old jape about my being able to come up at a moment's notice with a theory to fit anything. I've done a lot of thinking about this case, especially the planning that someone must have put into it, and the question I always come up against is this: What did Peplock want Sambord to do?"

"I haven't been exactly idle myself," he said. "I've asked the same thing. What's your answer?"

"Not an answer: just a reasonable theory. The events were planned for a Sunday afternoon when Peplock would in any case be at Ambourne. Right?"

"Right."

"Therefore the event, plan or scheme—call it what you like—was apart from Peplock's business as a private investigator. That would have been handled in town. Right?"

"Right."

"So Peplock was expecting a caller that late afternoon and he admitted that caller. The caller shot him, searched the house for something he wanted, or more likely to destroy any written evidence that would connect himself with Peplock. Then he took the gun and left. Right?"

"Could be."

"Now comes the tricky part," I said. "That caller should have come much later: at, say, half-past seven, when Sambord would have been there. But he came earlier and made some excuse, which Peplock accepted, for doing so. But that caller knew that Sambord was going to be present at that half-past seven interview, so he lay in wait. Sambord was the real evidence which the caller feared and he had to be disposed of. The caller—the third man, or woman—then had the happy idea of fastening the killing on Sambord by putting the gun in his pocket. He dumped him in the river to suggest suicide."

Jewle grunted. "Nice and snug the way you tell it. And who might this caller have been? You mentioned a woman."

"Right," I said. "We'll take her first. She'd have to be Trude Hayhill. She was the one who was so anxious to know where Sambord was. She didn't give a damn about him till not long before he was killed. But she hardly fits in with the man in the rubber-soled shoes. Unless she disguised herself as a man, and I'm not too sold on that. I admit she's big enough to have swiped Sambord over the head and later got him into the river. I prefer to think her husband was involved in all that. A pity his car wasn't the one that policeman saw."

I saw the suggestion of a smile. Some ironic comment was about to come. It didn't.

"Assume it *was* Hayhill in that car," he said. "That'd make him your killer, and our third man. But where does Sambord come in? What evidence could *he* have against Hayhill? The only connection between them, and you'll admit it's more than vague, is that Sambord married Trude bigamously and Hayhill married her later."

He glanced up at the clock. "You any ideas about that?"

"A few floating around," I told him. "As soon as they coalesce I'll let you know. If it's any help, some of them are connected with Dorlish. I'm not happy about that partnership. I want to know exactly why Trude called on him that evening when he was alone."

"We've got him in mind," Jewle said, and got to his feet.

"What I'm going to do now is give a lot of this a whole lot of publicity. A press conference in time for the morning papers. The public are going to be told just so much about Sambord, for instance. I hope the write-up men'll print a few questions: you know—why this and why that. Somebody might come up with some answers."

"If that's the case," I said, "you wouldn't object if I gave the news straight away to Trude?"

He thought for a moment. "No," he said. "It might even be a good idea. And to hear anything she has to say about an alibi. And possibly her husband's."

I stopped just short of the door. "Has she made any interesting moves since you began tailing her?"

"Not that we know."

"And Dorlish?"

"Nothing suspicious from him either. Only one thing. Far as we can make out, the firm isn't having many callers. Business is far from brisk."

He thanked me warmly. My wife was expecting me at the flat and I went straight home. We always have a service dinner and I asked if I could have it straight away as I'd probably have to go out. While we were waiting for it to come up, I rang Trude from my little den. She was in.

"Any chance of seeing me for a few moments?"

"A few moments?" she cried. "Why not have dinner here? I'll ring room service."

"No, no," I said. I'd had that early meal in mind just to forestall that kind of complication. "I've already eaten. Had to have dinner with a client who was leaving town. But I can see you? It's very definitely for your own good."

"Of course I'll see you. But you make it all sound very mysterious."

"Just a habit I've got into," I told her, and rang off.

Foreshadowed regrets are not much in my line but there's one thing I should say: partly in fairness to you and partly in fairness to myself. As I reiterate to the point of boredom, one of the hardest things in my job is the sifting of evidence: to listen to statements or take part in arguments and to know what is vital and what not. One longs, not necessarily for omniscience, but for a really superb keenness of discernment, even though if one had it, detection would ultimately descend to the level of the conveyer belt. That was why I felt so angry with myself some days later when I knew that that long afternoon with Jewle had given me every particle of evidence I needed to solve the Peplock-Sambord case.

The trouble was that the vital had been obscured by the not so vital, and the illusory. It wasn't all that consolatory to know that Jewle himself had fallen down as badly as myself.

11
A COUPLE OF REPORTS

THE lady admitted me and, after the words of greeting, let it be known that she'd been reading. She had a quick glance at the opened book on the settee, slipped in the marker, laid the book on the side table, and waved me to the place it had occupied.

"Sure you couldn't eat another dinner?"

"Positive."

"A drink then? What would you like? Whisky, gin and something?"

I cut short the catalogue. I didn't want a drink because post-prandial drinks always gave me a headache.

"A cigarette then? Or would you prefer a cigar?"

In my younger days I loved a cigar. Now I think them a bad investment and I haven't smoked one for years, even when they're free. All the same I thought I'd like to know just what kind of cigars Hayhill smoked. They looked good and were good. I didn't think Churchill himself would have turned up his nose at them. So there I was: Travers the epicurean: the corner of a soft settee at his back with the reinforcement of a silk cushion: in the other corner the lady herself, scented, smiling and, maybe under certain conditions, perfectly willing.

I shook all that off and tried to look stern.

"I ought to make it clear," I said, "that I'm here, as I said, in your interests. You were a client and we regard that as giving us a definite responsibility, especially when something happens arising out of the original commission."

"You sound very serious?"

"For a very good reason. I'll be blunt. This morning Sambord's body was fished out of the river. He'd been drowned." It caught her unaware. She didn't know what act to put on. "You'll read about it in your paper in the morning. I happened to get advance information."

She looked away. "I suppose I ought to shed a tear, or something, but I just can't. Even if I was so stupid as to think I might help him. Now I'm glad I didn't. I can't forget that filthy trick he played on me years ago."

A sudden idea came and she swivelled round. "In the river? You mean he committed suicide?"

"That's for the police to determine," I said. "But when people are fished out of rivers, nine times out of ten that's what it is. All the same we've got to be prepared for everything. That's why I'm here."

"I don't understand."

"Then I'll put it bluntly. The police have been enquiring into Sambord's past. They know by now that a Trude Layman went through a form of marriage with him. They'll go to Somerset House and look for anything else they can find about a Trude Layman or Sambord and that'll bring them to you through your husband."

She was so scared she couldn't speak.

"If it turns out that Sambord didn't commit suicide, then they'll want to know where you were that Sunday night. You'll have to have an alibi, both of you, for from, say tea-time to dinner-time. Five till seven.”

It might have been a bit feebly, but she smiled.

“But I was here the whole time. I had tea brought up—”

She frowned. “Yes, at about half-past five. I usually have it at about five but I’d been out for a short walk to try to clear a headache. I can tell you the maid who brought it up.”

“Not me,” I said. “Just be prepared to tell that to the police. And the evening meal?”

“At about half-past seven. I was here all the time.”

“And your husband?”

“He had work at the office. He spends most of his time there, even sometimes on a Sunday. He left me at about four o’clock. He got back in time for dinner with me. I can prove every word of that.”

“That’s fine,” I told her. “I don’t say the police *will* come—not for a day or two at any rate. They’re not so bad as they’re made out. Nothing whatever to fear if you tell them the truth. The last thing you want, or so I think, is for your husband to be involved in anything so unsavoury as all this. You admire all that work he’s doing?”

She looked almost angry. “Admire? Of course I do! I think he’s one of the finest men that—well, a really fine man. Other people do, too. You can’t know much about his work or you wouldn’t have asked me that.”

That sudden flare-up was so unexpected and so genuine, that it could only have been spontaneous and real. If Hayhill was a crook, then she wasn’t aware of it.

“Sorry,” I said, “but I didn’t mean it like that. I do know what he’s doing. But tell me about yourself. When you went to New York after your marriage, what did you think of it?”

“I only knew Manhattan,” she said, “but I just loved it. I wished we’d been able to stay longer but we had to leave suddenly after about six months because of business. We went to Chicago.”

“Not so good?”

She laughed. “Not so bad. We had an apartment on Lakeside Drive. It was delightful, especially in the summer. We were there about two years. I was really sorry to leave it. Toronto wasn't nearly so nice. In fact I was quite glad when Frank suddenly decided to come to England. His work you know, and the Refugee Year. He knew he'd be more in the heart of things over here."

Something was slightly wrong. She'd mentioned business in New York, though Hayhill was supposed to have retired. And twice she'd talked of *suddenly*. New York had been left suddenly and so had Toronto.

"What were people like over there?" I said. "Any real interest in this problem of displaced persons and refugees?"

"I think things were being done by large organisations. My husband was always very suspicious of them. More like big business than personal interest. That's what made him so dispirited about it finally and brought him over here. Here he really does feel at home."

"It must have been quite a feat getting that organisation of his started over here."

She smiled.

"It was. I helped, too, you know."

"You did!"

"Oh, yes," she said quite proudly. "As soon as we'd acquired the lease of a house. I was the first secretary. That was while Frank was in Europe, getting a branch opened in Austria. Later we were lucky enough to meet someone just as enthusiastic as Frank himself—a retired clergyman. He's a perfectly marvellous secretary."

"And now you do nothing?"

"I meet people who can help. Or go to receptions."

"But your spare time, so to speak. You must get very bored?"

"Bored?" She laughed. "I simply love the theatre. And dining out when Frank's away. And there's television. And books."

The telephone went. She gave me a look which I couldn't at the moment interpret, and reached out for the receiver. She hardly had to move an inch from the settee corner.

"Yes? . . . Yes. I'll take the call."

She was making signs to me, pointing frantically to something across the room, and twisting her free hand as if turning something. I spotted what she meant, so I nipped across the room and switched on the television. She was already taking the call.

"Splendid, darling . . . No. Nothing whatever . . . Oh, just reading my book and watching television at the same time. Some silly play or other. . . . Shall I meet you? . . . That'll be fine . . . And you, darling. . . . Goodbye, pet . . . Of course, of course. I'll see to it . . . Goodbye."

She made the most mischievous grimace. "That was Frank. He always rings me when he's away."

"Don't tell me he doesn't trust you?"

"Of course he does. Why shouldn't he?"

The cigar had gone out. I looked at my watch and scrambled up in alarm. "Good heavens! I've only about ten minutes to get back to town. An appointment."

She was fetching my overcoat. "What a shame! And just when I was beginning to enjoy our talk. But I mustn't forget to thank you. You've been very good—considering all that trouble I gave you."

"Forget it," I said. "We all of us make mistakes."

She'd been holding the overcoat for me. Now she gave me a critical look. She brushed some probably imaginary fluff from a lapel. I think I knew what was coming, but I just stood there like a rabbit confronting a stoat.

"You've really been very sweet."

Her arms went round my neck. She didn't have far to reach. Tiptoe did it. It was a warm, long kiss. The arms stayed there when we broke away.

"You're really sure you've got to go?"

"Unfortunately, yes."

"But you'll be coming again?"

"Well"—I smiled feebly—"what about that so devoted husband of yours?"

She tiptoed up again. But only to whisper, "He's going on tour again early next week!"

I could have told her she might be wrong. I just nodded knowingly. She laughed. And she blew me a kiss through the slit of the door just before it closed. . . .

Travers, the not-so-great Lover, made for the Tube and then thought better of it. The commissionaire stopped a taxi for me and I went straight to my club. I wrote a report for Jewle, took a taxi to the Yard and left the report with instructions to deliver it as soon as he was available. Then I walked home.

This is roughly what was in that report. Trude Hayhill had an alibi for the whole of that Sunday afternoon and evening, and I said how it could be checked. Hayhill was ostensibly at 103 from about half-past five till shortly after seven. If the premises were open at that time, then he had an alibi for the killing of Peplock. Even if they weren't, there was no proof that he wasn't there. He had every right to be. But he had an alibi, included in his wife's, for the Sambord killing.

I gave it as my very real opinion that Trude was unaware of any illegal activities. I didn't think she had any deep-down love for Hayhill, but I was positive she respected him very much as a man. In my judgment Hayhill had always kept her well away from any of his outside activities and had merely used her from time to time in a decorative way. Having her meet people, for example, whom he might want to impress.

I gave him the movements of the couple after their marriage and till the return to England in 1958. I particularly stressed Trude's use of that word *suddenly*. It looked as if on at least two occasions Hayhill had had to fold his tents and depart. I mentioned that she'd spoken of *business* in Manhattan, even though Hayhill always made it a plank in his public speaking that he'd retired some time before then.

I told him about Hayhill ringing her that night. I even told him, quite frankly, that the lady had tried to vamp me. It was hard to say whether or not it had been an act, and I was definitely not prepared to turn up some other night and put it to the test. But whatever her real intentions, I thought there was no doubt whatever about her motive. It was to keep me from ever letting it be known that she'd asked the Agency to make enquiries about Sambord.

"If you people ever confront her with a knowledge of her marriage to Sambord," were my last words, "then I'm dead sure she'll give you a reasonably true account of why she left him, and she'll swear she never heard of him or even thought of him since."

I slept sound that night, and the first thing I thought of at stirring time was what had happened at Jewle's press conference. I rang the hall porter and asked him to send me up a copy of the *Record*. My own two papers gave the Peplock-Sambord case a lot of prominence, and no wonder. The eyes of the reporters must have goggled when they'd heard what Jewle had to say.

The interest to me was in what had been omitted. Nothing was said about the man in the rubber-soled shoes, or a car-licence number ending in 33—that had been driven recklessly round a corner. That last surprised me. I'd have thought that at all costs Jewle would have wanted to learn a whole lot more about that American-type car.

Rodey had had the crime story of his life. He'd been given half the front page and banner headlines.

THE CASE OF THE DEAD MAN GONE
SENSATIONAL DEVELOPMENTS IN THE PEPLOCK MURDER

It was all there: details of Peplock's murder. Vingram's discovery, the missing body and the finding in the sluice. Peplock was tied in with Sambord. There was even the question of the gun and who'd used it. What had Peplock had in his house, asked Rodey, that his killer had used murder to obtain and then fire to eliminate? What was the role that Sambord had played?

From the paper's morgue Rodey had unearthed a picture of The Great Sambrino. There was also one of Granding's winter quarters that must have been obtained when Sambord had first been mentioned as wanted for questioning by the police. There was a short biographical sketch. There was so much that the story overflowed to a middle page. The whole thing, in fact, had been a crime reporter's dream.

Soon after breakfast Jewle rang me to thank me for that report. He'd had a good look at it, he said, and it would be most helpful.

"Matthews back?" I asked him.

"Came in late last night," he said. "Nearer morning, in fact. A most successful visit. I wouldn't be surprised if the wires don't start humming before the morning's gone."

I was a bit later than usual getting to the agency. I checked some reports with Norris and we'd just had mid-morning coffee when a call came for me.

"You're sure?" I asked Bertha.

"Yes," she said. "A Mr. Dorlish of City Investigations."

I asked her to put him through to my room as soon as I was there.

"Mr. Travers?" he said.

"Yes," I said. "What can I do for you, Mr. Dorlish?"

"I'm ringing from quite near your place, and I'd be grateful if I could see you for a couple of minutes."

"Why not?" I said, and thought I'd better clear the decks. "We met, I remember, at Ambourne. Sorry about having to mislead you about my name. Perhaps you'll allow me to explain that."

"No need for that," he said. "I know your agency's reputation. And your own."

I gave a chuckle. "That might have all sorts of meanings. Be seeing you then."

In five minutes he was being shown into the room. The same upright stance was there: the same brisk look of efficiency.

"Nice to run across you under more congenial circumstances," I told him as we shook hands. "Let me take your coat."

"I ought to apologise," he told me. "I've always been meaning to call. Yours must be practically the doyen of the London agencies."

"I won't say that. We may be getting a bit long in the tooth, but Paulings, for example, is far older. May I offer you some coffee?"

He'd had some already. I said that allowed me to plunge at once into an explanation of why I'd been at Ambourne that Monday afternoon and perhaps why Superintendent Jewle hadn't wanted to divulge my name. He seemed to be accepting it.

"What I've actually come to you for is advice," he said. "I'm fairly new to this game, as you heard me say, and nothing like this has ever arisen before. You've seen the morning papers?"

"If you mean the Peplock-Sambord case, I have. Pretty sensational. Even in my experience."

"This is, of course, in confidence, but my problem is something to do with that actual case. Or it might be. Mind if I lay my cards on the table?"

"Please do."

"Well, not long after the Yard announced they were anxious to get into touch with that man Sambord, I had an unusual call. A prospective client wanted to see me—privately. I said it was always privately, and apparently it didn't mean quite that. The call on me had to be private, in the sense that no one was to know. I asked for at least a hint of what was wanted, and all I was told was that a man had to be traced and the expense didn't matter."

"Just a moment," I said. "The client. Man or woman? I notice you're rather skating over that."

He pursed his lips. His eyes narrowed a bit.

"Well, let's assume it was a woman. I made an appointment for just after the time my staff would have left, and she duly turned up. She said she'd seen about Sambord in the papers and she wanted me to find him if I could before the police did. She pulled out some notes and said she'd be prepared to pay anything in reason."

He waited for a comment. I just shrugged my shoulders.

"What would you have done?" he wanted to know.

"Can't say off-hand," I told him. "Under the circumstances I'd probably have turned her down."

"That's what I did," he said. "I didn't like her story, for one thing, about her acting for some relation or other, and I didn't want an occasion to arise when I might be rapped over the knuckles by the police. But this is the real question. In view of what was in this morning's papers, what do I do about it? What are the professional ethics in this particular case?"

"Let me see if I've got you right," I said. "Are you asking my advice about mentioning her to the police?"

"Well, more or less—yes."

"Then I wouldn't. You're under no compulsion to do so. You didn't accept the assignment so you're under no obligation to her, but all the same I'd go careful. If by any chance the police should get word of it, and I don't see how they could, then that might be different." I spread my palms. "Purely my own opinion and for what it's worth."

"I'm sure you're right," he said. "Thanks for the advice. I shall certainly take it."

"How're things going now?" I asked him. "Have you thought of getting another partner?"

"I've thought of it, but somehow I can't imagine the place without George Peplock. He'd probably forgotten more about the game than I even knew. A real fine character, too. He kept himself to himself more than I thought was good for him, but that was the way he liked it. He loved it down there at Ambourne. And why he ever got into touch with that man Sambord, I can't even begin to think."

"But you'll have to do something," I said. "You can't run things entirely by yourself."

"Between you and me, I'm thinking of getting out. I more or less made up my mind at the funeral."

"He left you the agency?"

"Yes, and no," he said. "In connection with the partnership we had wills drawn up on the survivor-takes-all basis. He hadn't any relatives and I hadn't either. But the trouble was that his will was at Ambourne. One of the things that was burned. Mind you, I can get the evidence of the solicitors, but what the legal situation is, I haven't heard yet."

"Sounds to me as if you've got a pretty good case," I told him, and then he rose to go. I went with him to the door, and when we said goodbye I had to cut short his thanks. A few yards along the street he turned and gave me a friendly wave.

I went back to my room and it didn't take long to make me realise that that unexpected visit might have a very deep significance. I didn't like troubling Jewle again. It would look too much like poking a too-frequent nose into something that didn't all that much concern me. That was when I remembered something else. I'd have to tell Jewle. I couldn't help myself. He had a man on

Dorlish's tail. When the report came in, he'd know about that call. If I didn't make a report of my own, he'd be asking why.

I rang the Yard and I think I was a bit relieved when he wasn't available. I preferred not to talk to Matthews. There would have to be too much explaining and he mightn't be abreast of all that had happened the last couple of days, so what I did was to get down at once to writing another report:

"Thought you ought to know I had a visit this morning from, of all people, Dorlish. His excuse for the call was to ask my advice on a matter of professional secrecy. He said he'd had a possible client who'd read the police request for information about Sambord and who wanted him to find Sambord before the police did. Dorlish made a great point of being reluctant to reveal that the client was a woman. It was she, he insisted, who'd wanted to call on him after regular hours. He'd turned her down, but now, after what he'd read in the morning papers, ought he to tell the police about the woman? My advice was that the police couldn't possibly know about it and he ought therefore to do nothing unless a vastly different set of circumstances arose.

"You'll have spotted at once the significance of all this but I'd like to add some of my own deductions. Something is obviously going on between Dorlish and Trude Hayhill, and it's not necessarily to do with Sambord. When Matthews and I called on her, we'd let her know that we were aware of that very confidential call of hers on Dorlish, so she got into touch with him. Possibly she paid him to explain the visit away. Hence the call on me. And the pretext of asking my professional advice. Maybe you can lick some sense into it. I'm dead sure that Dorlish is deeply involved in both his partner's murder and the Sambord affair.

"He tried to draw me out by saying it was incredible to him that a fine character like Peplock should ever have wanted to have any contacts with a man like Sambord. I didn't rise to that particular bait. What may be equally significant is that he talked about selling the agency. Do you think he's intending to skip?

"Just one other thing may be worth mentioning. Don't you read into what I've told you that he knew about Trude's original visit to me? He might even have been trying to lure me, as a return for his own confidences, into telling him about it. But if he knew, who told him? It could only have been Trude. But why should she tell him? Surely it was something she wouldn't want him to know if, that is, there's any substance of fact in the way we've looked at things up to now.

L.T."

Bertha was going out to lunch so I asked her to take that report to the Yard. I'd marked it *Personal and Urgent*, so maybe Jewle would be ringing me in the course of the next half-hour.

I slipped out for a quick bite myself and then came back to wait.

12
FITTING THE PIECES

IT WASN'T till late that afternoon that Jewle rang. He apologised for the apparent rudeness but he'd literally had not a minute to himself.

"But thanks now for the report," he said. "We'd never have known about it otherwise. We're short-handed and we took our men off Dorlish's tail only this morning."

"Anything really vital in it?"

"Well, it's remarkably interesting. I wouldn't be surprised if it's the most useful piece of information we've had so far. Things are beginning to fit in."

"Any particular things?"

"Well, I'm still badly rushed so I can't give you details beyond that we had our first information this morning about Peplock. They've run him down at last as a very slick operator last using the name Dave Dilmore. His real name was probably Peter Lock-yer, and where do you think he last operated from just over two years ago? From Toronto. Have a crack at that." He gave a little chuckle. "And thanks again for the report."

It didn't take long to know what he was driving at. No wonder he'd chuckled at the way things were beginning to fit in. Hayhill had also left Toronto suddenly just over a couple of years back. If that didn't make a connection between the two men, what did? What that connection actually was it was useless to explore till Jewle had learned far more. There was only one thing that seemed to stand out. Nowhere during the whole case had we come across the slightest trace of any connection over here between Hayhill and Peplock. All that could possibly connect the two men up, and that far too vaguely, was Sambord. Both Hayhill's wife and Peplock had been interested in Sambord.

I went on with the work I was doing and it was just as I was thinking of going home that Rodey rang me. He was speaking from the news room at the *Record*.

"Congratulations on that feature of yours this morning," I said. "Don't think I'm patronising but it was a really good bit of work."

"Only because I had something to get my teeth into," he told me, "but it was about that I'm wondering if I could get your help. Peplock's far too drab. It's Sambord who's the really fascinating character, so I want to write a follow-up. Now you went down to Wishington and actually saw Sambord not long before all this business happened, so what I'd like to do is give your impressions."

"Hold on there," I said. "I couldn't possibly allow my name to be used in that connection."

"No, no," he said. "Your name wouldn't be used. I could use the old Someone-who-knew-him or just let it read like information unearthed."

"Oh, no," I said. "There's a far bigger snag. I'm under strict orders to keep my mouth shut. Maybe I know too much. I can't say. I can't think of anything I know as likely to prejudice anything whatever, but there you are."

"That's pretty bad luck on me."

"Why should it be? Where's the enterprise of the Press we're always being told about? There must be a score of people at Granding's place who could tell you enough to fill a front page."

"That's where you're wrong," he said. "A tight censorship down there. Granding's muzzled the whole farm."

"There ought to be ways and means. But what about the Waggoners?"

He grunted. "I sent a really good man down there and what he came back with you could have written on the back of a stamp."

"Listen," I said. "I'd like to help, but I can't. All the same, I'll give you a tip. Go down there yourself. Find out if Sambord had begun to get swollen-headed. And if he'd been talking of a come-back. And if he'd had more money than usual. They're just suggestions. Maybe the man you sent there didn't have any direct questions to ask. Now you have."

"That's very good of you," he said. "I'll do just that."

"Glad to help. All I ask is that my name isn't on any account to be mentioned. Oh, by the way, How's your boy?"

"Doing fine," he said, and his voice seemed somehow to light up. "Couldn't be doing better. We'll be having him home for Christmas."

"That's really great," I said. "No need for me to think of wishing you a Happy Christmas."

He didn't speak for a moment and then he thanked me again. If there was anything he could do for me at any time, I'd only to let him know.

I was thinking about Rodey when we were having dinner that night. Perhaps it's having a husband like myself—all over the place at all sorts of times—that accounts for Bernice's interests outside the flat. Work on the committee of one of the hospitals takes up quite a lot of her time, and that's why I told her about Rodey's boy. There wasn't a lot she could say. Until, that is, I mentioned the hard luck on parents suddenly having to spend a lifetime's savings.

"But surely he needn't have done any such thing," she said. "If the boy's at where I think he is—at the Arlsburg Clinic in Berne— it's been costing him an awful lot. But he needn't have done it. There're excellent clinics over here and they wouldn't have cost him a penny. The Welfare State includes all that."

"Maybe it's the old story," I said. "What you get for nothing, you don't value. Also I gather it's an only son. When it comes to a matter of being crippled for life or not crippled, any parent would want the best. If anything even remotely similar ever happened to you, do you think I'd be content with what I thought was only second best?"

"Well, perhaps not."

"Perhaps?"

She laughed. "Very well then. You wouldn't. Does that make you feel happier?"

That's about where we left it. It was unimportant in any case. And no business of mine how Rodey spent his money. Not, now I came to think of it, that he ought to be too hard-up. What the *Record* was paying him I'd no idea, but it couldn't be peanuts. It was just time for the headline news on television, so I switched the set on.

The morning brought me a personal, air-mail letter from Bob McGuffie.

"Not much to add to that cable we sent you but here are a few extra details, just in case. I had business in Harrisburg, so I thought it might be worth while to call on Grade Levitsky, as she now is. She turned out to be a great talker, but what I think concerns you is this. About two months ago someone who was almost certainly a New York enquiry agent called on her on the pretence that Sambord had died and left a fair amount of money. Under the very old will most of it would come to her as his then wife. Gracie's conscience got the better of her and she owned up that after Lambert's death—alcoholic poisoning, by the way—she'd only lived with Sambord. This smooth operator assured her that as a common-law wife, she was still entitled to inherit. He gave her a non-existent address.

"Grade made no bones about admitting what had happened with herself and Lambert's deputy for best part of a year, so she suggested marriage. My own opinion, for what it's worth, is that Sambord didn't want that. He said he'd been married years before and the woman had left him and he hadn't bothered about a divorce.

"The arrangement then was that Sambord was to try out the act in Europe—I have an idea it was as good as played out over here. All she got from him were hard-luck stories. She didn't hear from him at all for about six months and then she read about the success of the act in England. She immediately went over and confronted him, having discovered when she began to make enquiries that he'd married an English girl. There was nothing between her and Sambord on paper so he still had the whip hand. Also she by then had her present husband in mind, so she let the whole thing drop. Probably to convince Levitsky, the prospective husband, she got that Nevada divorce.

"I hope the above will be of help. If there's any other aspect you'd like us to investigate, please let us know. . . ."

It was a letter that couldn't be digested at one reading. A few minutes later I was sure of its importance and yet I couldn't put a finger on the precise spots wherein the importance lay. Unless, of course, it was inherent in the fact that Gracie Lambert had never married Sambord. and that somebody had been anxious to verify that fact.

The last thing I wanted to do at the moment was to tackle Trude again. She could have told me just what happened that day when Grade saw the erring Sambord, but all I could conjecture was that the word *wife* had been used. It was even possible that when Grade stepped into the outer office, she said something like, "So you're the one who's supposed to be his wife." The rest followed.

More important still, I now saw, was the fact that someone two months ago had been interested in discovering the real truth about the Gracie-Sambord marriage. I couldn't see why anyone in New York itself should have had that interest. Who then had employed that smooth operator? Trude, wondering after all those years about that morning at the Welland Street office? Hayhill, who'd caught Trude out in some indiscreet remark?

The whole thing was beyond me. And there was no point in getting Bob McGuffie to make further enquiries: in fact I didn't see what else he could do. And Jewle had infinitely better contacts in the States than I. And he'd talked overnight of pieces now slipping into place, and that all added up to a whole lot of reasons why I should simply put that letter for the moment into my private file. Something might emerge at any time to make it useful. Before the day was out, even more of Jewle's pieces might have slipped into place.

It wasn't to be long before I was to have a look at Jewle's jigsaw. Just after four o'clock that afternoon he rang me. Would it be convenient for me to see him for a few minutes?

I took Bob McGuffie's letter with me and the first thing I did was to hand it to Jewle.

"It came this morning. A follow-up on that cable."

He read it slowly through. He read it a second time, and asked if he might make a copy. I told him to keep it. There wasn't any reason I could see why I was likely to want it again.

"Extraordinary." he said, "how you keep popping up with odds and ends like this letter: things that keep on fitting in. Now I've got something to show *you*. What d'you make of it?"

It was a letter with its envelope attached by a clip. Paper and envelope were of fair quality. The letter had been posted at Ambourne the previous evening. The writing was upright and rather large, and the letters carefully formed. It had been addressed to "The Police Authorities, New Scotland Yard."

Dear Sirs,

I think I ought to tell you this, but about 7 o.c. on the evening when the murder took place I was in River Road, and there was a man walking in front of me. I think he was the Sambord you want to get in touch with, the dark over-coat and no hat which I thought was strange because it was a cold night. I was bigger than he was but he was walking as if he was in a hurry and he didn't hear me because I had crepe shoes on. At any rate when he was somewhere about where that Mr. Peplock was killed, I heard someone make a noise like a cough on the other side of the road and the man in front of me stopped and then crossed to where someone had been coughing. When I looked back there was no sign of him or anyone else.

Sorry I can't tell you my name as I wasn't supposed to be in River Lane at that time, but if you will put an advertisement in the Ambourne paper saying I shouldn't have to give evidence in court I would be willing to get in touch with you.

Mr. X.

"Seems genuine enough," I said. "Written by someone of quite fair education. Prints, of course?"

"Oh, yes. But you notice the real significance of it? Nothing has been allowed to get out about the man in the rubber-soled shoes. That means it wasn't written by some publicity-minded crank."

Somewhere, but just where I didn't know, there was something wrong with the letter but I couldn't put my finger on it. Jewle said he'd probably put an advertisement in the paper and see what happened, but if what was in the letter was all X had to tell, then there wasn't any great point.

"If it's genuine, we've got to find another third man," he said. "That's the one thing I've got against it. There was practically no one about in River Lane that night and if this letter identifies the man in the rubber-soled shoes, it means there was another man hanging around. Whoever it was that was supposed to be giving a cough as a signal to Sambord from the river side of the road, he doesn't fit the facts as we know them. If anything ever was a certainty, it's that the only person Sambord was anxious to meet was Peplock and that's why he was walking as fast as he could towards the house."

"That's right," I said. "If there was a man who coughed and if Sambord had expected to meet him, and knew him, then so far so good. All we're sure is that the coughing man wasn't Peplock. He was dead as mutton. What goes wrong is what must have followed. Presumably Sambord and the coughing man had a brief talk in the shadows and then they moved off towards River Cottage to the spot where Sambord was knocked out. That implies that the coughing man was not only known to Sambord but also that he'd convinced Sambord that he, too, had business at the Cottage. To my mind that's getting involved. Surely the assumption has hitherto been that Peplock was having a caller some time after seven and he wanted Sambord there as a witness. That argument only holds good now if the coughing man was also the caller. But if he was—"

I stopped. As I said, one could make objection after objection.

"Well," Jewle said, "you may be surprised but I'm disregarding that letter for the moment. That theory we arrived at still holds good and the McGuffie letter confirms it. I'm not in a position at the moment to tell you how. All the same, I think if you really got down to it, you could work it out for yourself." He picked up a paper from the desk. "Here's what we've got so far about Peplock, for instance. It goes back only as far as 1954.

"That was when Peplock, known as Dave Dilmore, skipped from San Diego, California, when the net began to close round a gang smuggling Mexicans into the States. Then in 1955, under the name of Henry Claire, he bought a partnership in an enquiry agency in Toronto, and when he'd thoroughly settled down he began working a blackmail racket unknown to his partner. He took one man for several thousand dollars. He skipped in 1957 and left a lot of trouble behind for his partner. Where he skipped to, of course, was over here. And he must have been well heeled."

"So that's it," I said. "He worked the same racket with Dorlish. Waited til something really juicy turned up and then operated privately from Ambourne."

"And that explains the burnt papers," Jewle said. "What happened was that the victim turned up too soon, made his way in at the point of a gun and then shot Peplock. Sambord, who was to have been at River Cottage at, say, seven-thirty, to help put the screws on, was himself disposed of by our third man."

He glanced up at the clock and got to his feet. "You think things over," he told me, "and you'll see why I'm not going to let Mr. X's letter draw me off into any side paths."

"Just one thing more," I said. "What's new about Hayhill?"

"Oh, yes," he said. "Here's a picture. Matthews took it as a press photographer. Caught him when he was wiping his glasses just after the lecture. He also got his prints when he got his autograph."

It was a fine picture, taken with a high-class lens.

"They're the other side of the ocean," Jewle said. "We ought to be getting some news at any time now. Sorry to kick you out like this but I'm due for a conference."

I'd got no further than Northumberland Avenue when I thought I was beginning to see what Jewle had been driving at. It was getting fairly late so I took a taxi to Streatham. The Montagu-Prince store was still open and a shop-walker told me where I might find Jack Ritcher. He was there—in the sports department.

He remembered me well enough. When I said I'd like a private word with him, he motioned me round behind a display stand.

"Now, sir, what can I do for you?"

"You'd like to earn a pound or two by answering some simple questions? The same case we talked about the last time we met."

He said he'd do his best.

"Right," I said. "Your assignment was to find Sambord's wife. Would you mind repeating exactly what Harry Frimmer instructed you to do?"

He'd given me a quick, surprised look when I'd mentioned Sambord. I gathered he'd read the papers and had done quite a lot of private thinking. If ever he was going to remember, this was the time.

"Well, sir, what it all amounted to was find the lady and try to recover the jewellery. Also I think Harry had some appeals in the Agony Columns."

"First question." I gave him a pound note. "The second's not too hard either. It's this: You were present with Sambord in Harry Frimmer's room when the disappearance was discussed. Right?"

"Yes, sir—right."

"Now in my judgement Sambord wouldn't have talked about a missing wife without giving some sort of reason why she'd left him. It might have been lies and you might have known it was lies; nevertheless, I'd like you to think back and tell me just what excuse she did have for leaving him."

His brow furrowed as he began thinking back. If he was going to tell me anything at all, it would have to be the truth. If he gave me one of the conventional reasons why wives leave husbands, I'd have to try from another angle.

I didn't have to. You could tell from his look that something had come back.

"I remember now, sir. He said his wife was under the impression that he'd a wife still living, which he hadn't."

"She'd thought he was a bigamist?"

"That's about it, sir. But, mind you, it didn't make any difference to us: I mean about finding her."

I gave him two more notes. It had been so easy that I was actually moving away before he could stammer out his thanks.

After dinner that night I really got down to thinking things out as Jewle had suggested. As far as I knew, I'd been perfectly frank with him: he, on the other hand, however willing, hadn't been in a position to be similarly frank with me. Considering everything, he'd taken a risk by telling me what he had.

It never was in Jewle's nature to display an enormous optimism, and so, when he'd kept talking of things slipping nicely into place, he must have been sure that the end of the case was definitely in sight. Similarly, when he'd assured me that I had enough facts at my disposal to arrive at the same conclusion, then I really did have those facts. I wasn't aware that I had them. Facts I certainly had, but I'd never got so far as to try to correlate them. And that was what I'd now made up my mind to do.

I began by thinking about Peplock, the man who'd used an enquiry agency in Toronto to work a blackmail racket; the man who'd made enough at it to buy Harry Frimmer's agency and that charming little place at Ambourne. It was only too obvious now that he'd bought the agency in order to work over here the racket that had been so profitable in Toronto.

That was when I knew something else. It wasn't making any kind of discovery: just arriving at a strictly logical conclusion. The events about which I'd questioned Ritcher had taken place years ago. If Trude Hayhill had been one of Peplock's victims, then he could have known about her in only one way. What, in fact, Peplock had really bought—though Harry Frimmer couldn't have suspected it—was not the actual business, even as a going concern. That had been merely a blind. *What Peplock had bought were Harry's old files.*

<h1 style="text-align:center">13
A SPOT OF HOMEWORK</h1>

I OWN that I was quite pleased with myself when I reached that conclusion. Peplock had bought all Frimmer's case files and all he had to do then was study them.

In our job blackmail's an ever-present risk, and what always amazes me is that far more operatives don't try the same racket. Norris and I, and a really trusted operative like Hallows, have enough secrets tucked away beneath our hats to bring in a fortune. A woman has had an illegitimate child; a man has done a prison term; a fire has turned out to be arson—you could add to that list a dozen more instances, and it had been Peplock's job to unearth them.

As I now saw it, he'd read the Sambord file and had been intrigued. Through Somerset House he'd discovered Trude's marriage to Hayhill, so he sifted the Hayhills and came up with Trude. The next thing was to get the low-down on the Sambord marriage break-up through an American agent. When that report reached him, he saw himself in a position to make the first real move. He could manipulate what he had, and what he had was enough to prove that in law Trude was still married to Sambord. To avoid any damage whatever to her husband's reputation, Trude would pay.

Maybe Trude did pay. Maybe she thought she might have to keep on paying, and that was why she came to the Broad Street Detective Agency. Her scheme was to get hold of Sambord and to induce him to admit that the woman who'd called that day at Welland Street had really been his wife, in spite of Peplock's apparent proofs to the contrary.

Did she get hold of him? It was possible that she did, and that the money he secreted in the caravan had been given by her and not by Peplock. If that were so, then Sambord had been playing a double game. In any case I didn't go into that possibility any further. I shifted to another one. I also took into account the fact that Peplock must have quite a few victims, and any one of them might have been the caller of that Sunday.

Still, as I said, I preferred for the moment to stay with Trude, and almost at once I came up against a snag. If she was supposed to be the one Peplock was expecting that Sunday evening, why didn't she keep the appointment? It *had* to be she who was expected at River Cottage; if not, why was Sambord to be there as a witness? His job was to swear that he'd never been married except to her, and so enable Peplock to put on the screws a second time. I couldn't imagine anything else about Sambord that would have been of the slightest use to Peplock.

The answer was that there had to be something wrong with Trude's alibi, and that was something I didn't really believe. It was far too capable of verification, and surely she wouldn't have gone so far as to bribe whoever it was that had brought in her tea? There was, of course, the possibility that she owned up at last to her husband, and he'd taken over the handling of things. He had no alibi for the time of the Peplock killing.

It was a solution I didn't like at all. I doubted if she'd have made such a confession, and then, as I began probing the matter further, I knew I was right. Trude must have kept everything under her own pretty hat and in her own pretty hands, or else there was no reason why she should have had that secret interview with Dorlish.

I took a look at Dorlish. Had his reputation on retiring from the Mainford police been as impeccable as, say, Norris's on retiring from the Yard, then I'd have had grave doubts about his involvement in that blackmail racket. Now I thought I knew what his role had been. His had been the legitimate business of City Investigations, with only spare time for the racket. He had known about that visit that had been arranged for Trude at Ambourne and this was the proof. When things had died down after Peplock's murder, he'd rung Trude, told her just so much, and fixed that secret, evening call at Whitmore Court.

So far, so water-tight. But what about Sambord? Had Trude paid him and had he double-crossed her? Had he promised her to write to Peplock and explain things, and had she been content to leave it like that? Then who'd killed Sambord, and why? Certainly not Hayhill. His alibi for that evening, like Trude's own, was easily capable of proof.

By that time I'd worn my brains almost to a frazzle. I'd done pretty well till I'd come up against that final brick wall. A change is as good as a rest, so I shifted to Hayhill. No picture of him had been in that literature Carnwell had given me, and it had been Carnwell who'd appeared on that brief television show featuring the Good Samaritans. But Matthews, posing as a press photographer, had secured a photograph without the disguise of the horn-rims, and by himself or through a collaborator, he'd also got prints. Both Canada and the States were now working on them, which meant that Jewle was pretty sure that Hayhill was a crook. I was also pretty sure that the Fraud Squad was making enquiries in order to be in a position to get a warrant to descend openly on 103 Gardener Road.

If Hayhill was a crook, then things were complicated by the fact that in my considered opinion Trude wasn't aware of it. Compared with the enormous swindle that Hayhill was getting away with, a simple confession of bigamy committed unaware, was just nothing at all. And there I stopped, once more against a solid brick wall.

I poured myself a stiff whisky as a guarantee of sleep. Bernice called from the bedroom that she hadn't wished to disturb me but she was going to bed. I looked at my watch. It was well after my usual time. Either that whisky was already freshening my brain or something in the way Bernice had called to me had brought back a something quite different, but suddenly I knew the answer to what had really been puzzling me—the reason for that drawn-out, almost anguished n-o-o! that I'd heard when I'd told Trude over the telephone that Sambord had been free to marry her.

What I thought I now knew was definitely startling. I saw that involuntary moan as a kind of horror at something that had happened but which needn't have happened if only she'd had that information before. And what had happened had been the death of Peplock. Not the death of Sambord. That hadn't been known. And if all that was true, then Trude had known both who had killed him and why he'd been killed.

I emptied my glass and hoisted myself from the chair. First thing in the morning I'd tell Jewle what I'd discovered, and it would be up to him to test a couple of alibis.

I didn't do it. Somehow I couldn't bring myself to pushing a nose once more into what didn't really concern me. And, since he'd spoken of things as going remarkably well, it was almost certain that he had no need of anything I'd be able to tell him. In fact, I was now having the suspicion that much of what I'd already been able to tell him had been either known or surmised, and that those little pats on the back he'd given me from time to time had been merely nice ways of concealing the fact. Old friendships die hard.

There was also the old illusion. Spectacles, rosy-tinted at eve, too often turn out to be ordinary lenses in a harsh morning light. All that day I attended resolutely to my own business, and if there was any intrusion by Peplock, the dead Sambord or the Hayhills, I managed to shoo it away. That evening I looked at television and when I woke next morning I was determined to pursue the course of the previous day.

It was during morning coffee that I began thinking about Trude Hayhill. I convinced myself that giving her a ring would be a kind of safety valve, and in the selfsame moment I found myself pressing the buzzer. Bertha got me Waterford Gardens.

"I'm afraid Mrs. Hayhill isn't available," I was told. "She left early this morning."

"Left?" I said. "She should have been lunching with me this morning."

"May I have your name, sir?"

"Wilson," I said. "Sir Charles Wilson."

"Just a moment, sir."

I waited two minutes.

"Mrs. Hayhill must have forgotten your lunch appointment, sir. She hasn't been feeling very well lately and she's left on a cruise. I believe it's to the Mediterranean."

I clicked my tongue audibly and annoyingly. "And Mr. Hayhill?"

"He's still at the apartment as usual. Shall I try him for you? He might be in."

"Don't bother," I said. "I'll probably see him at his office. And thank you for taking all that trouble. I expect Mrs. Hayhill will be writing me as soon as she reaches a convenient port of call."

I didn't hesitate then about getting Jewle. I had to wait only a couple of minutes before he was at the end of the line.

"Travers here," I said. "I think something's cropped up. Have you still got a tail on Trude?"

"No," he said. "When her husband got back we transferred to him."

"You know where he is now?"

"At Gardener Road, Highbury. If he weren't, then I'd have been told. Wait a minute and I'll try to check."

"Everything okay there," he told me when he came back. "He left at his usual nine o'clock and he's still there. Why'd you want to know?"

I told him. He let out a whistle.

"What's she doing? Really going on a cruise?"

"She looked fit as a horse the last time I saw her. If she's really gone on a cruise, the management at Waterford Gardens ought to have far more information than they gave me."

"You don't think so?"

"You should know," I said. "You know how far the Hayhill investigations have gone. If he's got a suspicion of what's in the wind, then I'd say he's parked her somewhere and will be joining her later. Then they'll both do another skip."

"Right," he said. "We're badly understaffed, but I'll get busy on it. And thanks very much for the tip."

"Just a moment," I said quickly. "Tell me just one thing. Those alibis. In order or not."

"In order. What she told you was dead right in every particular."

He rang off and a couple of minutes later I was back where I'd been two days before, puzzling my five wits over those two alibis. Hayhill might have killed Peplock, but as I'd already proved to my own satisfaction that he hadn't done it to protect his wife, then why had he done it at all? And neither of the Hayhills had killed Sambord. That could have been done only by our original and imaginary third man. I went further. If anyone wanted Sambord to keep alive, it was Trude. He was the only one who could really prove that the marriage with Hayhill hadn't been bigamous.

What about a double-cross? Had Sambord taken Trude's money and then let her down, and did his killer know it? The same old whirl began again and it looked like driving me crazy. That was when I decided on an early lunch and after it an afternoon at a cinema. When I emerged at four o'clock it wasn't till I was out in the street again that I remembered the case, and then I was wondering if Jewle had rang in my absence. That's why I took a taxi to the agency, only to find there'd been nothing from Jewle. It wasn't in fact till almost eleven the following morning that he did ring me.

"I'm in your neighbourhood," he said. "Fenchurch Street to be exact, and thinking about a cup of coffee. Will you join me or are you too busy?"

He mentioned a certain café and I said I'd be along at once. Ten minutes later I was there. It was past the usual coffee hour and easy enough to find a table.

"Thought, as I was so near, we might take a breather together," he told me. "Nice to get away for a bit."

"What brought you this way—or oughtn't I to ask?"

He smiled. "I don't think that would deter you. Still, the fact of the matter is I've been talking to two of the directors of a shipping company."

"About a certain possible Mediterranean cruise?"

"Oh, she wasn't lying," he said. "She's now off the south-west coast of Spain. It took us most of yesterday to check on cruises and, sure enough, she was there."

Somehow I couldn't believe it. I said it just couldn't be an ordinary pleasure cruise.

"Well, you can't call it ordinary," he told me. "It's pretty select. Includes the Holy Land, Greece, Egypt—the works. And all with professors and so on as guides. Even anyone so well-off as Trude Hayhill was lucky to be able to join it at almost the last moment."

There was something questioning in the way he looked at me.

"The last moment? Would you be relating that to Hayhill's return from his tour?"

"You've got it in one," he said. "He's suspicious. You can't throw a net as wide as we've been doing without something getting back to him. It's almost certainly what you said. He's laying his plans for a getaway."

He told me all sorts of things that might have happened. On a cruise like that, Trude wouldn't be pestered by Customs officials, so she might have with her quite a lot of loot. When she went ashore she could deposit it. If Hayhill did make his getaway, he could join her in some Mediterranean country, Egypt, for example, where extraditions either didn't apply or where palms could be greased.

"What about luggage?"

"Two large trunks and a smaller one. She probably took everything of personal value. Any loot, of course, needn't have been in the baggage. If you think of notes of large denominations in tight packages, you can get the very devil of a lot of money inside a girdle."

Something was suddenly striking me. "You're talking as if you were dead sure about Hayhill."

"We are," he said.

He took out his notebook and found a page. "Here we are. This is briefly what we got last night on the strength of the photographs and prints. Under the name of Harold G. Hayes he worked a big swindle in surplus war materials. Sold the same stuff to different customers and then skipped. That was from Regina in 1947.

"Next he turned up here, as you know. I'd say he saw no immediate prospects and was on his way elsewhere when he met Trude in Southampton. He was then Frank Hayhill."

He left the notebook for a minute.

"I rather think you're right about Trude not knowing what he was up to. If he'd ever taken her into his confidence, then he could have gone on operating under aliases. But he didn't. When the newly married couple went to New York, he opened an office in 38th Street: Hayhill Incorporated, importers and general agents. All he did isn't known but he definitely took two supposed-to-be hard-bitten business men from Argentina for twenty-five thousand dollars. Before they knew it, he'd skipped.

"That wasn't bad work for only six months. He was heard of, again too late, in Chicago: still as Frank Hayhill but working largely under cover in collaboration with a doctor who was later apprehended in Alberta. We haven't any fuller details but it was some sort of orphanage racket. Surreptitious disposal of babies to people who wanted to adopt.

"It looks as if that was the germ of what he's doing over here, because when he was next heard of, which was when he skipped from Toronto just over two years ago, he was working the same racket but very much under cover. The front man was another doctor."

Somehow I couldn't help smiling.

"You've certainly got to hand it to him as a shrewd operator. And if you can recover all the money he's helped himself to over here, he'll have been working this time for a real good cause without knowing it."

Jewle didn't see the joke. "Oh, yes, he was smart enough. And he must have been pretty besotted about his wife to run the risk of using his marriage name. Or am I wrong? Was she only a really good asset? Someone to introduce a customer to? A good-looker like her could create a good impression."

"Anyone flying over here to identify him?"

"It's more tricky than that," he said. "We could hand him over in no time and be rid of him. The thing is we don't want him for that. We want him for the Peplock killing."

"You've really got something on him?"

"We've had it for some time," he said. "It's the car—the one he was driving until the day after the killing. It answers the description and the number ended in 33. Easy enough to find that out, and that's where he went wrong. When he went on with his lights out, he was sure the number hadn't been seen. All the same, he drove the car to Oxford on the Monday and managed an exchange at a used car lot for the car he's driving now, and he was shrewd enough to drive a hard bargain."

He went on to explain just how tricky it all was.

"We don't want him out of the country, even if they jail him for fraud. We can nab him ourselves on a holding charge for fraud if we have the time, and we don't want all the business of getting him back here again. What we've got to do is substantiate the murder charge, and that's going to be damn difficult. The only line we have at the moment is the fact that Peplock and he were both in Toronto at the same time."

"Birds of a feather flock together," I said. "They might have got acquainted somehow. When Peplock got everything ready to put the screws on Trude, he also ran an eye over her husband to see any other potentialities. That's when he recognised him."

"That's how I see it," he said. "Proving it is a different matter. Peplock's the only one who might have had the answers."

"So what now?"

"Well, there's a conference for two o'clock this afternoon and then it'll be decided. Strictly between ourselves, I think the fraud boys have enough for a holding charge, coupled with a bit fuller information on his activities over there. Plus identification."

The coffee had long since been drunk. I paid the small bill and we went out to hail a taxi.

"I know you too well to think you're going to sit tight and wait for what you read in the papers," he said, "so if you want to work your wits, why not see if you can connect Peplock and Hayhill?"

"Some hopes," I told him. "If you people can't—"

He was stopping a taxi. The last I saw of him was a cheerful wave as the taxi moved off.

It was not till the late afternoon that I was able to do any thinking at all about the half-hour I'd spent that morning with Jewle, and I couldn't help a little pleasurable glow. He'd wanted no talk at the Yard about my frequent appearances there, so he'd virtually gone out of his way to arrange the morning's talk and bring me up to date. As I've said, old friendships die hard.

As for that final challenge to find a connection between Peplock and Hayhill, I thought that a bit of a leg-pull. In any case it had happened so quickly that I hadn't been in a position to judge. But what else could it be? When one considered the means at his disposal and at mine, it couldn't be anything else.

It had been that insatiable curiosity of mine that had kept me hovering around the fringes of the case so far, but after a few minutes another side of me was, like sex, rearing its ugly head, and that's a certain obstinacy. All my life I've never liked to be licked by something I know ought to be well within my powers and, above all, a challenge has always been something of a spur.

Ten minutes later I was temporarily beaten. For the life of me I could find no possible means of arriving at a connection between Peplock and Hayhill that would help to convict Hayhill of murder. To put Bob McGuffie on the job seemed a waste of time. Jewle must already have asked the F.B.I. and the Canadian authorities to get busy over that. All the same, I wanted to be doing something and that was why, after Bertha had brought in some tea, I thought I'd review the whole case again.

Straightaway I came up against that mysterious character whom we'd called the third man. Since neither Trude nor Hayhill had killed Sambord, there just had to be that third man, so what I then decided was to have a new look at every person even remotely connected with the case and find, perhaps, the one who fitted. It was a very long shot and another quarter of an hour's work produced only two—the Rev. Herbert Carnwell and the anonymous writer of a certain letter.

I didn't have to think long about Carnwell. For the life of me I couldn't see him as the murderer of Sambord. As for Mr. X—and I'd forgotten that morning to ask Jewle about him—he looked just as bad a misfit. If he'd been Sambord's killer, then why should he so gratuitously have drawn attention to himself, and when a man in crepe-soled shoes had never been publicly mentioned? And that left me with just no one. I'd thought for a moment of Granding, but only for a moment.

It was when I was thinking of Trude and trying to imagine her on that cruise, that I did have another idea. Trude had had a brother. Everything was mysterious about that brother. Naturally I'd never mentioned him nor had she. I thought of that hour I'd spent at Highgate with Victor Lang and his widowed daughter. Lang had mentioned the brother, but only vaguely. "A brother," he'd said when I'd asked about relatives. "A brother. He went away."

There'd been something else before that and I began putting down the fragments I remembered. The son of Martin Rubenstein had been called Martin, after his father. The mother had later married a Sam Layman and he and young Martin hadn't got on well together. Martin had finally left and Layman had accused him of taking some money. Martin was Trude's stepbrother and the difference in their ages would be about ten years. Lang hadn't got on well with Layman either, and that might be why he'd known no more of the whereabouts of Martin than that he'd gone away. The two Laymans had been killed in the blitz not long after Martin had left them.

Those were all the facts I had and I wondered if another visit to Highgate would produce more. Lang was a pipe smoker, so I bought a tin of the brand I smoked myself and got hold of a taxi. It was about six o'clock when I was once more knocking at the door of 15 Brownlow Avenue.

Mrs. Foster didn't recognise me for a moment, then she asked me to come in. I followed her through to a warm kitchen. I asked her if her father was available.

"I'm sorry to say no," she said. "He has a very heavy cold and the doctor's keeping him in bed. He's not so young as he was, you know."

"I do know," I said. "Quite a lot of us, including myself, were born too soon. But will you give him this as soon as he's able to enjoy his pipe again?"

"That's very kind of you." she said. "I'm sure he'll enjoy it. You wanted to see him?"

"It's the same old business of that legacy. I've as good as found Trude—"

"You have!"

"Yes," I said. "As soon as I've really got in touch with her. I may be able to let you know more. Now I want to find that stepbrother of hers, Martin, the one who couldn't stand living with Sam Layman. I gathered the last time I was here that Trude never mentioned him."

She smiled. "I think I told you that because I didn't want father to be upset. He thinks Trude's treated him so shabbily, he hates even to hear her mentioned."

"Then she did occasionally talk about Martin?"

"Well, not really that," she said slowly. "She knew we didn't like Martin much. His mother had spoiled him and I think he resented the fact that his parents had been employed by my father."

"And you've no idea where he went to after leaving the Laymans?"

She smiled. "Oh, yes, I know that. If Trude was telling the truth, that is. He went to America. You could get there very cheaply in those days, you know."

"You've any idea what part of America?"

"I'm almost sure it was New York."

I thought that over. I asked her if I might put another question or two. I didn't want to be a nuisance.

"Wasn't Martin supposed to have stolen some money from his stepfather and wouldn't you think he took it to pay his passage?"

"No, I don't," she said. "I never trusted Trude where her children were concerned. You know what things were like in nineteen thirty-nine."

She paused for a moment, shaking her head.

"I hardly know how to explain this, but what I mean is that Trude was really a foreigner, a European, and they felt even more than we did there was going to be a war. I think she took the money herself and sent Martin to America like a lot of English people did. She just doted on that boy. He must have been about eighteen at the time. Young Trude was only eight."

I thought she was right. And, if so, it might be possible to pin things more closely down.

"Then Trude would have been too young to send to America. Martin, of course, was old enough to earn his living. You never heard of any relatives over there to whom he might have gone?"

"It's all very complicated," she said. "After that marriage to Layman we lost touch with her. Also Trude's people were all Jewish and they were very sensitive about it at that time. You remember there were all those troubles in the East End."

"But later, when the Laymans were killed, you did get into touch with young Trude again. Didn't she ever mention her brother? Jewish families are very clannish."

"That may be," she said, "but you must remember that what I'm telling you I heard at second hand, from my mother. But Trude hated being a Jew. I suppose she got the idea it wouldn't do her any good in the world."

"So she never talked about her brother."

I didn't see the connection, but there it was.

"Look," she said. "I'm just going to take some hot milk up to my father so I'll see if I can get him to say something. Just what was it you wanted to know?"

"Only the two things. If Martin went to a relative in America, and if Trude ever had a letter from him."

It was over ten minutes before she came down. She smiled as she told me what had happened.

"He took a lot of managing but I think I got what you wanted. He says young Martin went to one of his father's relations. He doesn't know what he was. He also says he asked Trude once about Martin and she put him off. He thinks she did know where he was."

I rose to go. "I'm most grateful to you, Mrs. Foster. Oh, and before I forget it, you never heard Trude mention Toronto?"

"I didn't. That's in Canada, isn't it?"

"Yes, and not all that far from the United States border."

14

ALARUMS AND EXCURSIONS

I WENT straight home. Before the evening meal came up I arranged for a person-to-person call in New York. I knew I'd have to wait quite a time and it was just after Bernice had gone to bed that

Bob McGuffie came on the line. You can't say a lot in just under three minutes, so I had to talk fast.

"I'm asking you to do the impossible," I said. "A Martin Rubenstein, aged about eighteen, came to New York in nineteen thirty-nine. Jewish by birth, and he went to a relative, probably named Rubenstein. That's all I have on him but try to find him and anything about him. Your immigration authorities might have records."

He read it back to me and said he'd do his best. He couldn't promise results, and definitely not quickly.

"Put in, say, a week, and then drop it," I said. "And thanks for your letter. It was most helpful. We'll be seeing you here soon?"

That was that. I felt much easier but it didn't take the whole case from my mind. As I lay on the borderland of sleep, I began to see something like a connection: a vague one, it was true, but something, if I'd then known it, that I ought to have mentioned to Bob McGuffie.

Trude had been sent to an aunt, now dead, after her parents had been killed. Surely the aunt must have had Martin's address and been able to inform him of what had happened. Or the secretive Trude may have had the address. There was no certainty about any of that but I thought it did bolster up what Ellen Foster had learned that evening from her father.

More important then, was this. Trude Hayhill had been brought up as a snob, and she'd added to it her own brand of racial snobbery. That was all very well in England, but it needn't have held good in America. There she had nobody to impress and nothing particularly to conceal. And so, when she'd gone to New York in 1952 my guess was that she'd almost certainly looked her brother up.

Where did that get me? I didn't exactly know. I was merely exploring the vaguest of theories. I wasn't sanguine about dividends, even if still wilder hunches had paid some pretty hefty ones in the past. If I'd been frank with myself, of course. I'd have admitted that what I was doing was for little other reason than a feeling of doing: taking a long chance while waiting for something really to happen. A kind of *Waiting for Godot*, except that in this case it was *Waiting for Jewle*. Travers the bletherer, yammering away to himself as audience, and keeping a weather eye on the Yard.

One of these days I'll really have to take myself in hand and try to damp down that curiosity of mine, and the restlessness that goes with it. Nothing happened that day but as soon as I woke the next morning I had the same urge to be doing something. It was a wonderful day. The cold had lessened appreciably and the sun was shining. I drove my own car to the agency and, as the sun struck my cheek, it felt almost warm. If I'd still been playing golf, I'd already have been heading the other way.

The upshot was that soon after ten o'clock I was driving towards Ambourne. I didn't quite know why, unless it was that I wanted to get the feel of the place and to get away from the smell of town. In a way that's the schizophrenic in me: born and bred a countryman but thinking London the best place on earth, till it happens to be a fine day.

I slowed the car as I neared the town. Far to my right was a line of willows that marked the course of the river as it made a bend. When the river began to close in, I took a turn on the right and then went right again. In a couple of minutes I was at the far end of River Road. I slowed the car again and crawled past River Cottage. Except that the curtains were drawn, it was just as I'd last seen it. A few yards along, a constable was patrolling. He turned and came slowly back and I guessed he was keeping an eye on the house. He gave me a quick look as I passed him.

The elms made a wonderful sight with the tracery of boughs against the clear sky. "Bare, ruined choirs," I said to myself, "where late the sweet birds sang." Boughs that might have made a deep shadow for a man who'd coughed as another man neared. I went on to the turn where a man in a hurry had cut a corner and then switched off his lights. I had the road ahead of me along which a man had hurried that Sunday night to keep an appointment at River Cottage. I turned into the High Street and the Hare and Hounds. The lights had been against me but when they turned to green. I went right. Maybe all the time I'd intended to go to the Griffin.

I parked my car in the open space in front of the pub and went in. The landlord was behind the main bar, polishing a glass.

"Morning, sir. A nice morning."

"Couldn't be better. I think I'll have a light ale."

He poured one for me and I paid him. I took out my agency card and let him take just a quick look at it. It's a trick that works two times out of three. He made a face.

"Oh my Gawd! Not you fellers again. What d'you want me to do? Die of a sore throat?"

"Pour yourself a drink," I said. "What I want won't take a couple of minutes. Just that we're approaching this business at a new angle."

I was wondering if the luck would hold, and it didn't. Another customer came in.

"Just a minute, George. I'll send Mary in. Might as well attend to you first. The usual?"

He drew a pint of old and mild. He motioned to me and I followed him into a back room. I guessed it was the small lounge where Sambord had taken his nap and looked at the Sunday papers. He went through another door and I heard him calling for Mary.

"Now, sir," he said, "just what is it you wanted to know?"

"We'll go back again to that Sunday morning," I said, "when Mr. Peplock came in and a man with him. Did he approach you confidentially or did he just speak in the ordinary way?"

"Well, we were pretty well full up. I was behind the bar trying to serve two customers at once and I saw him sort of elbowing his way through and the other man, that Sambord, just behind him. There was a bit of an empty space and he leaned across and asked me if I did lunches. He gave me a pound note and said his friend—that was Sambord—wanted lunch. 'He's under doctor's orders,' he said, 'and he's not to have more'n a pint.' He was making a kind of joke of it, if you understand. 'If you do,' he said, 'I'll be back for the change.' I didn't believe him at first and then I saw he meant it."

"He was speaking confidentially, or how?"

"I've told you all that before," he said. "He had to speak up or I wouldn't have heard him at all. You ought to know what a bar's like on Sunday morning. Then he said his friend hadn't anywhere to go and would I look after him and he'd be picking him up when we opened at seven. I reckon I looked a bit surprised but he gave me another pound note and just sort of waved his hand and that's the last I saw of him."

"Sambord," I said. "This is where he had an afternoon nap, isn't it?"

"That's right, sir. He was still on that couch there when I brought him in some tea at five o'clock."

"He could have gone out if he'd wanted to?"

He looked surprised. "Why not? He was a free agent, as they say. You go through that door and turn left and you're in the back yard."

"Just asking," I said. "Later on, at seven, he had a pint."

"That's right. Only it was before seven: say about five or ten to. I stretched a point and drew him a pint seeing as how he was a sort of guest. He had it down before you could say knife."

"I know," I said. "He was expecting Mr. Peplock at seven, and he went out to wait. You didn't see him again?"

I'd brought my drink in with me and I finished it, then held out my hand.

"That's all at the moment. And I'm much obliged."

I went through the bar and out to my car. I looked along the road and tried to calculate the distance. Sambord, at the rate he'd been walking, could easily have got to the place where he'd been killed at just about the time Vingram found him.

I thought I'd make a day of it so I left the main road for a side road that would bring me to Wishington. I was hungry by the time I'd reached the Waggoners. The landlord asked if he hadn't seen me before and I said I'd had lunch there not so long ago. This time he found me cold ham, cheese and celery, and I had a pint of bitter to wash it down. One or two men were there whom I'd seen before.

I left at just short of two o'clock. I took the side road that led me past Granding's place, then reversed. I didn't go back by the

Waggoners but took another side road which ultimately brought me out near Epping Forest. I went left at the Finsbury Park four-cross roads, and on into Gardener Road. I slowed past the offices of The Good Samaritans and, for all that was happening, the staff might have been taking a siesta. I turned right through Islington, and it was still short of four when I drew up outside the agency.

It had been a long time since I'd enjoyed a day so much. And I'd learned an enormous deal. I'd seen things for the first time in perspective and my mind was fresher than it had been for days. One character at least was still unknown but the modus oper-andi was clear.

Peplock had picked up Sambord that Sunday somewhere near the farm and almost at once a waiting man had been cautiously on their tail. When Peplock drew in at the Griffin, the man drew in too. He might have been behind them when they walked in or he might have guessed what they'd do and gone in ahead. In any case he'd been in a position to hear every word that Peplock had said to the landlord.

Much later he'd reconnoitred River Cottage and almost certainly from the back. He must have been astounded to find Peplock dead. But Peplock's death didn't vitiate what had to be done to Sambord, so, for some reason I didn't know, he slipped the gun into his pocket and went out to wait. What happened then depended on whether or not that letter from Mr. X was genuine or a fake.

So much for what I'd call the trail of the third man. And that's where I left things. That night I slept like the dead and for the next couple of days the case didn't worry me. I'll own I thought Jewle perhaps might ring, but he didn't. Not until later on the afternoon of that second day, and then what he had to tell me didn't seem to have any immediate bearing.

"That Mediterranean cruise," he said. "We got into touch by radio and flew Matthews out to Marseilles. He's boarded the boat and is working under cover. I thought if you knew it might relieve your mind."

"I don't know," I said. "I've been thinking and there are things that don't fit. If she genuinely hasn't known what he's been up to, then why this cruise? What did he do? Own up to everything and get her to help?"

"Not necessarily. He could have kidded her into taking the cruise. Not that she'd need a lot of kidding. Would your wife jib at it? I'm damn sure mine wouldn't. As for any loot, she could have that without knowing it. In a false bottom to a trunk, for instance. If so, it means he's now scheming some way to join her. That'd surprise her but there'd be plenty of ways of explaining it away."

I agreed that was how things might be, but wouldn't it all mean forcing his hand?

"Don't worry," he told me. " Everything's under control."

Two days later things really happened. I'd heard nothing from Jewle and it was almost by luck that I saw the brief notice in the paper. A Frank Hayhill of Waterford Gardens, Hampstead, had been formally charged under the Fraudulent Practices Act with operating a charitable agency known as The Good Samaritans with intent to defraud. Hayhill's passport had been impounded but the police strongly opposed bail.

I gathered that the magistrate had not been convinced about the possibility of the defendant's ability to leave the country and the police had had to go further than they'd wished. Bail was strongly opposed, they said, because Hayhill might later be charged with a much more serious offence. I underline that because, as a printed phrase it was to be the one thing that ultimately unravelled the whole affair. At any rate, Hayhill was remanded in custody.

I read that in the final edition of an evening paper. Jewle rang me later and asked if I'd seen it.

"Weren't you rather forced to overplay your hand?" I said.

"Oh, you mean about the more serious charge," he said. "I don't think so. Too vague for one thing, and who's going to connect it with Peplock?"

"Any more on that?"

"Oh, odds and ends. But the D.P.P."—Director of Public Prosecutions—"thinks we've as good as got a case. The Canadian authorities are hard at it in Toronto trying to get a link-up between Hayhill and Peplock. If they do, that'll clinch it."

The morning papers didn't make too much of a splash. Perhaps I've given the wrong impression about The Good Samaritans. Compared with the big organisations, they were hardly a ripple in the ocean of the International Refugee Year. Hayhill had been operating a nice little cosy organisation, the sort that always appeals to the great British sentimental heart. Even those tours of his had been local and trivial compared with, say, the rallies in immense public halls. And he had been careful not to make of himself any kind of public figure. It was Carnwell who'd been eased into whatever little limelight there was.

Not that Hayhill hadn't made money. His hadn't been the cheques of great corporations or foundations. He'd been only too content with the morsels that came steadily in through postal appeals; a source always expanding instead of drying up; and, of course, the steady income from regular tours. And all the time he'd been able to keep himself comfortably installed behind the scenes.

That morning I didn't go straight to the office but made a big detour round through Gardener Street. There were no sightseers: nothing but a queue of unobtrusive police cars drawn up in front of 103, and a large CLOSED where the notice had been by the front door. I wondered what Carnwell was thinking of it all. My guess was that he'd still be prepared to swear that the police were making an enormous mistake.

When I moved on, I wondered what had appeared in the more sensational papers, so I stopped at a newsagent's and bought a *Record*. What I'd expected I don't quite know but the notice there was virtually no different from that in my own staider *Telegraph* and *Times*. I thought I knew why. Whatever they might have liked to print, papers were chary of comment with things as vague as they were. The law can be pretty severe on those who try to anticipate its own judgments. And an acquitted Hayhill could mulct them heavily in damages for libel. Hayhill had been remanded for a week. At its expiration he'd almost certainly be remanded again, which wasn't much consolation to myself. As I saw it, what the police intended was this: Maybe by a fortnight's time they'd be ready to bring Hayhill to trial on the minor charge. In other words, they had three weeks in which to find the final evidence. The prospect of that wait didn't please me in the least. If I'd been hunting for that vital evidence, that would have been different, but I wasn't. I'd done all my hunting. Now I'd nothing to look for and nowhere to look. Jewle did give me a ring a day or two later.

"You might like to know that Trude's back." he told me. "Not at the apartment. She's incommunicado at a private hotel."

"But why's she back? What happened?"

"The boat publishes the usual daily news-sheet. They all have much the same sources so we arranged to radio a paragraph about Hayhill's arrest and then to have it printed. Trude saw it in Naples and at once left the boat and arranged to fly home. Matthews came earlier and was waiting for her here."

"How'd she take it?"

"Definitely couldn't believe it, even when we found about twenty-eight thousand pounds in the false bottom of one of her trunks. She's glad to be where she is. Couldn't face going back to that apartment and all the publicity."

"And the Hayhill trial?"

"Coming on earlier than we'd hoped. With his record it's largely a matter of course."

"And nothing else on the more serious charge?"

"It'll come," he said. "We're not worrying."

So there it was. Patience, as I see it, isn't a virtue, it's an affliction, and I hated crawling back into my own private cosmos. That was why I was so surprised an evening or two later when Matthews rang me at my private number.

"You busy?"

"No. Why?"

"Could you meet me by the National Portrait Gallery in, say, ten minutes?"

"I could, but mightn't you tell me why?"

There was a quick, impatient click of the tongue.

"Dorlish," he said. "Someone's done him in."

15

ENTER A CORPSE

I'D NO idea where Dorlish lived. Hallows had kept him under observation for too short a time and there'd never been anything like a written report because he'd been working directly for me. I did know that the car was heading for Tottenham Court Road, but traffic was thick and Matthews was driving and I just sat there till we stopped at the lights.

"Far to go?"

"No distance at all. Just off Finsbury Park."

We moved on. There's a long, straight stretch as you near Holloway Road and traffic was thinning out.

"Why me?" I said.

"The Old Man was in conference when we got the news," he said, "and from what I was told I thought your opinion might help. You'll soon see why."

"When was he found?"

"That's interesting too. His receptionist found him."

"Then what's he doing at Finsbury Park?"

"Sorry," he said. "I've given you the wrong idea. He wasn't killed at his agency. He was killed at his flat."

"Oh," I said lamely and I didn't say anything more. The lights were with us at the busy junction and we were going through. Short of the Tube station we turned left. A couple of dingy streets and we were in a residential road. Towards the end of it Matthews slowed.

"Tamar Avenue. Should be on the left here somewhere."

We found it and turned. Not far ahead of us, still on the left, were the usual cars and an ambulance. There wasn't any crowd: just two or three people on the far pavement. I looked at my watch. It was a quarter to eight and a fine clear night. All was well in Tamar Avenue, except perhaps for Dorlish.

I didn't know then what the layout was, but it didn't take long to get the hang of it. The road was largely Edwardian, and when it was built, no doubt considered modern. The houses one might have taken for detached, were closely spaced, but they weren't houses at all: merely double flats. The lower one had the usual front door and a side door led to the upper. Dorlish's was a ground floor—14A.

A plain-clothes man let us in. Doors opened out from a tiny hall. All lights were on and there wasn't any need to ask what door to take. Old Doc Anders was there and a divisional inspector whom I didn't know. A couple of plain-clothes men were standing by.

Anders gave me what no one else would have considered a smile. There were brief introductions. The inspector's name was Howlett. Anders was always what's known as a dry old stick: pig-headed, cantankerous, impatient, but a first-class man at his job.

"So you got here," he said. "Damn lucky we didn't have him buried."

"Plenty of time," Matthews told him. "That blond of yours'll keep. Where is he?"

The room we were in was a conventional lounge. The room we went into looked as if it had once been a bedroom: now it was a study. On the right was a reproduction Georgian flat-topped mahogany desk and Dorlish lay by the front. He was on his back, head slightly sideways, one arm against the desk and the other flung out. That was all I saw before Matthews went forward and stooped.

I'd halted just inside the door. I looked round at the room. It had a small bureau-bookcase, every shelf of which was filled with books, mostly paper-backs. There was an easy chair facing a fireplace built into a chimney-breast that served the fireplace of the lounge, and the grate was so filled with blackened strata of burnt paper that, except for a faint glow at a corner, the fire might have been out. In the left-hand corner was a large, old-fashioned safe of the type that opens with a key. It looked the very spit of the one in Peplock's den at Ambourne.

Matthews was getting to his feet. "Have a look at him." he told me.

Howlett drew back and I got down on a knee. Blood disfigured Dorlish's face as it had done to Peplock's, but Peplock had been shot clean through an eye. The bullet that had killed Dorlish had gone through the forehead, just below the hair parting. The outflung arm had almost overturned the chair at which he might have been sitting, so that now its top was tilted back against the wall.

"Well?" Matthews said as I got to my feet.

"Almost as if we might be back at Ambourne again." I said. "What about that safe? Is it open?"

"Open all right." Howlett said. "Clean as a whistle inside."

"Everything done here that you want to do?" Matthews asked him.

Howlett thought so. Matthews turned to Anders.

"What's the time of death. Doc? Near as you can get."

"Don't know. Six. Half-past. That secretary says he had a cup of tea and a chocolate cake at about half-past four."

"Right." Matthews said. "Make a rush job of it. Close as you can to time of death, and we'd like the bullet."

"A rush job." Anders told me. "He takes an hour getting here and now he wants a rush job."

"All right. Doc. You've got it off your chest, so take him away. Where's that secretary?"

Howlett said she was in the kitchen. She'd had a long wait and had been very upset and he'd told her to make herself a cup of tea. No other place to park her except the bedroom. Matthews got out his notebook.

"What's her name?"

"Miller. Clarice Miller."

"Right," he said. "I'll see her. You get Dorlish away and later we'll compare notes in here."

He'd nodded back at me so I went with him to the kitchen. The plain-clothes man got another nod, and left.

It was a smallish kitchen that had been recently modernised. Clarice Miller was seated at an enamel-topped table, a tray in front of her on which were a couple of empty cups. She was a good-looking brunette, about five-six and with a fine figure. She'd done a first-class job on her face for there wasn't a sign of the upset that Howlett had mentioned. She wore a perky little black hat with a red feather and a red jumper just showed where she'd partly opened the black coat with a fur collar.

"Don't get up," Matthews said. "All I want to do is ask you a few simple questions and then you can go home. You smoke?"

"Well, occasionally."

He passed his case, lighted her cigarette and his own, and drew up another kitchen chair. I took the one that was left.

"Let me see. Your name is Clarice Miller. What's your address, Miss Miller?"

"Two thirty-five Milton Terrace. That's Harringay. It's a flat. I share it with another girl."

The voice had just a faint trace of Cockney. Lower middle-class upbringing, I thought; general schools' certificate and then a secretarial school.

"Now about this evening." Matthews was using the old avuncular handling. "Just why did you come here?"

"Well, I used to work with him sometimes of evenings. Private work."

"That must have been interesting. What kind of private work?"

"Well, records and things. He used to dictate them to me."

"I see. And this was one of those nights. You got here when?"

"Just about seven. That was always the time. It gave him time to get himself a meal before I got here."

"How'd you get in?"

"Oh, I had a key. He gave me one in case I ever got here first."

He made a note or two, thought for a moment and nodded. "Well, we're grateful to you for what you did. A lot of women would have panicked but you kept your head. You dialled 999."

She smiled slightly. "I only did what was right. I knew what I ought to do. You see it's part of my work, in a way."

"Exactly," he said. "You can't have been working at City Investigations without picking up a thing or two. How long have you been there?"

"Just over a year."

"Business pretty brisk?"

"Well," she smiled slightly again. "Mr. Dorlish didn't seem to worry. I was receptionist as well as secretary but I didn't really know."

Matthews smiled. "Still, I take it you always got your salary, plus overtime so you weren't worrying. By the way, who did for Mr. Dorlish here, as they say?"

"No one," she said. "He always looked after himself. He told me he always had. He didn't like breakfast much but he always had his big meal in the middle of the day and then supper at night."

"I see." He got to his feet. "Well, we're much obliged to you, Miss Miller. It's getting late, so you might like to go home. You'll be going to the office as usual in the morning?"

It was something that apparently hadn't struck her. As she rose, the handbag that had been on her lap fell to the floor. I retrieved it for her.

"I don't know," she said. "I suppose so."

"What time do you usually arrive?"

"Well, about nine."

"And you have a key?"

"Yes, it's in my bag."

"Tell you what then. You let me have the key and I'll get there a bit earlier in case anyone comes. You turn up just as usual. That be all right?"

She gave him the key. He shook hands and thanked her again. She'd glanced more than once at me, and I gave a nod and a smile.

"What about us driving you home?" Matthews said.

"Oh, no. It isn't far really. And there's a bus stop just along he road."

"Well, thank you again and good-night. You know your way about."

She went straight to the door: the door in the kitchen that must have been a kind of tradesmen's entrance. Just as she opened it—he was reaching for it from close behind her—he remembered something.

"Oh, just a moment. Miss Miller. Shan't keep you more than a second or two. There's something I've got to ask Inspector Howlett. Just make yourself comfortable again."

She looked far from comfortable: undecided whether to sit or stand. I held the chair for her. What Matthews was up to I hadn't an idea, unless it was to arrange for a man on her tail. Even then I didn't see just why.

"Lucky it's a nice night," I said. "It would be pretty nasty if you had to go home in a fog."

"Yes," she said. Her tongue went slowly over her lips. "Was that another inspector who was here?"

"That's right," I said. "Inspector Matthews. A very nice man indeed. I've known him for years."

"He seemed a bit kind. And you're an inspector, too?"

"For my sins."

If it was a joke, it was one she didn't quite follow.

"I was concerned with the other murder," I said. "Mr. Peplock's murder. That must have been a shock to you, too." I should have kept my mouth shut. She bit her lip and then the tears flooded her eyes. She groped in the bag for a handkerchief and then turned her head away. Another minute and she was just dabbing her eyes.

"I'm sorry. I was just upset, that was all."

"My fault," I said. "You smarten yourself up again before you go."

I took the tray over to the sink and pottered around for a moment or two, and then Matthews came in.

"All clear now." he said. "Sorry to have kept you hanging about."

He took her arm solicitously and this time he opened the door. He said another good-night as she went through.

"What was the matter with her?" he wanted to know. "Looked as if she'd been crying again."

"Well," I said, "she started to make conversation and I happened to mention Peplock: you know, coming before all this. That upset her again. What'd you go out for?"

He seemed to switch the conversation.

"Which would be the normal way for her to go out of the house?"

"Don't know. Probably the front door. If that's the way she came in."

"That's what I thought," he said. "But let's have a dekko at the bedroom. Something you'd like to see."

We went out to the tiny hall and through a door to the left. The bedroom was L-shaped. the lower arm being a bathroom-lavatory. It had a wardrobe, a chest of drawers and a chair. The bed was full-sized. It had been made, but up near the central pillow the overlap of a sheet was slightly rumpled.

"Now come in here."

I followed him into the bathroom. Ho opened the hot-press door. On the top shelf was a pillow.

"You see?" he said. "There're pillow cases but only that one pillow. What she did before she dialled the police was to take one of the pillows from the bedroom and put it in here, and then re-arrange the bed."

"Looks like it." I said. "And that's why she was here to-night?"

"Why not? She's a mighty smart piece. I don't know as we'll be able to prove it. Unless . . ."

"Unless you get her to talk?"

"Maybe." he said. "But let's get back to Howlett. It's too damn cold in here."

Howlett was crouching over that remnant of fire in the study, gently stirring the burnt paper with the poker. He looked up as we came in.

"Still nothing there?" Matthews said.

"Not even a speck of white. Whoever burnt that paper put it on piece by piece."

"Give it a rest." Matthews told him. "Soon as it's cold you can get it out here. Tell me about Clarice Miller. What time did she leave the office tonight?"

"Five o'clock, so she said."

"And Dorlish?"

"She didn't know. He said he'd be leaving early. According to her, that'd be about half-past five."

"What about the top flat?"

"I went up there myself," Howlett said. "One of the first things I did. It's occupied by a retired couple, name of Geary. Television fans, Children's Hour and all. They'd had it on from five o'clock. Soon as I left them they had it on again. You can just hear it out there in the hall. They wouldn't have heard a rocket, let alone a gun."

A plain-clothes man looked in and then came through.

"Any luck?" Howlett said.

"Yes, sir. Soon as she came out she looked as if she was listening, then she nipped back to the other side of the door and got something out from back of the dustbin. It might have been a flat sort of parcel or a little case. I couldn't see, but she slipped it under her coat. It was all done so quick."

"And then?"

"Well, sir, I gave her a nice little start and then I crossed the road and went along to the far end where she was waiting for a bus. Whatever it was she took from behind that dustbin, she still had it under her coat. She had her arm pressed against it, like this. When the bus did come, she went on top."

"Good work," Howlett said. "Now you'd better get back and lend a hand."

Lending a hand was asking questions all along Tamar Avenue.

"That was smart deduction on your part," I told Matthews. "What're you going to do with her now?"

"Only two choices," he said. "Let her get away with it or be waiting for her when she gets home. All that's worrying me is it mightn't have been just nightie and toothbrush. It might have been a flat package of case records. What do you think?"

Howlett reckoned every record, if there'd been any, would have been already burnt when she'd arrived. I didn't think she was the sort in whom Dorlish would confide.

"Don't think I dare risk it," Matthews said. "Better hurry if I'm going to head her off. You two'd better search the whole flat. The Old Man ought to be along soon."

It was nearer ten o'clock than nine. Howlett hadn't eaten since lunch so he brewed a pot of tea while I searched the kitchen. After that I took the bedroom and he the lounge. Just as I joined him, Jewle arrived. A brief report and the three of us got to work in the study. Howlett and I tackled the books, flicking over the pages in case any slip of paper should be inside. The paper-backs, almost without exception, were crime stories, quite a few dating from Dorlish's Mainford days. The rest were a mixed lot: books on famous criminal cases, Weber's *The Pinkertons*, and reference books like Hans Gross's *Criminal Investigation* and Glaisher's *Toxicology and Medical Jurisprudence*. Now and again we found slips of paper, put to mark a place, but never a one had the least bearing on Dorlish himself.

"Well, somebody made a pretty good job of it," Jewle said. "No correspondence, no cheque book, no paying-in book, no nothing."

He listened suddenly. A car was drawing up. A couple of minutes and Matthews was back.

"I picked her up just as she got off the bus," he told us. "This is what she had."

It was a little flat brief case, almost new. The leather was good and the impressed gold monogram was C.M.

"A present from Dorlish," he said. "Nothing in it but what she might want for a night, so I took her home. Left her crying her eyes out. Her room-mate wasn't there. She's away for a long weekend."

Howlett went off to check up on the Tamar Avenue enquiries. Jewle said it was time we talked things over. The study fire was now out so we went to the lounge. Matthews switched on an electric fire.

"You see now why we wanted you to come along here?" Jewle said to me. "Even the preliminary report we had from Howlett seemed to show some sort of a tie-in with Ambourne, let alone the second of the partners getting done in. You got any ideas?"

I said I hadn't any, that is, that were likely to be different from their own.

"Well, it might be the same case all over again," Jewle said. "Not the same gun, of course. That doesn't matter. It doesn't even matter what calibre it was. The fact remains that Dorlish was killed just like Peplock. Both were shot in the head."

"Yes," I said. "In both cases it looks as if the killer was someone expected, especially so here. Otherwise he wouldn't have been admitted. And the killer came for the same reason—to destroy certain evidence."

"Isn't there a little more to it than that?" Matthews said. "Peplock was killed and Dorlish knew how he was killed. He was in this blackmail racket just as deep as Peplock, so wouldn't he have taken precautions?"

It was a good point Peplock had probably opened the door expecting maybe to see a far too early Sambord. and had then been forced back to his study at the point of a gun. That theory had been made public. Dorlish knew about it. Why then had he opened the door without making sure?

He couldn't have been expecting Clarice. Matthews had got out of her that she was to arrive at seven o'clock as near as she possibly could. And that's when she had arrived. If that precision showed anything, it was that Dorlish really was taking precautions. He wasn't going to open that door unless he was sure.

And yet he had opened it. Why? Could the caller have been a friend who was implicitly trusted? That'd mean the laborious job of finding out if he had any friends. Or could the killer have made an appointment by telephone just before arriving, which again would mean that he was someone whom Dorlish was perfectly willing to see?

"There's another possible solution," I said. "Thanks to the destruction of all the records, we'll never know just how many people were being blackmailed. Tonight's caller may have been one of them. Someone who had been here before. Someone of whom Dorlish wasn't in the least scared."

"No," Jewle said. "Let's say four people were on the books when Peplock was killed. I think that's a liberal estimate. Dorlish knew all about them. He knew who was supposed to call on Peplock that Sunday evening. It was a report on the results of that, that he expected to get from Peplock personally when he returned from Brighton on the Monday. That's fact. Dorlish was definitely at Brighton.

"Very well then. Dorlish had a choice of the same four people for the killing. What'd he have tonight? Only two. If Hayhill was being blackmailed, then he's in custody. Trude, as far as he or anyone else knows, is on a cruise. Dorlish wasn't a fool. If one of those people had tried to get in here, he wouldn't have had a chance. Also Dorlish would never be unprotected. We mayn't even be able to prove it, but I'll bet anything you like he had a gun."

"Let's take another look at the Peplock killing," Matthews said. "What was Hayhill doing there if he wasn't the one? Why'd he get rid of his car?"

Jewle gave one of his wry smiles.

"I thought it'd come. There's something we're going to have to face up to, but let me give you my ideas about Hayhill, then you'll see what I'm getting at. I think now that he went to River Cottage that evening with the intention of killing Peplock, but he got there too late. He found Peplock already dead. That's why he got rid of his car."

"But the killer was in the house," I said. "He was searching the place."

"Didn't make any difference. As soon as Hayhill saw Peplock lying there, he got out of that house like a bat out of hell. That's the only thing he could have done."

So there it was. If Jewle's reasoning was correct, then Hayhill would never be charged with the Peplock killing. When one came to look things squarely in the eye, there was a far better reason for Jewle's being right. Hayhill didn't kill Dorlish, and yet the second killing was virtually a replica of the first. When we did face up to that, it was pretty disheartening. Both the partners must have been killed by a person unknown, and, since the records had all been destroyed, there didn't seem much likelihood of our discovering who that unknown was.

"We're back at the third man," I said. "The man who disposed of Sambord. What about that anonymous letter? Did you follow it up?"

"Yes," he said, "and there wasn't any answer. Either Mr. X got scared, or else the whole thing was a fake."

After that the talk did go on but it seemed a bit useless. I asked about Trude. What exactly was meant by saying she was incommunicado?

"Well, it was her wish not to go to the apartment," Matthews told me, "so she was offered a hotel. She didn't want to see anybody and we could keep an eye on her. She's been out only once, when we took her to Brixton to see her husband. Just five minutes and the usual precautions. In fact they were very closely watched."

As far as I was concerned, that was the end of the evening. Jewle thanked me, and his driver took me home. Jewle and Matthews were staying on. I was probably tired that night but my brain didn't know it, and it was a long time before I could get to sleep. When I woke in the morning, it was in the same fog of disappointment. I felt as I'd once done as a boy when I'd been picked for the first and only time for a first eleven and then the match had been scratched. As far as I was concerned, the bottom had fallen out of the whole case. Trude had done nothing and Hayhill was only a crook, and who the mysterious third man was who had killed both Peplock and Dorlish, I just didn't care.

16
DAYLIGHT

THAT curiosity of mine might be dead but it refused to lie down. I drove to the agency that morning and happened to get held up at Chancery Lane. When the Strand traffic moved again, I turned left towards Whitmore Court. Maybe some little inner voice had whispered that Matthews or Jewle might be at City Investigations. Just a minute or two and loose ends could be neatly tucked in and the whole case decently interred.

The place was closed. Nobody seemed to be there but I pushed the bell. A minute and Matthews opened the door.

"It's you, sir. Come along in. Just about finished but you might like a look."

"Where's Clarice?"

"She couldn't tell me anything I didn't know, so I sent her home."

Everything inside was much as Hallows had described it. On the desk in the waiting-room was a pile of records.

"All the regular case files they've had." Matthews said. "They'll have to be gone through, of course. The one operative on the books arrived at nine. He's gone, too. We'll have a word with him when we've examined those files."

"I thought you people were keeping an eye on Dorlish." I said.

"So we were. Then we had to rob Peter to pay Paul."

"Well, no use crying over spilt milk," I said. "No fault of yours being short-handed. Nothing else here at all?"

"Only what you see. But there *was* something. Fact of the matter is that if you hadn't dropped in just now, I was going along to see you. Don't know if you'd be prepared to do it. but the Old Man thinks it'd be a good idea if you paid a call on Trude."

I stared. "What on earth for?"

"We don't know. It's just an idea. You'll be the same old friend." The smile was more of a leer. "From what I've been told you really are an old friend. Just let her talk. Make out you had the devil of a time getting permission to call. I don't need to tell you what to do."

"That's where you're wrong," I said. "What exactly do you want to know? Or am I to let her cry on my shoulder and collect a few tears for the back-room boys?"

"Look," he said. "We don't know. Just get her to talk. Tell her about Dorlish, for instance. The news won't be out till this afternoon. For all we know, she might let something slip."

He grabbed a sheet of paper from the desk, cut off the heading and took out his pen.

"Here we are. Lanchester Hotel in Gayford Street. Just across from Harrods. She's in a little suite, number seventy-four. Our man's in seventy-seven, just across the corridor. Give him this and Bob's your uncle."

"Very well." I said. "Ill see what I can do. but don't blame me if it's a waste of effort. What's the best time to see her?"

"Oh. about eleven. Say just before. She might offer you coffee."

He locked the outer door and I held that collection of while he brought his car round from the other side of the Court. It was a flagrant sort of wink he gave me as he drove off.

London has scores of hotels like the Lanchester. You never see them advertised but a hard core of clientele know they're there. They're the sort of places in which you get really good food, quiet and comfort and, when you come up to the desk, the chances are the clerk remembers your name. He didn't ask for mine. I went straight to the lift.

The Yard man gave me a quick look when I tapped at the door of seventy-seven, took the chit I held out, then drew back to let me in.

"All right, sir," he said. "The door's probably locked but she'll let you in."

"Has she had any other callers?"

"No, sir. She keeps herself to herself. Has all her meals brought up and anything she wants."

I knocked at the door of seventy-four. I was about to knock a second time, and then it opened. Her face went a violent red at the sight of me.

"May I come in?"

She didn't speak. I went into a tiny lounge. Through an open door I could see a bedroom. I turned and held out my hand as she came toward me.

"So sorry to hear about all your worries. I had a great deal of trouble getting here but I just had to come and see if I could help."

"That's really kind of you," she said. "I feel ashamed of myself, really But do sit down."

I took an easy chair that faced a fireplace with an electric fire. Above the mantelpiece was an old-fashioned mirror. Vases stood at each end.

"But why ashamed?" I said. "You were perfectly ignorant of what was going on."

"I ought to have known. I'm so angry with myself for being such a fool."

"You're far from the only one he fooled," I said. "But what are you going to do? That's what I wondered if I could help you about."

"Would you like some coffee? And do take your overcoat off. I'll speak to room service."

She rang for the coffee. I drew a chair up just across from my own.

"I was asking what you were going to do with yourself." I reminded her as I held the chair. She gave a little toss of the head.

"Well, I'm absolutely finished with him, of course. I shall get a divorce and I may go abroad. I've some money of my own and I'm sure I could always find a job. Under my maiden name, of course."

"I think you're wise. I don't see what else he can expect."

"Oh, he knows," she said. "I was allowed to see him the other day. I made it all perfectly clear."

There was a tap at the door. It was a waiter with the coffee. She rose, maybe to place a small table, and it was then that I saw something in the tall mirror above the fireplace. The waiter glanced at me and then at her. She shook her head. "Put it here, Charles, will you? On this table."

He placed the table between us and the tray on it, asked if there was anything else, and withdrew. I asked for black with one lump. Hers was white with no sugar.

"The service is so good here," she told me. "The police want to spare me any annoyance and it's really rather nice being here alone. A chance to catch up with one's reading. And there's the wireless, of course. A pity there's no television. I can always turn the wireless off if there's anything unpleasant."

"That reminds me." I said. "Don't be surprised if you hear some unpleasant news when you turn your set on later in the day. I got a private tip about it this morning."

"Unpleasant?" She flushed again slightly. "You mean for me?"

"Heavens, no!" I said. "Well, only remotely. You remember that dreadful man Peplock? The one who was mixed up with Richard Sambord? The one who nearly got you involved with the police? Well, it turns out he was a blackmailer. But that isn't what I was going to tell you about. He had a partner named Dorlish who was with him in the blackmail racket, and last night this Dorlish was killed, too. Shot through the head, like Peplock."

"But how horrible!"

"Maybe, maybe not. Murder's a crime but people like those two deserve what they get." I shook my head. "The police had an idea I might know something since I was mixed up with Peplock through making those enquiries for you about Sambord, and that's why I had to see them this morning and how I learned about Dorlish."

I gave a little start of surprise.

"Wait a minute. You went to Dorlish some time later and asked him to find Sambord, too. I wonder if the police will find a record of that in his files."

"Oh, but he wouldn't do it for me. He said he couldn't take on anything when the police were doing it as well."

She poured me a second cup when I asked her what she'd thought of Dorlish. That was to make time.

"I hardly remember him," she said. "After all, I was only with him a minute or two. He just seemed an ordinary sort of man. Very business-like. And a bit abrupt." She smiled. "Well, does that set your mind at rest?"

"Not at all," I told her. "I wasn't all that uneasy. But there is a something else the police might mention to you. You don't mind if I have to be a bit blunt?"

She frowned.

"This doesn't concern you," I said. "It really concerns your husband, so let's forget about it."

"But I'd like to know."

"Well, apparently your husband was operating some sort of racket in Toronto—you didn't even suspect it, of course—and at the same time Peplock was running a crooked enquiry agency there. The police are wondering if he and your husband knew each other there. Peplock was known as Henry Claire."

"I never even heard of him," she said. "As for my husband. I'm really not interested. After what he's done I'm prepared to believe anything. You're not going already?"

"Afraid I must. I virtually sneaked out of my office to come and see if I could help."

I hastily grabbed my coat and put it on.

"You're really a darling," she told me. "As soon as all this horrible business is over, we must try to see each other more."

"Nothing I'd like better," I told her as I went through the door.

I went straight back to the agency and rang Matthews. He was in. I told him I was just back from that call on Trude.

"How'd you get on? Pick anything up?"

"How could I?" I said. "You people don't allow her to communicate with anyone, so what could she know? I did learn that you're on the wrong track."

"What d'you mean?"

"This," I said, "and I'm not grumbling about your using me as a stalking horse. How do you know that Trude isn't in contact with outside?"

He laughed. "Because she isn't. We have her watched."

"What about any letters? She's got every facility there for writing."

That time he didn't laugh. "What if she has? She could only post them through the hotel."

"That's what you think," I said. "A waiter named Charles brought in coffee this morning. He looked the sort to me who'd post a letter if the lady asked in the right way. If I were you people I'd ask him some questions."

I left it like that. Just as I was going out to lunch, Jewle rang. He was quite perturbed.

"What you told Matthews about a waiter. Was there anything in it, or just guesswork?"

I told him precisely what I'd seen in the mirror. He granted, thanked me and rang off.

Nothing much happened that early afternoon. The evening papers came in as usual. Both gave prominence to the Dorlish story, even if it was little more than a padding out of what they'd been handed. There was also an appeal for witnesses of anything unusual in the neighbourhood of Dorlish's flat that night.

At five o'clock I was thinking of going home when Bertha buzzed through to ask if I'd take a person-to-person call from New York: It was Bob McGuffie.

"Thought I'd report to you direct," he said. "Afraid we've got to a dead end and we'd like your opinion about further instructions. This is what we've got. Your Martin Rubenstein landed on May 16, 1939. The sponsor who was guarantee for his support was a David Rubenstein, his great uncle, age given as sixty-four, occupation enquiry agent. The Brooklyn address doesn't matter because most of the block was pulled down in forty-eight. The point is, do you want further enquiries. So far we can get nothing on either of the Rubensteins. Twenty years over here is a long time ago."

"Better wash the whole thing out," I told him. "It wasn't all that important. Thanks in any case."

He just had time to say he'd be seeing me personally early in January, then we had to ring off. I didn't feel any particular disappointment: it had been far too long a shot. I could even convince myself once more that the case, as far as I was concerned, was over. Not that I wouldn't like to know if Jewle had managed to pin anything on that waiter, Charles. I even took a chance and rang him, and he happened to be in.

"Any luck with that waiter?" I asked him.

"We haven't done a thing," he said, "except to have him watched. Better to catch him out in something than do any questioning. All the same, would you mind telling me something? I don't doubt your word about there being something going on between him and the lady, but suppose he did post a letter for her, to whom would it be? She's got money. She can order anything she wants, so why write letters surreptitiously? Who's she writing to?"

That was a facer. I said I didn't know. She couldn't get anything through to her husband: also she'd told me she was divorcing him.

"Well, this Charles isn't all that bad-looking," he said. "What you saw might have been for quite a different reason. I wouldn't put it past her."

If it were ever in question, I suppose I'd pride myself on being a good husband: the kind, that is, who'd never given his wife a moment of anxiety. Maybe it was a kind of dog-in-the-manger attitude, but when I thought of the comparatively little that had happened between Trude and myself, and even what possibly could have happened, I couldn't bring myself to think what Jewle had even so tactfully suggested. All the same, he'd had a certain amount of logic on his side. However much I thought, I couldn't think of a single soul to whom the lady would want to smuggle out a letter.

Bernice came in a bit late that evening: a hospital committee meeting had been rather protracted. During dinner she brought up again that question of treatment of polio.

"I mentioned what we were talking about the other evening." she said, "and Doctor Mandelbaum was telling me about that Swiss clinic. It probably is the best in Europe but it's frightfully expensive. There must be a lot of moneyed people because it's always full."

"Then we were both right," I said. "A whole lot of people don't think about money when a child's rehabilitation is concerned. Did you learn anything else?"

She told me about various new treatments and then, with the ending of the meal, that particular conversation petered out. The television programmes looked good for once, so I switched the set on. It made me remember the couple above Dorlish's flat, and then I got interested in what was on the screen. We actually sat up till past our normal time.

In the morning I had a good look at the papers in case there'd been any developments, but there hadn't. I rang down to the hall porter again and had a *Record* sent up, and. as soon as I saw the front page, I knew that Rodey had once more revelled in a crime reporter's dream. There was a picture of Dorlish's flat and another, which I'd seen before, of the outside of City Investigations, but, as I began reading, that wasn't what intrigued me.

There's no law against speculation and little risk of libel when a killer is unknown, so Rodey had produced a theory. It wasn't even remotely a new one to me but it must have taken quite a bit of shrewd thinking. I could imagine him firing questions during the press conference and maybe getting some answers; at any rate he'd come up with the suggestion that Peplock's killer and Dorlish's were the same person. Much of what he'd written had been said in Dorlish's lounge when Jewle and Matthews and I had tried to thrash the whole thing out.

Rodey hadn't thought along the same lines—there was no mention, for instance, of Dorlish taking precautions—but he'd arrived at the same conclusions.

The two men had been partners in what was really a blackmail racket; each had been killed in the same way and clearly for the same reason, and it could only have been by one and the same man. He made a suggestion. If some other victim of the racket would come forward, then, given a guarantee of absolute secrecy, that victim might be able to throw some light on the killer.

There was a third leader on the middle page that looked as if it, too, had been inspired by Rodey. It said blackmail was a heinous crime that could flourish only by the cowardice of its victims. Who knew how many people were being blackmailed at that very moment by scoundrels of the type of Peplock and Dorlish. What was needed was greater publicity, and the *Record* was determined there should be such publicity. The public had to know that cowardice in approaching the law was the one thing on which the Peplocks and Dorlishes had always battened.

Rodey, I thought, had done pretty well, I wouldn't go so far as to say that what he had written would appear in future school text-books as a prize specimen of English prose, but he'd done a first-class job of reporting. That was all I thought about it. By the time I'd finished what little there'd been for me to do at the agency, I was feeling a bit restless. Then, by sheer luck, Matthews rang me. He said he might be coming my way and could he drop in for a minute, say in ten minutes' time. I told him there'd be some coffee.

In the old days he'd have breezed in. That morning he was looking a bit subdued. Things weren't going any too well, he said, not that there wasn't plenty of time. Where he'd actually been that morning was to a city bank and that was the only thing that was new.

"We got Dorlish's bank through Clarice," he told me. "Something she remembered. I've been having a look at his bank statements. Can't give you the details, but one or two quite big payments in. One about three weeks ago. Always in cash."

"Did you ever get Peplock's?"

"Never," he said. "Our guess is he always worked on a cash basis, too. We're still trying, though, far as we've got the men. The trouble is he might have been using an alias. Whoever burnt all his papers did a pretty good job, just as they thought they'd done with Dorlish. Lucky for me Dorlish had once sent Clarice to his bank."

I asked him if he'd seen that morning's *Record*. The look on his face told me he had.

"Rodey's a bit too clever for his boots." he told me. "One of these times he's going to trip over himself and I hope I'm there to see it."

He'd got up to go and I asked him why the hurry.

"Got to see Dorlish's brother," he said. "He's coming in from Mainford about midday."

I've often thought it queer how ideas can flap loosely around in one's mind for days, and then suddenly and for no apparent reason, coalesce. I've said before that I even run up against something of the sort in the matter of crosswords, and I mean the really hard ones. I've been absolutely stumped overnight for a clue and then woke in the morning to find the answer there. The subconscious, maybe. I wouldn't know. I'm no psychologist.

That was what happened that morning after Matthews had left. That brief call had started me off again, reviewing the case, and, before I'd been at it more than a couple of minutes. I all at once had the germ of an idea. I grabbed a sheet of paper and made a note in case it should slip away, and by then I'd another idea that seemed to bolster the first one up. Another minute or two and I was leaning back. The whole thing was too preposterous. Things just couldn't have happened that way. Or could they?

I began again. This time I tried a method that'd served me pretty well before. I wrote down a fact: an undeniable fact, and asked myself what various things might have happened then. They radiated like spokes from a wheel and I explored each one till it seemed to join up with another possible fact. On the basis of those two facts I tried other radiations. By midday I was beginning to get excited. Half an hour later I thought I knew who had killed whom, and why.

Somehow it made for an enormous easing of the mind. I stood myself lunch at my club and sat on afterwards in the lounge with coffee and a headful of ideas. To know was one thing; to prove was another. Given unlimited time I knew I could get that proof, but time was something I didn't want to live with till the proof came. What I needed was a short cut or two, and for that I needed help.

I went back to the agency and saw Norris. Hallows was doing nothing from which he couldn't be spared for a couple of days. Late that afternoon he came in and I brought him bang up to date with the Peplock-Dorlish case. He, too, was now of the opinion that both had been killed by the same man. I set to work to *try* to disprove him. He nodded now and again as he listened, and I could see he was coming my way.

"No time to ring New York?"

"It isn't that," I said. "It's how long they take to find out"

"What about that Mrs. Hayhill? Couldn't she help?"

"Too risky," I said. "One little slip and we'd blow the whole thing sky-high."

"Why not pretend to make a slip," he said. "Something that wouldn't matter. Something that'd make her use that waiter, Charles, again. Give the Yard the tip and have them pick him up."

"That'd only touch the fringes," I said. "There'd still be all the rest to prove."

I said we'd play it my way. Give it at least a chance. I reached for some paper.

"Let's write it down and see how it works out. Soon as it looks good enough to you, then you can get to work."

17
"IT'S UP TO YOU"

BY THAT evening Hallows had the photograph we needed. It was only a picture cut from a newspaper, but a rush job gave us a half-dozen prints. Hallows had another job to do in the morning while I went to Wishington. Granding was in his office with his secretary. I told them we thought we had a line on the man who had been seen leaning on his motor-bike in the road by the gate on the Saturday before Sambord had gone away. What we wanted was help in identifying him.

I asked Jane Bewley, the secretary, to try to describe the man's face, especially the beard. She'd seen the face for only a moment. She'd been walking on the grass verge and hadn't been heard till she was quite near, and then the man had whipped on his goggles. The beard was quite a close one, starting just below the ears, then coming to a point just below the chin. And there'd been a moustache that merged into the beard.

I sketched in beard and moustache on a photograph and let her see it. She said it looked too rough and asked if she might try it herself. The second photograph pleased her. She said she wasn't sure, but thought it was the man. If she could see the actual man, she'd really be sure. That wasn't much good to me but it'd have to do. I thanked the pair of them and moved on.

This time it was back to the Griffin at Ambourne. The landlord didn't look too pleased at the sight of me. I just showed him the photograph that Jane Bewley had titivated and asked him to think back to that Sunday morning when Peplock and his friend had approached the car. Did he remember any such man near the bar at the time?

He looked at the photograph and he looked at me. "Funny, but I do remember someone," he told me. "You don't often see people like that, not in this bar."

He had another look. "Yet it's funny. I can't remember serving anyone like him with a drink."

"He didn't need one," I told him. "He'd found out what he'd come for, so he probably went straight out."

Hallows was there when I got back to the agency. He also had what we wanted, so we made a final check in case there was anything else that might fit in, and then I called Jewle.

"Travers bothering you again," I said, "but I'd like to see you. It's rather important."

"You can't tell me now?"

"It's far too long. And I don't like talking on the 'phone."

"Just a minute," he said, "and I'll try to fit you in. . . . Two o'clock do? I'll have a few minutes then."

I said I'd be there on the dot, and I was. No sooner had I hung up my overcoat than Matthews came in.

"This is going to be a bit difficult," I said, "but I want to convince you that I'm almost certain I know a short cut to solving all this business. All I want is your co-operation." Jewle looked at Matthews and Matthews at Jewle.

"Did I hear you right?" Jewle said. "You can solve the Peplock business?"

"No," I said. "All I said was I knew a short cut. I don't actually need your co-operation except to get your permission to go down to River Cottage with a friend."

Jewle was trying to be patient.

"Look," he said, "start again and tell us just what you want. What sort of co-operation. What has River Cottage got to do with it."

"The basis is this," I said. "I've found someone who might know more than anyone about this Peplock business and I'd like to talk with him, and the ideal spot would be River Cottage. If I may suggest it, you could have a microphone installed and overhear the conversation and, if you do, then you'll know as much as either of us. After that it'll be up to you. All I want is for you to listen."

"Why River Cottage particularly?" Matthews wanted to know. "Because that was where everything started and because it's one of the few places the man I've been talking about will want to see. He knows a whole lot of things. That's what I'm certain about and that's what I can get him to talk about."

"Who *is* this man?"

"Someone who'll talk to me and not to you."

"Look," Jewle said, still patiently, "let's not start going all mysterious about this. We know each other, or we ought to. You say you know a way to help us, and that's fine. We're not too proud to be helped. We're only too glad to be. You should know that, so put your cards on the table."

"I will," I said. "I've discovered purely by chance that Max Rodey has unearthed a whole lot of information which he's planning to make use of. I've had proof more than once recently that he rather likes confiding in me. and I'm dead sure he'll do it again, at Ambourne. I'm equally sure he'll never talk to you."

"Sounds good," Jewle said slowly. "Max Rodey, eh?"

"Max gets about," I told him. "Maybe he's planning to solve this business himself in the *Record*: sort of let the solution out by driblets. That's why he'll never talk to you. But he'll talk to me, provided it's in Peplock's study at River Cottage." Jewle grunted. "You mentioned a microphone. I suppose one could be rigged up. That garden shed's quite handy as a listening post."

"I'd want something to start the ball rolling with." I said. "So tell me one or two things. At what time did Dorlish die?"

"As near six as makes no difference."

"And the gun?"

"Probably a nine millimetre Luger."

"And Dorlish's safe? What was the make?"

Matthews answered that one. A Grover and Trench. Both had been bought at the London showrooms in 1958. Perhaps there hadn't been all that much money available after various heavy expenses, so the key type had been bought. The combination-lock variety cost a great deal more.

"Everything depends on whether Rodey takes the bait or not." I said. "I think I ought to ring him now, from here."

Two or three minutes and he was on the line.

"Hallo, Rodey," I said. "How are you? This is Travers."

"Ah!" he said. "I'm fine. How're you, Mr. Travers?"

"At the moment, in a position to do you a favour." I let my voice drop. "You've asked me to pass on anything I can. and now I think I'm on to something big. I've got permission to have a look inside Peplock's place at Ambourne tomorrow morning. Something there I very much want to see, and I wondered if you'd care to join me. I can wangle the pass to include a friend."

"Sounds good," he said. "Like to give me a clue?"

"Well." I told him reluctantly, "seeing it's you. You haven't been in Dorlish's flat, have you?"

"Don't think anybody has, except the police."

"Then it arises out of the safes they had. Can't tell you more at the moment There is one other thing. On no account is my name to be mentioned."

"It won't be." he said. "And what time's your visit?"

"I want to be there at about eleven. I'll wait for you there or you can wait for me. I've got business first in North London or I'd offer you a ride."

"Right" he said. "I'll be seeing you. And thanks a lot."

Jewle put his own receiver back. "Sounds as if it's all set. You'd like me to write you a permit?"

I said no. Mightn't it be better for him to let the local police know I'd be coming to them in the morning and asking for a permit.

"I'll be waiting for you." he said. "A permit for self and friend. And the microphone's to be in the study?"

"You might make sure and have one in the lounge as well. It's easier to talk when you're comfortable and there's an electric fire I can switch on in there. Anything else?"

There wasn't, so we left it at that. If anything whatever went wrong, we'd let each other know.

The next morning I collected my permit and just before eleven I parked my car in the road just beyond River Cottage. Rodey drove up a few moments later, in what was probably one of his newspaper's cars, and parked just beyond me. He was holding out his hand and I went to meet him.

"Glad you could make it," I said. "Lucky we had a nice morning."

We talked about the weather as we walked the few yards to the house. Along the road the patrolling constable saw us making for the door and called to us to stop. I gave him the permit. He read it, looked at me. looked at Rodey and put the permit in his notebook. Then he opened the door.

"Any idea how long you two gents'll be staying?"

"Can't say." I told him. "Twenty minutes? Perhaps a little more. Why d'you ask?"

"Only that I have to make a note of when you leave." He drew back to let us in. "I'll be about, sir, if you'll let me know."

The lounge, as I told Rodey, wasn't any too warm. If the electricity was still on, we might as well light that electric fire. It was on, so I carried it over in front of the grate. I looked round.

"Hasn't changed since you and I were here that Monday morning." I smiled. "Don't think I'll ever forget the shock when Superintendent Jewle handed me that card of mine they'd found in Peplock's fob pocket. But let's have a look at the study. That's where the safe is."

"The study? Where's that?"

"Oh, just through here."

We crossed the cloakroom-hall. I opened the study door and drew back and waved him through. He halted just inside and looked round.

"So this is where he was killed."

"That's right. You can still see the chalk that marks the spot." He had a good look. "Just as they gave out. Shot at his desk. And that's the safe you were talking about?"

I simulated a little excitement as I skirted the desk. The safe door wasn't locked and I got down on one knee and looked carefully inside. I wiped a finger on the one shelf and had a look at it. I examined the name plate on the front of the door and got to my feet.

"Just what I wanted. It's the absolute spit of the one in Dorlish's room at his flat."

He was looking puzzled.

"I don't see it. What difference does it make?"

"Well," I said largely, "even in the most elementary way it ties the two men up. But there's more to it than that. I think I can make it prove something."

I nodded back. "Let's go back to the lounge and I'll tell you. Might as well be comfortable while we're at it."

We went back. He took a chair near the fire and I passed him my cigarette case. He smiled.

"Given up smoking. Can't afford it these days."

"I always preferred a pipe," I told him.

I got it going, then looked suspiciously round.

"I don't think we'd better talk too loud. Looks as if that copper is hanging around outside."

He looked round too. "Probably thinks we're going to walk off with something. But you were saying something about the safe."

"Perhaps I'd better explain. The police tried to tie me up with Peplock on account of that card, and apparently they never quite believed in the explanation, so, when Dorlish was killed, they had me round at his flat the same evening. Yesterday morning I was asked pretty early to go to the Yard and I told them bluntly I wasn't going to be humbugged about. I had my agency to run and if necessary I'd complain to the Commissioner. I think they wanted to placate me. Also, and don't get me wrong, I think they had the idea of using my brains, and that's why they told me a whole lot of things. This is going to be strictly confidential?"

"Of course."

"Then you may have noticed one very peculiar remark the police made when Frank Hayhill, the Good Samaritans crook, appeared before the magistrate. They wanted bail refused because there was the likelihood of a much more serious charge. Now do you get it?"

He shook his head, but his eyes never left my face.

"There isn't a doubt about it," I said. "They're sure that Hayhill killed Peplock. They have proof that Hayhill was on the spot at the time and that Peplock was blackmailing him."

"But that's nonsense! Anybody but a fool could see that the two murders were committed by the same person. Hayhill couldn't have killed Dorlish. He was in Brixton jail!"

"Fool or not, I know they're right. I admit Hayhill couldn't have killed Dorlish, but he certainly killed Peplock. I know it. You ought to know it, too."

"I?"

"Listen," I said, "and don't talk so loud. What I'm going to tell you I swear to God I haven't said a word about to the police. This is the first time I've said a word about it to a soul. Maybe I like you. Maybe I want to help you. I don't know, but I had to have this private conversation with you, even if you haven't exactly played fair with me."

"What in God's name are you talking about? This is all Greek to me!"

"Then why didn't you tell me you were Trude Hayhill's step-brother?"

It hit him clean in the wind. He stared at me, moistening his lips. "Who told you that?"

"Nobody," I said. "It happened to fall into my lap. I'd happened to see Victor Lang for one thing, and you told me the rest. You said you'd been in the enquiry business in the States. Well, a Martin Rubenstein went to New York in 1939 and a David Rubenstein, an enquiry agent in Brooklyn, was his guarantor. Martin's sister Trude was a racial snob and my guess is that Martin changed his named to Max Rodey before he came back to England in 1952. People always try to stick to the same initials. In any case the whole thing could be proved."

"All right. Suppose she's my step-sister. What then?"

"You really want me to tell you? It'll take quite a time."

"Keep on talking. Time's one thing I've plenty of."

I knocked the cold pipe out in the grate and put it in my pocket.

"Very well," I said. "I'll tell you the way I've worked things out. I don't think you ever suspected Hayhill was a crook. You'd left New York before the police were looking for him there. Trude didn't know either. Hayhill was a mighty slick operator. I know; I've heard him talk. You must have met the Hayhills in New York and whenever you subsequently heard from Trude, you thought she was doing just fine. You were probably very glad when she came back here a couple of years ago.

"The trouble was that you soon found out that Trude in that handsome apartment wasn't quite the same. I don't say she cold-shouldered you, but she preferred to keep herself to herself. All right then. You got the idea. But Hayhill was different. He wasn't a snob. He was the warm-hearted, open-handed man he was making himself out to be. When you had that dreadful trouble with your boy, he said you'd have to have the best. He said he'd pay everything, and he did. You didn't, of course, know he wasn't spending his own money. I'm telling the truth so far?"

He gave that ironic smile. "Carry on talking. It's a pleasure to listen."

"Right." I said. "Still strictly between me and you. but something happened not so long ago. Peplock was just about ready to put the bite on Trude: to prove she'd committed bigamy in marrying Hayhill. The only person she could turn to was you. She was supposed to see Peplock here at seven-thirty on that Sunday night and he was having Sambord here to swear he was a single man when he'd married her. You told Trude not to worry and she wasn't to keep that engagement. You had ways and means to shut Peplock's mouth. It'd be dangerous for you, however, to try to discover Sambord's whereabout's, so you arranged for her to see me. There wasn't much time, so you chose a reliable agency.

"Once you knew just where Sambord was, you got to work. You reconnoitred the ground and. when Peplock picked Sambord up on that Sunday morning, you followed on your motor-bike. I don't know if you changed the number-plates, but you were in the Griffin when Peplock made arrangements with the landlord about Sambord. All you had to do then was get some lunch elsewhere for yourself and park the motor-bike. I'd say you got a bit tired of keeping an eye on the Griffin so you thought you'd have a look at this place. The lights weren't on. which was queer, so you tried a door or two and you found one that wasn't locked. Then you found Peplock's body. You'd like me to prove that?"

"I'm still listening."

"This morning I deliberately took you into the study. A person going into a strange room looks ahead, at the room itself and what's in it. You didn't. You looked down before you looked up. What you were looking for was a section of the parquet flooring that had worked its way up. Jewle took a toss on it on the Monday morning and I stubbed my toe against it and nearly had a nasty fall. You weren't so lucky. You fell pretty heavily and hurt your wrist. It still hurt pretty badly when you were in here on that Monday afternoon.

"And you didn't sprain it through cranking a neighbour's car. Your street is all semi-detached houses: no garages and no cars. If a neighbour had had a car, he'd have kept it at a garage and it'd have been started up there. All there's room for between the houses is a path to the side door and on to the back garden. Just room to wheel your motor-bike through to the shed where you keep it.

"I don't know if you recognised the gun. I don't think you did. I think it had been left against Peplock's hand to prove he'd committed suicide. You're one of the few persons who'd know how damn silly that was, so you put the gun in your pocket and went out. But Sambord could still make trouble.

"You knew you'd been seen walking behind him that night, so you later wrote a letter about a coughing man who attracted Sambord's attention across the road out there. Unluckily for you, it didn't throw the police off the scent. Mind you, they haven't the faintest notion it was you. Then Vingram scared you after you'd knocked Sambord out. When he'd gone and Sambord got to his feet, you knocked Sambord out again, slipped the gun into his pocket after a quick search and dumped him in the river. That was to give the appearance of a remorse suicide after he'd killed Peplock.

"All that made Trude safe enough and maybe she didn't want to ask any questions. Then Dorlish began making a bit of trouble and you were called in again. I think you must have told her he couldn't make any real trouble and, if he did, you could handle him. Then the Hayhill story broke and you must have read what was said in court about a more serious charge. You knew Trude was far from trustworthy and, whatever she might have sworn to you, she might have told her husband about Peplock. After all, only you and she and Hayhill could possibly have known. It didn't take you very long after that to guess that Hayhill had killed Peplock, and not because of Trude but because Peplock had discovered that Hayhill was a crook he'd known in Toronto."

I paused for a moment to collect my thoughts.

"That's all?"

"No," I said, "but now things get very personal. Hayhill might get three to five years, say, for fraud, but he'd get at least life for murder. You owed him an enormous debt. You're a good father, Rodey. You love that boy of yours and, but for Hayhill, he might have been a cripple for life instead of what he'll be now. It was a debt you wanted to repay, and soon you saw how. You'd already killed one person, so another didn't matter all that much, but you saw, when you'd thought it all out, that you were the one person probably in all London who could get into Dorlish's flat and have his complete confidence.

"I think you watched him home that evening, then rang him from a call-box.

"'This is Rodey of the *Record*, Mr. Dorlish. Could you do me a favour and see me for just a couple of minutes? Something confidential I've unearthed about your late partner.'

"Dorlish must have known you by reputation. I don't say those were the words you used, but he certainly had no bones about letting you in. After that you'd only to make the murder look exactly like the one here and you'd killed two birds with one stone. You'd got Dorlish off Trude's neck and you were in a position to prove in your paper that Hayhill could never have killed Peplock."

He was still keeping up the ironic pose as he asked if that was all.

"Almost," I said. "Just one rider to add. You thought Trude was on that Mediterranean cruise and then you had a shock. The police were holding her virtually incommunicado in a hotel, and you learned that because she got into touch with you through a hotel waiter named Charles. She was going to see her husband and wanted advice. You got word to her to tell him to swear that he had been here that Sunday afternoon and had found Peplock already dead and that's why he panicked and sold his car. After the Dorlish killing, the police would accept that as truth, provided only that you could convince them that both Peplock and Dorlish had been killed by the same man."

I got to my feet. "That's all, Rodey. Time we were going, or that copper'll be getting suspicious."

He got up, too, but he didn't move away. "And all this beautiful theory is entirely your own?"

"It is," I said. "All the same I'd really like to warn you that the police have almost reached the same conclusions. At any moment you may be talking to them instead of me."

He was game to the last: still that ironic smile, and he actually held out his hand.

"Well, good luck to them. And thank you for an interesting morning."

There were other things I might have mentioned but it was too late: that attempt, for example, to run another eye over River

Cottage on that Monday after the murder, and the real reason behind his call on me at Broad Street, and the telephone call he'd made. Somehow that made me think of Rodey the man, divorced from all those things, and suddenly I was making for the door. Rodey must have stopped for a word with the policeman for he'd only got as far as my car. I called to him.

"Mind if I ask you a personal question?"

"Why not?" he said.

"Well, are you insured?"

"I am. Why d'you want to know?"

"Think it over for yourself," I said, and turned back towards the house. Then I stopped him again.

"Just one other thing. I don't know why I'm telling you this but you ought to know it. Every word you and I said in the house there was overheard by the police. But not what I've been saying to you out here."

As I turned quickly away I heard the sudden catch of his breath. I went on back to the house and watched from the lounge window till he drove off. A moment or two and Jewle was coming in from the garden. He was holding out his hand.

"That was great," he told me. "Just great. But you don't look too pleased."

"Just reaction," I said. "And maybe I'm not so happy about these Judas roles as I used to be in the old days."

"You're too sensitive," he told me. "Rodey wouldn't have been the same about you if he'd guessed what was going on. Our only worry was about you."

"Sorry," I said. "You mean you didn't think I could pull it off?"

"Never doubted it," he said. "All the same you must give us credit for having ideas. After you left us yesterday we did quite a lot of thinking about Rodey. That's why we had our man hovering round and Matthews handy at the back door. Rodey isn't a fool. If you did know anything and he was sure we didn't, he wouldn't have hesitated about using a gun."

I hadn't thought of that but now it didn't somehow seem to matter. When Matthews came in, they were asking if I could come round that afternoon to the Yard. I said I'd rather they made it the morning. That'd give me time to get things sorted out.

A few minutes later I was on my way back to town. I didn't feel like hurrying, and at Epping I pulled up at a hotel for lunch.

I was feeling, too, a bit mentally tired, but a drink cleared most of that away and by the time I was sitting over coffee in the hotel lounge, I could think once more about that morning.

It was Rodey, Rodey: Rodey all the time. I couldn't get his face out of my mind. Jewle had been right. There'd always been something queerly likeable about him, and even now a furtive sympathy kept breaking through.

Maybe, I told myself, I'd been unjust. That ironic smile of his might not have been for himself but for me—Travers the self-righteous who hadn't really troubled to think. Now even I could think of characters like Peplock, Dorlish and even Sambord as far better dead, so maybe that was the way in which Rodey had always regarded them. There hadn't been killings: just executions. What the law thought didn't seem to matter.

What I myself knew was that all these thoughts had suddenly coalesced as he'd left that lounge and it was they that had prompted me to hurry after him. Had he gathered what I'd been trying to make him understand? I didn't know, but I did know what in his case I'd probably have done myself. On the way back to town I'd have jammed the accelerator clean down and hurled that car at a brick wall or a tree. Dead men don't get accused. Dead men's wives can get by for a time on insurance.

As I drove home later that afternoon I began to have the curious certainty that the law would never touch Rodey. As I went on through the dingy suburbs I slowed the car every now and then to look at the placards of the evening papers outside the little newsagents' shops.

FATAL CAR CRASH
WELL-KNOWN JOURNALIST KILLED

That, perhaps, was what I kept expecting to see and somehow I felt in my bones that something like that would soon be there.

I'd have had never a doubt of it if he'd known what I'd been saying to myself when I'd finally turned back to my car.

"It's up to you now, Rodey," I was telling myself. "It's up to you."

THE END